The Little White Horse

The Little White Horse

Elizabeth Goudge

· A YEARLING BOOK ·

Published by
Dell Publishing
a division of
Bantam Doubleday Dell Publishing Group, Inc.
666 Fifth Avenue
New York, New York 10103

ISBN: 0-440-40734-6

Reprinted by arrangement with the author

Printed in the United States of America

December 1992

10 9 8 7 6 5 4 3 2 1

OPM

Dedicated to Walter Hodges
With my thanks

THE LITTLE WHITE HORSE

It was under the white moon that I saw him,
The little white horse, with neck arched high in pride.
Lovely his pride, delicate, no taint of self
Staining the unconscious innocence denied
Knowledge of good and evil, burden of days
Of shame crouched beneath the flail of memory.
No past for you, little white horse, no regret,
No future of fear in this silver forest—
Only the perfect now in the white moon-dappled ride.

A flower-like body fashioned all of light,
For the speed of light, yet momently at rest,
Balanced on the sheer knife-edge of perfection;
Perfection of grass silver upon the crest
Of the hill, before the scythe falls, snow in sun,
Of the shaken human spirit when God speaks
In His still small voice and for a breath of time
All is hushed; gone in a sigh, that perfection,
Leaving the sharp knife-edge turning slowly in the breast.

The raised hoof, the proud poised head, the flowing mane,
The supreme moment of stillness before the flight,
The moment of farewell, of wordless pleading
For remembrance of things lost to earthly sight—
Then the half-turn under the trees, a motion
Fluid as the movement of light on water . . .
Stay, oh stay in the forest, little white horse! . . .
He is lost and gone and now I do not know
If it was a little white horse that I saw,
Or only a moonbeam astray in the silver night.

Chapter One

1

The carriage gave another lurch, and Maria Merryweather, Miss Heliotrope, and Wiggins once more fell into each other's arms, sighed, gasped, righted themselves, and fixed their attention upon those objects which were for each of them at this trying moment the source of courage and strength.

Maria gazed at her boots. Miss Heliotrope restored her spectacles to their proper position, picked up the worn brown volume of French essays from the floor, popped a peppermint into her mouth, and peered once more in the dim light at the wiggly black print on the yellowed page. Wiggins meanwhile pursued with his tongue the taste of the long-since-digested dinner that still lingered among his whiskers.

Humanity can be roughly divided into three sorts of people—those who find comfort in literature, those who find comfort in personal adornment, and those who find comfort in food; and Miss Heliotrope, Maria, and Wiggins were typical representatives of their own sort of people.

Maria must be described first, because she is the heroine of this story. In this year of grace 1842 she was thirteen years old and was considered plain, with her queer silvery-grey eyes that were so disconcertingly penetrating, her straight reddish hair and thin pale face with its distressing freckles. Yet her little figure, small as that of a fairy's child, with a backbone as straight as a poker, was very dignified, and she had exquisitely tiny feet, of which she was inordinately proud. They were her chief beauty, she knew, which was why she took, if possible, a more burning interest in her boots than in her mittens and gowns and bonnets.

And the boots she had on today were calculated to raise the lowest spirits, for they were made of the softest grey leather, sewn with crystal beads round the tops, and were lined with snow-white lamb's-wool. The crystal beads, as it happened, could not be seen, because Maria's grey silk dress and warm grey wool pelisse, also trimmed with white lamb's-wool, reached to her ankles, but she herself knew they were there, and the thought of them gave her a moral strength that can scarcely be overestimated.

She rested herself against the thought of those beads, just as in a lesser degree she rested herself against the thought of the piece of purple ribbon that was wound about her slender waist beneath the pelisse, the little bunch of violets that was tucked so far away inside the recesses of her grey velvet bonnet that it was scarcely visible, and the grey silk mittens adorning the small hands that were hidden inside the big white muff. For Maria was one of your true aristocrats; the perfection of the hidden things was even more important to her than the outward show. Not that she did not like the outward show. She did. She was a showy little thing, even when dressed in the greys and purples of the bereaved.

For Maria was an orphan. Her mother had died in her babyhood and her father just two months ago, leaving so many debts that everything he possessed, including the beautiful London house with the fanlight over the door and the tall windows looking out over the garden of the quiet London Square, where Maria had lived throughout the whole of her short life, had had to be sold to pay them.

When the lawyers had at last settled everything to their satisfaction, it was found that there was only just enough money left to convey her and Miss Heliotrope and Wiggins by coach to the West Country, a part of the world that they had never seen, where they were to live with Maria's second cousin, her nearest living relative, Sir Benjamin Merryweather, whom they had never seen either, in his manor-house of Moonacre in the village of Silverydew.

But it was not her orphaned state that had depressed Maria and made her turn to the contemplation of her boots for comfort. Her mother she did not remember, her father, a soldier, who had nearly always been abroad with his regiment, and who did not care for children anyhow, had never had much hold upon her affections; not the hold that Miss Heliotrope had, who had come to her when she was only a few months old, had been first her nurse and then her governess, and had lavished upon her all the love that she had ever known. No, what was depressing Maria was the wretchedness of this journey and the discomfort of country life that it surely foreboded.

Maria knew nothing about the country. She was a London

lady born and bred, and she loved luxury, and in that beautiful house looking out on the London Square she had had it; even though it had turned out at her father's death that he really oughtn't to have had it, because there had not been the money to pay for it.

And now? Judging by this carriage, there would not be many comforts at Moonacre Manor. It was an awful conveyance. It had met them at Exeter, and was even more uncomfortable than the stage-coach that had brought them from London. The cushions on the seat were hard and moth-eaten, and the floor had chickens' feathers and bits of straw blowing about in the icy draughts that swept in through the ill-fitting doors. The two piebald horses, though they had shining coats and were obviously well loved and well cared-for, a fact which Maria noticed at once because she adored horses, were old and stout and moved slowly.

And the coachman was a wizened little old man who looked more like a gnome than a human creature, clothed in a many-caped greatcoat so patched that it was impossible even to guess at its original colour, and a huge curly-brimmed hat of worn beaver that was so much too large for him that it came right down over his face and rested upon the bridge of his nose, so that one could scarcely see anything of his face except his wide toothless smile and the grey stubble upon his ill-shaven chin. Yet he seemed amiable and had been full of conversation when he tucked them up in the carriage, covering their knees tenderly with a torn and tattered rug, only owing to his lack of teeth they had found it difficult to understand him. And now, in the thick February mist that shrouded the countryside, they could scarcely see him through the little window in the front of the carriage.

Nor could they see anything of the country through which they were passing. The only thing they knew about it was that the road was so full of ruts and pits that they were jolted from side to side and flung up and down as though the carriage were playing battledore and shuttlecock with them. And soon it would be dark and there would be none of the fashionable new gas-lamps that nowadays illumined the London streets, only the deep black awful darkness of the country. And it was bitterly cold and they had been travelling for what seemed like a century, and still there seemed no sign of their ever getting there.

Miss Heliotrope raised her book of essays and held it within an inch of her nose, determined to get to the end of the one about endurance before darkness fell. She would read it many times in the months to come, she had no doubt, together with the one upon the love that never fails. This last essay, she remembered, she had read for the first time on the evening of the day when she had arrived to take charge of the motherless little Maria, and had found her charge the most unattractive specimen of a female infant that she had ever set eyes upon, with her queer silvery eyes and her air, even in babyhood, of knowing that her Blood was Blue and thinking a lot of herself in consequence. Nevertheless, after reading that essay she had made up her mind that she would love Maria, and that her love would never fail the child until death parted them.

At first Miss Heliotrope's love for Maria had been somewhat forced. She had made and mended her clothes with grim determination and with a rather distressing lack of imagination, and however naughty she was had applied the cane only very sparingly, being more concerned with winning the child's affection than with the welfare of her immortal soul. But gradually all that had changed. Her tenderness, when Maria was in any way afflicted, had become eager; the child's clothes had been created with a fiery zeal that made of each small garment a work of art; and she herself had been whipped for her peccadilloes within an inch of her life, Miss Heliotrope caring now not two hoots whether Maria liked her or not, if only she could make of the child a fine and noble woman.

This is true love and Maria had known it; and even when her behind had been so sore that she could scarcely sit upon it, her affection for Miss Heliotrope had been no whit abated. And now that she was no longer a child but a young lady in her teens, it was the best thing in her life.

For Maria from babyhood had always known a good thing when she saw it. She always wanted the best, and was quick to recognize it even when, as in the case of Miss Heliotrope, the outer casket gave little indication of the gold within. She was, perhaps, the only person who had ever discovered what a dear person Miss Heliotrope really was; and that, no doubt, was why Miss Heliotrope's feeling for her had become so eager.

Miss Heliotrope's outer casket was really very odd, and it just shows how penetrating were Maria's silvery eyes, that they had pierced through it so very soon. Most people when confronted with Miss Heliotrope's nose and style of dress stopped there and could not get any farther. Miss Heliotrope's nose was hooked like an eagle's beak, and in colour was a deep unbecoming puce which aroused most people's instant suspicions. They thought she ate and drank too much and that that was why her nose was puce; but, as a matter of fact, Miss Heliotrope scarcely ate or drank anything at all, because she had such dreadful indigestion.

It was the indigestion that had ruined her nose, not overindulgence. She never complained of her indigestion, she just endured it, and it was because she never complained that she was so misunderstood by everyone except Maria. Not that she had ever mentioned her indigestion even to Maria, for she had been brought up by her mother to believe that it is the mark of a True Gentlewoman never to say anything to anybody about herself ever. But Miss Heliotrope's passion for peppermints was in the course of time traced by the discerning Maria to its proper source.

So distressing was Miss Heliotrope's nose, set in the surrounding pallor of her thin pale face, that the great beauty of her forget-me-not-blue eyes was not noticeable, nor the delicate arch of her fine dark eyebrows. Her scanty grey hair she wore in tight corkscrew ringlets all around her face, a mode of hairdressing which had been suitable when she had adopted it at the age of eighteen, but was not very becoming to her now that she was sixty.

Miss Heliotrope was tall and very thin, and stooped, but her thinness was not noticeable because she wore her old-fashioned dress of purple bombasine over a hoop, and winter and summer alike she wore a black shawl over her shoulders and crossed over her chest, so that she was well padded. Out of doors she always carried a large black umbrella and wore a voluminous shabby black cloak and a huge black poke bonnet with a purple feather in it, and indoors a snow-white mob-cap trimmed with black velvet ribbon. She always wore black silk mittens, and carried a black reticule containing a spotless white handkerchief scented with lavender, her spectacles and box of peppermints, and round her neck she wore a gold locket the size of a duck's egg, that held Maria did not know what, because whenever she asked Miss Heliotrope what was inside her locket Miss Heliotrope made no answer. There was not much that Miss Heliotrope denied her beloved Maria, if what Maria wanted was not likely to injure her immortal soul, but she did consistently deny her a sight of what was inside her locket. . . . It was, she said, a matter that concerned herself alone. . . . Maria had no chance to have a look on the sly, because Miss Heliotrope was never parted from her locket; when she went to bed at night she put it under her pillow. But, in any case, Maria would not have looked on the sly, because she was not that kind of girl.

Maria, though decidedly vain and much too inquisitive, was possessed of the fine qualities of honour and courage and fastidiousness, and Miss Heliotrope was entirely made of love and patience. But it is difficult to draw up a list of Wiggins's virtues. . . . In fact impossible, because he hadn't any. . . . Wiggins was greedy, conceited, bad-tempered, selfish, and lazy. It was the belief of Maria and Miss Heliotrope that he loved them devotedly because he always kept close at their heels, wagged his tail politely when spoken to, and even kissed them upon occasion. But all this Wiggins did not from affection but because he thought it good policy. He was aware that from Miss Heliotrope and Maria there emanated all those things which made his existence pleasant to him—his food, always of good quality and served to him with punctuality in a green dish to which he was much attached; his green leather collar; his brush and comb and scented powder and soap. Other mistresses, Wiggins was aware from the conversation of inferior dogs met in the park, could not always be relied on to make the comforts of their pets their first consideration. . . . *His* could. . . . Therefore Wiggins had made up his mind at an early age to ingratiate himself with Maria and Miss Heliotrope, and to remain with them for as long as they gave satisfaction.

But though Wiggins's moral character left much to be desired, it must not be thought that he was a useless member of society, for a thing of beauty is a joy for ever, and Wiggins's beauty was of that high order that can only be described by that tremendous trumpet-sounding word 'incomparable'. He was a pedigree King Charles Spaniel. His coat was deep cream in colour, smooth and glossy everywhere upon his body except upon his chest, where it broke into an exquisite cascade of soft curls like a gentleman's frilled shirt-front. It was not then the fashion for spaniels to have their tails cut, and Wiggins's tail was like an ostrich feather. He was very proud of it and carried it always like a pennon in the wind, and sometimes when the sun shone through the fine hairs it scintillated with light to such an extent that it was almost dazzling to behold.

The only parts of Wiggins that were not cream-coloured were his long silky ears and the patches over his eyes, that were the loveliest possible shade of chestnut brown. His eyes were brown, too, and of a liquid melting tenderness that won all hearts; the owners of the said hearts being quite unaware that Wiggins's tenderness was all for himself, not for them. His paws and the backs of his legs were most delicately feathered, like those of a heraldic beast. Wiggins's nose was long and aristocratic, and supported fine golden whiskers that were always well under control. His nose was jet black, shining, and cold, and his beautiful rose-pink tongue was never unpleasantly moist. For Wiggins was not one of those emotional dogs who let themselves go with quivering whiskers, hot nose, and dribbling tongue.

Wiggins was aware that excessive emotion is damaging to personal beauty, and he never indulged in it. . . . Except, perhaps, a very little, in regard to food. Good food did make him feel emotional, so intense was his delight in it, so deep his thankfulness that the good fairies who at his birth had bestowed upon him an excellent digestion had also seen to it that over-eating never seemed to impair the exquisite slenderness of his figure. . . . That dinner that he had had at the inn at Exeter had really been excellent, the chop, greens, and baked potatoes that had really been meant for Miss Heliotrope, but which she had not felt equal to. . . . Thoughtfully his beautiful pink tongue caressed his golden whiskers. If the food of the West Country was always going to be as good as that meal at Exeter he would, he thought, be able to put up with cold mists and draughty carriages with calm and patience.

Presently it was quite dark, and the queer old coachman got down, grinned at them and lit the two antique lanterns that swung one on each side of the box. But they did not give much light, and all that could be seen from the coach windows were the drifting mist and steep precipitous banks covered with wet ferns. The road grew narrower and narrower, so that the ferns brushed against the carriage upon either side, and bumpier, and bumpier and more and more precipitous, so that they were always either crawling painfully uphill or sliding perilously down what felt like the side of some horrible cliff.

In the darkness Miss Heliotrope could no longer read, nor Maria contemplate her boots. But they did not grumble at all, because True Gentlewomen never grumble. Maria clasped her hands tightly inside her muff, and Miss Heliotrope clasped hers under her cloak, and they set their teeth and endured.

·: 2 :·

Perhaps in spite of the cold, they all three dozed a little from sheer weariness, because it was with a shock of complete surprise that they discovered that the carriage had stopped. And it must have been that between their loss of consciousness and its return they had come a long way, because everything was completely different. For one thing, the mist had gone and the moon was shining, so that they could see each other's faces quite plainly.

Their depression had completely vanished and their hearts were beating fast with a sense of adventure. With the eagerness of small children Miss Heliotrope and Maria let down the carriage windows upon either side and leaned out, Wiggins pushing himself in beside Maria that he might lean out too.

The fern-covered banks that had been on each side of them

had disappeared, and in their place, close up against the windows of the carriage, were walls of solid rock of a beautiful silvery grey, and in front of them, too, completely blocking their passage, was solid rock.

'Can we have come the right way?' asked Miss Heliotrope.

'There's a door in the rock!' said Maria, who was leaning so far out of the window that she was in danger of falling headlong into the narrow lane. 'Look!'

Miss Heliotrope also leaned out at a perilous angle, and saw that Maria was quite right. There was a door of weathered oak set in the rock, so old that it was of the same colour as the stone and hardly distinguishable from it. It was very large, big enough to admit a carriage. Close beside it there hung a rusty chain that issued from a hole in the wall.

'The coachman is getting down!' ejaculated Maria and with eyes shining with excitement she watched the gnome-like little man as he scurried to the rusty chain, seized hold of it, lifted both legs off the ground, and swung there like a monkey on a stick. The result was a deep hollow clanging somewhere within the recesses of the rock. When there had been three clangs the coachman dropped to the ground again, grinned at Maria, and climbed back upon the box.

Slowly the great door swung open. The coachman clucked to the old piebald horses, Miss Heliotrope and Maria sat down again, and they moved forward, the door closing behind them as noiselessly as it had opened, shutting out the moonlight and leaving them once more with no illumination but that of the flickering lantern light gleaming upon the wet moss-grown walls of an underground tunnel. It gleamed also, Maria fancied, over some sort of shadowy figure, but of this she could not be sure, because the carriage moved forward before she could get a proper look.

'Ugh!' said Miss Heliotrope, not quite so happy as she had been, for it struck very clammy and cold, the tunnel seemed to go on for a very long time, and the echoing of the coach wheels made a roar like thunder. But before they had time to get really frightened they were out in the moonlight again, and in a place so beautiful that it seemed hardly to be of this world.

It was all silver. Upon each side of them the trunks of tall trees rose from grass so silvered by the moonlight that it glimmered like water. The trees were not thickly planted, and beautiful glades opened between them, showing glimpses of an ebony sky set with silver stars. Nothing moved. It was all quite still, as though enchanted under the moon. The silvery tracery of twigs and branches above the silver tree trunks was so delicate that the moonlight sifted through it like a fine film of silver dust.

But there was life among the trees, though it was life that did not move. Maria saw a silver owl sitting on a silver branch, and a silver rabbit sitting up on its haunches beside the road blinking at the lantern light, and a beautiful group of silver deer. . . . And for a fleeting instant, at the far end of a glade, she thought she saw a little white horse with flowing mane and tail, head raised, poised, halted in midflight, as though it had seen her and was glad.

'Look,' she cried to Miss Heliotrope. But when Miss Heliotrope looked she could not see anything.

They drove on for a long time, over a thick carpet of moss that deadened the sound of the carriage wheels, until at last they found themselves driving through an archway in an old grey wall; not natural rock this time but a manmade wall crowned with battlements. Maria had just time to notice the battlements with a throb of excitement, and they were within the walls and the beautiful park had given place to a formal garden, with flower-beds and paved walks surrounding a water-lily pool, and yew-trees cut into strange fantastic shapes of crowing cocks and knights on horseback.

The garden, like the park, was all silver and black under the moon, and a little tremor of fear seized Maria as they drove through it, for it seemed to her that the black knights and black cocks turned their heads to look very coldly at her as she went past. Wiggins, though he was down on the floor and couldn't see the shadowy black figures, must have felt a bit queer too, because he growled. And Miss Heliotrope also must have felt not altogether happy, because she said in quite a quavery voice, 'Aren't we nearly at the house?'

'We *are* at the house,' rejoiced Maria. 'Look, there's a light!'

'Where?' demanded Miss Heliotrope.

'There!' said Maria. 'High up behind that tree.' And she pointed to where an orange eye of light was winking at them cheerfully through the topmost branches of a huge black cedar that towered up in front of them like a mountain. There was something wonderfully reassuring about that wink of orange, set like a jewel in the midst of all the black and silver. It was a bit of earthliness amongst so much that was unearthly, something that welcomed and was pleased to see her in place of those cold black shadows who had not wanted her to come.

'But it's right up in the sky!' ejaculated Miss Heliotrope in astonishment, and then the carriage took a wide sweep round the cedar-tree and they knew why the light was shining so high up. For the house was not the sort of modern house they were accustomed to, but a very old house, almost more of a castle than a house, and the light was shining in a window at the top of a tall tower.

Miss Heliotrope let out a cry of dismay (quickly stifled, because only the ill-bred cry out when confronted by an alarming prospect), thinking of mice and spiders of both of which she was terrified; but Maria gave a cry of delight. She was going to live in a house with a tower, like a princess in a fairy-tale.

Oh, but it was a glorious house! It towered up before them, its great walls confronting the shadowy garden with a sort of timeless strength that was as reassuring as the light in a window of the tower. And though she had never seen it before, it gave her a feeling of home. For Merryweathers had lived in it for generations, and she was a Merryweather. She was ashamed of her previous dread of coming here. This was home, as the London house had never been. She would rather live here austerely than in the most luxurious palace in the world.

And she was out of the carriage almost before it had stopped, and running up a flight of stone steps that were built sideways against the wall and led up to the great oak front door, and beating upon it with her fists to be let in. Neither her light feet nor her small fists made much sound, but someone inside must have been listening for the sound of the carriage wheels, for the great door opened almost at once, revealing the most extraordinary-looking elderly gentleman Maria had ever set eyes upon, standing upon the threshold with a lighted lantern held high in his hand.

'Welcome, Cousin,' he said in a deep, rich, fruity voice, and held out his free hand to her.

'Thank you, Sir,' she replied, and curtsied and put her hand into his, and knew that she would love him from that moment on for always.

But her cousin was really very odd to look at, and once she started looking at him she found it very difficult to leave off. He was so tall and so broad that he seemed to fill the big doorway. His face was round and red and clean-shaven, and his big hooked nose put Miss Heliotrope's entirely in the shade. He had three double chins, a large smiling mouth, and twinkling eyes of a warm tawny-brown, almost lost beneath bushy white eyebrows. His clothes, most scrupulously cared for, were very old-fashioned and most oddly assorted.

He had a huge white wig like a cauliflower on his head, and his double chins were propped by a cravat of Honiton lace. His waistcoat was of pale-blue satin embroidered with yellow roses and crimson carnations, and was so beautiful that it contrasted oddly with his faded and patched riding-coat and breeches and the mud-splashed top-boots. He was slightly bow-legged, as men are who have spent most of their life in the saddle. His hands were big and red like his face, with palms as hard as leather from much holding of the bridle, but beautiful lace fell over the wrists, and on one finger was a ring with a great ruby in it that flashed like fire.

Indeed, everything about Sir Benjamin Merryweather was warm and glowing; his round red face, his smile, his voice, his tawny eyes, his ruby ring. After he had taken Maria's hand he looked at her very attentively, as though he were asking himself some question about her. And she trembled a little under his scrutiny, as though she feared herself lacking in some quality he looked for; yet she looked steadily up into his face and did not blink at all.

'A true Merryweather,' he said at last in his deep rumbling voice. 'One of the silver Merryweathers, straight and arrogant and fastidious, brave and the soul of honour, born at the full moon. We shall like each other, my dear, for I was born at midday; and your moon Merryweathers and your sun Merryweathers always take a fancy for one another. . . .'

He broke off abruptly, suddenly aware of Miss Heliotrope and Wiggins, who by this time had got themselves out of the carriage and up the steps, and were standing behind Maria.

'My dear Madam!' he cried to Miss Heliotrope, after subjecting her to one long keen glance. 'My dear Madam! Allow me!' And bowing very low he took her hand and led her ceremoniously over the threshold. 'Welcome, Madam!' he said to her. 'Welcome to my poor unworthy home.'

And his words rang out like a note that strikes true. He did really and truly think his home unworthy to house Miss Heliotrope.

'My dear Sir!' cried Miss Heliotrope, all of a flutter, for owing to her unattractive appearance gentlemen seldom bestowed upon her these flattering attentions. 'My dear Sir, you are *too* kind!'

Maria, picking up Wiggins, who was snorting disagreeably because no one was paying the least attention to him, pushed the great door shut and turned to follow her elders with a sigh of content. For she was aware that Sir Benjamin had seen at a glance of what fine stuff her dear Miss Heliotrope was made. . . . They were all going to like each other.

But no, perhaps not, for a low disagreeable growl from under her arm, where she had Wiggins, was echoed by a rumble like thunder from the hearth of the great log fire which was burning in the stone-paved raftered hall into which Sir Benjamin had led them.

An animal of sorts, a rather alarmingly large animal, whose body seemed to stretch the length of the hearth, had raised a huge shaggy head from his forepaws and was gazing at Wiggins's exquisite little face peeping out from beneath Maria's arm. He sniffed once loudly, got the aroma of Wiggins's character, thought apparently little of it, blinked once contemptuously, and laid his head back on his paws. But he did not go to sleep. Through the cascade of reddish hair that fell over them, eyes like yellow lamps shone disconcertingly upon the assembled company; disconcertingly because they were so terribly penetrating.

If the eyes of Sir Benjamin had seemed to see a good deal, the eyes of the shaggy creature on the hearth saw infinitely more. What sort of a creature was he, Maria wondered. She supposed he was a dog, and yet, somehow, he wasn't quite like a dog. . . .

'The dog Wrolf,' said Sir Benjamin, answering her unspoken question. 'There are those who find him alarming, but I assure you that you need have no fear of him. He is an old dog. He came out of the pine-wood behind the house on Christmas Eve more than twenty years ago, and stayed with us for a while, and then after some trouble in the household he went away again. But just over a year ago—also on Christmas Eve—he came back, and has lived with me ever since, and never to my knowledge harmed even a mouse.'

'You have mice?' whispered Miss Heliotrope.

'Hundreds,' boomed Sir Benjamin cheerfully. 'But we keep 'em down with traps, you know. Traps, and Zachariah the cat. Zachariah is not here just now. Now, dear ladies, you must see your rooms and lay aside your wraps, and then you will come down to the hall again and we will eat together.'

Sir Benjamin took three large brass candlesticks from a table beside the fire, lit their candles, handed one each to Miss Heliotrope and Maria, and led the way with his into an adjoining room that Maria guessed was the parlour, though in the dim light she could scarcely see anything of it.

He opened a door in the wall, passed through it, and they were on a turret staircase. The steps were of stone, worn in the middle because so many feet had trodden them during the centuries, and wound round and round the central newel in a fashion that poor Miss Heliotrope found most dizzying; though Sir Benjamin, going on ahead with his candle, mounted them as merrily as a boy, in spite of his age and bulk, and Maria, bringing up the rear, stepped up them with the agility of a happy monkey.

'Six hundred years old,' said Sir Benjamin cheerfully. 'Built in the thirteenth century by Wrolf Merryweather, armour-bearer to King Edward I, and the founder of our family, on land ceded him by the king in gratitude for Wrolf's valiant bearing in battle. In our family, Miss Heliotrope, we spell Wrolf with a W, for we are of Viking ancestry, and great fighters.'

'Yes,' sighed Miss Heliotrope. 'When Maria was little, I had great trouble in getting her to eat rice pudding.'

'Did you call the dog that came out of the pine-wood after that Wrolf?' asked Maria. She had hesitated a little before she spoke of that great beast down in the hall as a dog, because she still somehow could not think that he was.

'I did,' said Sir Benjamin. 'For tradition has it that Wrolf Merryweather was auburn-haired, and Wrolf the dog, as you may have noticed, has a reddish mane.'

'Yes, I noticed,' said Maria.

Sir Benjamin had stopped outside a door. 'Here, ladies, I leave you,' he said. 'This is Miss Heliotrope's room, over the parlour. Maria's is higher up still, right at the top of the tower.' And he bowed to them and went away down the stairs with his candle.

Miss Heliotrope, who had thought that perhaps she would have to sleep on a straw pallet on a rush-strewn floor, gave a gasp of relief upon seeing her room. It was a fair-sized room, and its oak floor was almost entirely covered by a crimson carpet. It was a very shabby carpet with large holes in it, but it was a carpet and not rushes.

There was a big four-poster with a flight of steps leading up to it, and crimson velvet curtains to keep the draught out. There was a bow-fronted mahogany chest of drawers, a huge mahogany wardrobe, a dressing-table with a chintz petticoat, and a winged armchair with a foot-stool for her feet. The stone walls had been panelled in warm dark wood, and the window was closely shuttered, with chintz curtains covering the shutters. All the curtains needed mending, but the furniture was well polished and it was all scrupulously clean.

And someone, it seemed, had been giving much thought to her comfort, for a log fire was burning brightly on the hearth, candles were burning on the chest of drawers and the dressing-table, and there was a warming-pan between the sheets. And their luggage was already here, piled neatly at the foot of the four-poster.

But Maria did not linger in Miss Heliotrope's room. She waited only to see that she was happy, and then she went quietly off with her candle and pursued her way up the turret stairs, up and up and round and round for quite a long way. A room of her own! She had never had a room of her own before. She had always slept with Miss Heliotrope and, loving her as she did, she had not minded that; but yet, just lately, she had thought it would be nice to have a room of her own.

•: 3 :•

The turret stairs ended at a door so small that a large grown-up could not possibly have got through it. But for a slim girl of thirteen it was exactly right. Maria stopped and gazed at it with a beating heart, for though this little, narrow, low door was obviously hundreds of years old, yet she felt as though it had been made especially for her. For if she had been able to choose her own door, this was the door she would have chosen. It was more like a front door than a bedroom door, like the door of her very own house. It was of silvery grey oak studded with silver nails, and it had a knocker made of the smallest, daintiest horseshoe Maria had ever seen, polished so brightly that it shone like silver. At sight of it Maria thought instantly of the lovely little white horse she had thought she had seen in the park and that she had pointed out to Miss Heliotrope . . . only Miss Heliotrope hadn't been able to see it. . . . The door was opened by a silver latch that clicked in a friendly sort of way, when Maria lifted it, as though it was welcoming her.

She went in, latched the door behind her, put her candle carefully down on the floor, leaned back against the door and gazed and gazed, with her lips parted and her usually pale face glowing like a pink rose, and her eyes like stars.

No pen could possibly do justice to the exquisite charm and beauty of Maria's room. It was at the top of the tower, and the tower was a round one, so Maria's room was circular, neither too large nor too small, just the right size for a girl of thirteen. It had three windows, two narrow lancet windows and one large one with a window-seat in the thickness of the wall. The curtains had not been drawn across the windows, and through them she could see the stars. In each of the windows stood beautiful silver branched candlesticks with three lighted candles burning in each of them.

It was the light from one of these, Maria realized, that she had seen from outside shining through the branches of the cedar-tree. The walls had not been panelled with wood, as in Miss Heliotrope's room, but the silver-grey stone was so lovely that Maria was glad. The ceiling was vaulted, and delicate ribbings of stone curved over Maria's head like the branches of a tree, meeting at the highest point of the ceiling in a carved representation of a sickle moon surrounded by stars.

There was no carpet upon the silvery-oak floor, but a little white sheepskin lay beside the bed, so that Maria's bare toes should meet something warm and soft when they went floorwards of a morning. The bed was a little four-poster, hung with pale-blue silk curtains embroidered with silver stars, of the same material as the window curtains, and spread with a patchwork quilt made of exquisite squares of velvet and silk of all colours of the rainbow, gay and lovely.

There was very little furniture in the room, just a couple of silvery-oak chests for Maria's clothes, a small round mirror hung upon the wall above one of them, and a stool with a silver ewer and basin upon it. But Maria felt that she wanted no more than this. Heavy furniture such as Miss Heliotrope had, would have ruined this exquisite little room. Nor did she mind that the fireplace was the tiniest she had ever seen, deeply recessed in the wall. It was big enough for the fire of pine-cones and apple wood that burned in it, filling the room with fragrance.

But when Maria started to explore her room she found that it was not without luxuries. Over the fireplace was a shelf, and on it stood a blue wooden box filled with dainty biscuits with sugar flowers on them, in case she should feel hungry between meals. And beside the fireplace stood a big basket filled with more logs and pine-cones—enough to keep her fire burning all through the night.

It was all perfect. It was the room Maria would have designed for herself if she had had the knowledge and skill. For she realized that very much knowledge and skill had gone to the making of this room. Fine craftsmen had carved the moon and stars and fashioned the furniture, and an exquisite needlewoman had made the patchwork quilt and embroidered the curtains.

This way and that she stepped, putting her pelisse and bonnet and muff away in one of the chests, smoothing her hair before the mirror, washing her hands in the water that she poured out of the little silver ewer into the silver basin, touching all the beautiful things with the tips of her fingers, as though caressing them, saying thank you in her heart to the people who had made them, and whoever it was who had arranged them. Was it Sir Benjamin? But it couldn't have been, because he couldn't have got through the door.

A knock on the door, and the startled voice of Miss Heliotrope outside, reminded her that her governess, with her height and her hoop, would not be able to get through the door either, and in spite of her love for Miss Heliotrope she felt a little thrill of glee. . . . This room was indeed her own. . . . When she opened the door there was a mischievous dimple in her left cheek that had never been there before.

'My dear! My dear!' lamented Miss Heliotrope, who had now removed her outdoor garments and was wearing her mob-cap and her black shawl folded across her chest, 'what a ridiculous little door! I shall never be able to get inside your room!'

'No!' giggled Maria.

'But what shall we do when you're ill?' asked poor Miss Heliotrope.

'I shan't *be* ill,' said Maria. 'Not here!'

'I certainly think that the air here is salubrious,' agreed Miss Heliotrope, and then her eyes fell upon the inside of Maria's room and widened in horror. 'What an extraordinary little place! So very odd! Oh, my poor darling Maria! However are you to sleep in a place like this? It'll give you the creeps!'

'I like it,' said Maria.

And Miss Heliotrope, looking at Maria's rosy cheeks and sparkling eyes and that entirely new dimple, could not doubt that she spoke the truth. And looking again, more attentively, at the extraordinary little room, she saw that it suited Maria. Standing there so slender and straight in her grey dress, her room seemed to curve itself about her like the petals of a flower about its heart; they completed each other.

'Well, well!' said Miss Heliotrope. 'So long as you are happy, my dear. And now, I think, we should go down to supper.'

Carrying their candles, and with Wiggins following them, they made their way down the winding staircase again.

'I wonder,' said Miss Heliotrope, 'who does the work of this house? I have seen no sign of a maidservant, and yet everything is scrupulously neat and clean. A darning needle is wanted everywhere, as no doubt you have observed, but apart from that I have no fault at all to find, so far, with the household staff. . . . But where are they?'

'Perhaps they'll wait on us at supper,' said Maria.

·: 4 :·

But no one waited on them. They waited on themselves. The supper was delicious. There was home-made crusty bread, hot onion soup, delicious rabbit stew, baked apples in a silver dish, honey, butter the colour of marigolds, a big blue jug of warm mulled claret, and hot roasted chestnuts folded in a napkin.

Miss Heliotrope confined herself to eating bread and butter

and sipping a little claret, but she did it with an appetite that surprised her. Maria ate everything there was to eat, very daintily, as was her habit, but with an enjoyment surprising in one so ethereal-looking. Her cousin greeted her good appetite with a chuckle of appreciation. 'A digestion of cast iron, like all the Merryweathers,' he noted with approval. 'Your little dog, also, I note, is a good trencherman.'

Wiggins had been provided with a plateful of stew, and was doing full justice to it. He was sharing the hearth with Wrolf, if not with any show of friendship yet with no enmity now. He and Wrolf, it seemed, had decided simply to ignore each other. . . . And the huge hearth was quite wide enough for them both.

'I have always heard that West Country women are wonderful cooks?' said Miss Heliotrope with a faintly questioning note.

'You and Maria are the first members of the fair sex to set foot in this house for twenty years,' Sir Benjamin informed her.

'But why, Sir?' asked Maria, her silver spoon arrested in mid-air. 'Don't you like females?'

'Not as a general rule,' said Sir Benjamin. Then he bowed very gallantly, first to Miss Heliotrope and then to Maria. 'But there is always something particularly delightful about exceptions to a rule,' he said.

He spoke with such sincerity that neither Miss Heliotrope nor Maria felt any sinking of the heart at the thought that they had come to live in an anti-feminine bachelor household. Yet they looked at each other in stupefaction. It was hard to believe any mere male capable of such superb soup and such a princely stew.

But they asked no more questions, because at this point Wiggins created a diversion. Overcome by greediness, he splashed a bit, and a small piece of carrot shot out of his dish and landed upon Wrolf's nose. The indignity was too much for Wrolf. Outraged, he arose, and slowly and with measured gait left the room, lifting the latch of the front door with his nose. So majestic was his exit, so incomparable his dignity, that it was not so much an exit as a royal progress that compelled all eyes.

There was a momentary cessation both of conversation and mastication as he departed, and for the first time Maria got a real good look at the whole of him. A dog? Whatever Sir Benjamin might say, she could not believe that he was a dog. She had never seen a dog with such a huge head and massive chest, so strangely combined with such a slender waist; or such a glorious flowing sable mane. His tail, too, with that queer tuft of hair at the end of it, was not like a dog's, nor his gait, nor—

'Are you a good horsewoman, Maria?' asked Sir Benjamin abruptly, and in duty bound she turned her attention back to her host.

'I love horses, but I have not been taught to ride, Sir,' she said.

'Not been taught to ride!' ejaculated Sir Benjamin in horror. 'Whatever was your father thinking of? No Merryweather, male or female, is ever really happy out of the saddle.'

'My father was so little at home,' explained Maria.

'Maria has no habit,' Miss Heliotrope put in anxiously; for the thought of her precious Maria galloping about on horseback terrified her.

'That is not of importance,' said Sir Benjamin cheerfully. 'What is of importance is that I have a pony just the right size for her.'

Maria's pale face flushed again and her eyes sparkled. 'The white one?' she asked with quite extraordinary eagerness.

Sir Benjamin looked startled. 'White? No. Dapple grey. Had you especially set your heart on a white mount?'

'No-o,' said Maria, not quite truthfully. 'Only—I thought I saw a little white horse in the park as we drove through.'

If she had startled her relative before, she had now dumbfounded him. He set down his wineglass rather suddenly, spilling a little of the beautiful claret, and gazed at her with the queerest expression on his face, a mixture of astonishment, relief, and profound tenderness that made Maria feel quite queer. She was glad when he stopped staring at her, drained his glass and got up.

'Two such weary travellers—three if we include the little dog—must be longing for their beds,' he said.

They had been abruptly dismissed, Miss Heliotrope and Maria realized, yet they went bedwards with no sense of outrage, for a little oddness of behaviour was only to be expected in a man who had been for twenty years bereft of the civilizing influence of female companionship. . . . Also he had been startled.

'You must be careful not to startle him, my dear,' said Miss Heliotrope, as they once more mounted the steps of their tower, with their candles in their hands and Wiggins pattering behind. 'He is a man of considerable age and full habit, and perpetual shocks to his system will do him no good at all.'

'But I didn't mean to startle him,' said Maria. 'I only said I'd seen—'

'You see very odd things,' Miss Heliotrope interrupted her. 'I myself have been considerably startled, at times, by the things you've seen and that I couldn't see. There was the time you saw the cuckoo fly out of the cuckoo-clock and sit on top of it and preen his feathers, and that peculiar imaginary playmate of yours that you made up for yourself when you were only a little thing, that boy with the feather in his hat who used to play with you in the Square garden.'

'But he *wasn't* imaginary,' said Maria hotly. 'He was a real boy. He *is* a real boy. I know he's alive somewhere still, even though he does not come to play with me any more. His name is Robin, and he looks like a robin, with bright dark eyes and rosy cheeks and—'

'My dear,' interrupted Miss Heliotrope again, somewhat sternly, 'you have told me a thousand times what he looks like, or what you imagined at the time that he looked like, and I can only repeat that there was, and is, no such person.'

Maria said no more, because she did not want to quarrel with Miss Heliotrope. The only subject upon which she and her governess had ever really disagreed with any heat was this subject of the existence or non-existence of Robin. Miss Heliotrope had been deeply distressed at Maria's inability to draw the line between fiction and fact, and Maria had been equally distressed because her word was doubted; for Maria was very truthful, and when she said a thing was so nothing distressed her more than to hear people say it wasn't.

At the little door with the silver knocker Miss Heliotrope and Maria kissed each other good night affectionately, the tiny momentary rift between them quite forgotten.

'You'd better have Wiggins at night,' said Maria. 'And then if any mice come he can chase them away.'

But Wiggins thought differently. Through the open door he had caught sight of the little four-poster with the patchwork counterpane, and it struck him that it was a much softer bed than Miss Heliotrope's. . . . Also he thought he could smell biscuits. . . . He trotted in, took a flying leap, and landed on the bed.

'Now isn't that touching!' said Miss Heliotrope, tears of sensibility coming into her eyes. 'He knows that you are his little mistress. He feels that he must guard you now that you are to sleep by yourself for the first time.'

Wiggins, curled up on the bed, wagged his plume of a tail, and his beautiful eyes shone softly in the candlelight.

'Oh, my Wiggins, aren't you sweet!' cried Maria, running to kiss him after Miss Heliotrope had shut the door and gone away. 'Such a loving, devoted little Wiggins. You shall have a biscuit, Wiggins. You shall have the largest of the sugar biscuits.'

Maria, fetching Wiggins the largest biscuit, the round one with the pink sugar rose on top, noticed that the fire had been made up afresh, the silver ewer had been filled with hot water, and that a glass of milk had been put on the shelf beside the biscuit-box. Now who had done that? Not the old coachman, surely. He was little enough to get in through the small door, perhaps, but there seemed no way to get to her room except through the hall, and she had not seen him pass through while they were at supper.

Well, whoever it was, it gave her a lovely warm happy feeling to find herself so cared for. As she undressed, she sipped the milk, and it was warm and sweet, just as she liked it. And the sugar biscuit that she ate with it, a long-shaped one decorated with a green shamrock, was delicious too. So life in the country was not going to be so comfortless, after all. That ramshackle carriage had been quite misleading.

She undressed, washed, put on her long white nightgown and her white nightcap with the lace frills, blew out the candles, and climbed into bed. One of the windows was open, and the night air that blew in was not cold but fresh and sweet. Her mattress, she found, was stuffed with the softest feathers, and her sheets and pillow-cases were of the finest linen and smelt of lavender. Earlier in the evening there must have been a warming-pan in her bed as well as Miss Heliotrope's, because it felt lovely and warm when she put her toes down. It was a lovely bed, and with sighs of content she and Wiggins crunched up the last crumbs of their sugar biscuits and snuggled themselves down for repose.

Wiggins was deeply asleep at once, but Maria lay for some time between sleeping and waking, thinking of the beautiful park through which she had driven to this lovely house and imagining herself running up one of its glades. And then her fancy became a dream and she was in the park, with the scent of flowers about her and spring trees talking to each other over her head.

But in her dream she was not alone, Robin was with her,

running beside her and laughing. And he was just the same—just as he had been when in her childhood she had been sent to play in the Square garden, and had felt lonely, and he had come running through the trees to companion her loneliness. He was just exactly her age—or perhaps a little older, because he was a head taller than she, and much broader.

There was nothing ethereal about Robin—very much the opposite; which fact in itself proved to Maria that he was a real boy and no mere creation of her imagination. He was sturdy and strong and red-cheeked, with a skin tanned brown by sun and wind. His dark eyes sparkling with fun and kindliness were set in thick short black lashes beneath strongly marked dark eyebrows. His nose was tip-tilted and a little impudent above his wide, laughing, generous mouth and strong cleft chin. His thick chestnut hair grew low on his forehead, curled all over his head as tightly as a lamb's fleece, and at the back of his neck the final curl formed a comic sort of twist like a drake's tail. He was dressed all in brown, a rough brown jerkin the colour of fallen beech leaves, brown leather breeches and leggings, and he wore upon the side of his head a battered old brown hat with a long green peacock's feather in it. . . .

Such was Robin when he had come to play with her in the Square garden; such was he as he companioned her dreams during this first night at Moonacre Manor, strong and kind and merry, warm and glowing like the sun, and the best companion in the world. . . .

In the little room at the top of the tower moonlight and firelight mingled their silver and gold, and Maria smiled as she slept.

Chapter Two

·: 1 :·

She woke up abruptly with the sun in her eyes, and lay for a moment a little puzzled by the light, the quiet and the freshness. Then she remembered, and with one swift excited movement flung back the patchwork counterpane over the top of the still sleeping Wiggins and slid out of bed, her bare toes sinking gratefully into the warmth and softness of the little sheepskin rug.

Though it was still very early her room was quite warm and, looking round, she saw to her astonishment that the fire had been lit, and that bright flames were leaping up the chimney. It was obviously a very skilfully made fire, and only someone as soft-footed as a fairy could have managed to creep in and lay and light it without waking her. Warming her hands at the flames, she looked about her, wondering what else this fairy person had done for her comfort.

As she had expected, there was once again hot water in the ewer, and—what was that lying on the top of one of the oak chests? A new dress? She picked it up, and it was a beautiful riding-habit, made of the finest dark-blue cloth trimmed with silver braid. There was a hat too, a dark-blue one trimmed with a white ostrich feather. And there was a riding-crop, a pair of gloves, and a strong little pair of riding-boots. . . . And lying on top of the pile of garments was a bunch of snowdrops, still wet with the morning dew.

She dressed in a sort of tremor of excitement which was increased when she found that the habit fitted her perfectly. She knew it had not been made for her, because it was old-fashioned in style (not that that mattered in this timeless place) and because she could see that it had been worn before; down by the hem a three-cornered tear had been exquisitely mended with thread as fine as a spider's filament. The gloves and the boots, too, were a little rubbed in places, and in one of the pockets of the coat there was a gossamer handkerchief worked in one corner with the monogram L. M.

Yet the fastidious Maria found that she did not mind that someone else had worn these clothes first. She had a queer feeling, as she fastened the coat of the habit and pinned the bunch of snowdrops in the front of it, that L. M.—whoever she was—put loving arms about her; almost as her mother might have done, had she not died. 'I'll always be safe when I'm wearing this habit,' she thought. 'People are always safe in their mother's arms.'

Standing in front of the little round mirror, she brushed out her straight carroty hair and pinned it up on top of her head, and then she was free to look out of the windows.

She went first to the wide one with the window-seat, the south window that looked out towards the formal garden. It was the window whose light had welcomed her upon arrival, and it looked straight out into the topmost branches of the great cedar-tree.

It would be perfectly possible for anyone agile to climb out of the window and into the tree and then down to the garden. She got on to the window-seat, flung the window wide and leaned out. She could not see a great deal, because of the tree, but she was conscious of floods of silver sunlight, of a pale-blue cloudless sky. And, looking downwards, she could see through the cedar branches a garden no longer ebony and silver, but bright with the white and gold of snowdrops and aconites, with here and there brilliant spots of colour where the first gold and purple crocuses were holding up their cups to catch the sun.

The yew-trees, those strange fantastic shapes of cocks and knights, were not frightening this morning, because their sombre darkness was entirely eclipsed by the loveliness of the spring flowers. The garden, she could see now, was not very tidy. The yew-trees needed clipping, the flower-beds about the water-lily pool needed weeding, and the paving-stones of the paths that wound between them were overgrown with bright green moss. But somehow the untidiness added to the charm of it all, giving it a look of easy friendliness that warmed one's heart. In her childhood she had been scolded if she had stepped on any of the immaculate flower-beds in the Square garden, when she had been playing with Robin, but here no one would mind what she did.

'Oh, if only Robin would come back and play with me here!' she whispered to herself.

But Robin had disappeared out of her life quite a couple of

years ago; as soon as she had started pinning her hair on top of her head and putting on grown-up airs, he had gone away.

She climbed down from the window-seat, and turned to the lancet window that looked west, framing a picture that took her breath away with its loveliness. Just below her was a tangled rose-garden, with a rose-coloured arbour in the middle of it, and grass paths winding between heart-shaped rose-beds.

It was lovely, even though there were as yet only a very few tiny leaves on the thorny overgrown briars, and she could just imagine how wonderful it would be in June, with a mass of blossom and perfume sweeping right up to the old battlemented walls beyond, and breaking against them in a wave of colour and light. Though even now there was plenty of colour, because the rose-garden was full of birds, tits with blue on their wings and chaffinches with rose-red breasts, gay little creatures whose beauty caught at Maria's heart.

But these little creatures were not the only feathered things about this morning. A sound over her head made Maria look up, to see a flock of white seagulls flying over the manor-house from east to west. One after the other they came, their great beating wings catching the morning light most gloriously, their strange high cries making her heart beat fast with excitement. They were telling her that the sea could not be far away, to the east behind her, and she had never seen the sea. . . .

For a little while the glory of the morning light on their wings dazzled her, so that she could not see properly. Then she rubbed her knuckles in her eyes and feasted them again on the loveliness outside the window.

Beyond the battlements, she could see right over into Moonacre Park. Never in all her short life had she seen such wonderful trees; giant beeches clad in silver armour, rugged oaks, splendid chestnuts, and delicate birches shimmering with light. They had no leaves as yet, but the buds were swelling, and there seemed a mist of pale colour among their branches—amethyst and chrome and rose and blue, all melting into each other like the colours of a rainbow that shines for a moment through the clouds and then changes its mind and goes away again.

The trees did not grow too close together. Between them opened the glades that last night had been silver and now were clothed in the tawny grass of very early spring. Soon, Maria guessed, the grass would be bright green and full of primroses. The gorse was already in flower, glorious clumps of gold that shone almost as triumphantly as the flowers in the formal garden. In the open spaces of the park, sheep were feeding, with their lambs gambolling about them, and she saw a few deer. Yet though she strained her eyes, and looked this way and that, she did not see the little white horse.

Beyond the park the hills began, those gently rounded green hills of the West Country that presently she would come to love so passionately. They seemed to encircle the valley, rather as the battlemented walls encircled the manor house. Among the nearer hills there was one that she especially liked, a tall conical-shaped hill, with a group of trees on the top, that was like a friendly presence. Against the background of the hills she could see a tall grey church tower, and guessed that the village of Silverydew nestled at its foot.

Then she went to the north window. Below her was a jumble of old weathered moss-grown tiles, the manor-house roof ending in the northern battlements, and immediately beyond them was a pine-wood, stretching away up the slope of a hill; and the pine-wood frightened her. It was so dark and dense and mysterious. . . .

The mysterious alarming Wrolf, she remembered, had come out of the pine-wood. . . . As she stood there, she heard a cock crowing somewhere in the depths of the wood, and the usually reassuring sound was oddly frightening.

An imperious bark behind her brought her attention back to the room. Wiggins had awakened, and was demanding his morning run. At home in London he had always had an airing in the Square garden before breakfast, and he saw no reason why a change of abode should be allowed to interrupt his routine. An airing before breakfast was of great assistance to his digestion.

'Come along, Wiggins,' said Maria, and, seizing her hat, crop, and gloves, she opened the little door, ran down the tower steps with Wiggins at her heels, opened the door at the bottom of the staircase, and found herself in the parlour.

·: 2 :·

Last night she had not seen it properly, but now the light flooding in through the western windows, and the light of the log-fire in the grate, revealed it to her in all its pleading beauty. For it was a lovely little room, but a room that was obviously never used. And it wanted to be used. Every lovely thing in it was simply crying out to be used; only, as this was a lady's room, and no female had set foot in Moonacre Manor for twenty years, the cries had not been heard. . . . But they were heard now. . . .

Almost without realizing what she was doing, Maria flew like a bird to the old harpsichord and alighted on the stool before it, her hat, gloves, and crop flung on the floor, her fingers running up and down over the keys. There had been a harpsichord in the London house, and Miss Heliotrope had taught her to play very prettily, and to sing too. Now, as she played, she looked about her in delight.

The pretty room was panelled in oak, and the western window, with its deep window-seat, looked out on to the rose-garden. Perhaps because of this, the person who had furnished the parlour had made it a rose room. The cream-coloured brocade curtains at the window, torn but beautiful, had little flame-coloured rosebuds scattered over them, and the winged armchair beside the fireplace was upholstered in the same brocade. The Persian rug upon the floor was patterned all over with full-blown golden roses upon a sea-green ground. The six Sheraton chairs that stood stiffly round the walls had seats worked in petit-point, white wild roses with golden hearts, upon a background that echoed the sea-green of the carpet. There were no pink roses anywhere. The creator of this room had not, apparently, been fond of pink.

'Now isn't that a good thing,' said Maria to herself. 'Because I'm not, either. I hate pink. It looks awful with my hair.'

Her eyes went on travelling round the room as she played. There was a lovely graceful Adam fireplace, with the carved woodwork of the mantel sweeping up to form a picture frame, with delicate pillars at the sides and some words carved above. 'The brave soul and the pure spirit shall with a merry and a loving heart inherit the kingdom together.' Within the frame was a queer dim oil painting. Maria had to stare at it for some while before she could make out the subject of it, but when she did make it out her heart suddenly missed a beat. For it showed a little pure-white horse and a brave-looking tawny animal rather like Wrolf cantering along a forest glade together.

Though the painting was so dim that it was hard to see their figures, yet they looked merry, as though they loved each other and liked being together. There were no ornaments upon the mantelpiece, and no other picture over it; the little white horse and the tawny animal reigned there supreme. But upon a table against the wall stood a carved cedarwood workbox, with the lid shut so firmly down that one felt it had not been lifted for years, and a chessboard with its ivory pieces all set out in neat array. The chessmen were beautifully carved, and in this particular set the knights were represented by plumed helmets, while the red pawns had heads like dogs and the white pawns were little white horses. But it was such a long time since anyone had played with them that they looked frozen.

Maria was seized with a great longing to lift the lid of the workbox and to set the chessmen galloping out to battle once more. But she could not leave off playing. A lovely rippling tune that she did not know at all was singing away under her fingers. She had always been good at extemporizing on what Miss Heliotrope called 'the instrument', but she did not feel that this tune was one that she had composed herself; she felt it was a tune that had got shut up inside the harpsichord the last time it had been played, and now it had flown out freed. It was a grand little tune, and Maria abandoned herself to it with joy, until suddenly she left off abruptly. . . . Someone was listening. . . .

There had been no sound, but she was conscious that someone was listening intently to her playing. She got up and ran to the open window and looked out, but she could not see anyone in the rose-garden; only the birds. Then she ran to the door that led from the parlour to the great hall and opened it, and saw that Wrolf was sitting before the fire and that Sir Benjamin, dressed this morning in dark-green riding-clothes, was just entering the hall through a door at the far end. He gave a smile that for geniality and warmth was like the sun rising on the first warm day of the year, but he made no reference to her playing, and she did not think he had heard it.

'How did you sleep, my dear?' he asked.

'I slept well, Sir,' said Maria, and curtsied to him, and then stood on tiptoe to kiss him. This was perhaps rather forward of her, for at that time the young did not kiss their elders unless commanded to do so. But she felt that she loved him so very much. And Sir Benjamin did not seem to mind. On the contrary, he seemed pleased, for, nearly-grown-up young lady of thirteen though she was, he picked her up and gave her a great bear-hug. Then he set her down and, feeling something wet and warm against her hand, she looked round and saw to her astonishment that Wrolf had risen to his feet and was standing beside her licking her hand, his great tail swishing slowly from side to side.

'Look at that now!' cried Sir Benjamin in triumph. 'Wrolf knows it. You're the true Merryweather steel, my dear, and Wrolf knows it.'

Shyly Maria laid her hand upon Wrolf's great head, and with a beating heart dared to look straight into his strange burning yellow eyes. They looked back at her, taking possession of her. She was his now. Suddenly all fear of him vanished, and she flung her arms round his neck and buried her face in his tawny mane.

Then she looked up again at Sir Benjamin. 'I've been looking at the lovely views from my windows, Sir,' she said. 'Which way does your room look?'

'South and east, my dear,' he said. 'There is a second tower, and my room corresponds to the one Miss Heliotrope has. It was my mother's room, when she was alive, but now I use it. The little room above, rather like yours but without the carvings and with a normal-sized door, was mine when I was a boy. But it is too small for me now and is not used any more.' And then with a charred stick he traced the plan of the house on the ashes before the hearth.

The ground floor of the manor was composed only of storerooms and the room where Digweed slept. The great hall, with raftered ceiling reaching to the roof, the kitchen leading out of it on one side and the parlour on the other occupied the first floor. Miss Heliotrope's bedroom was over the parlour and Sir Benjamin's over the kitchen.

'And now,' said Sir Benjamin, 'I'll show you the lie of the land.'

He opened a drawer in the old writing-desk that stood against the wall and pulled out a rolled parchment, let down the flap of the desk and spread it out. 'You can take this and examine it at your leisure whenever you like, my dear,' he told her. 'It shows you the whole of your Royal Highness's Kingdom of Moonacre. But for now just take a quick glance at it and learn the lie of the land.'

It was an old map of the estate, and Maria bent over it with a beating heart; for though it showed her only a few square miles of England's West Country, they were a few square miles that Sir Benjamin said were her very own—her kingdom. And at the right-hand edge of the map was a half-moon of blue that was the sea—Merryweather Bay. . . . It seemed that Maria Merryweather, who had never seen the sea, actually owned a whole half-moon of blue water. . . .

And then to the left was the church that she had seen from her west window, called the Church of Mary the Virgin, and the lovely hill behind it was called Paradise Hill. The names on the map, quite ordinary names though they were, sounded in her head like the notes of some beloved familiar piece of music. She looked up into Sir Benjamin's face, smiling but speechless, and he nodded understandingly.

'You've come home, my dear,' he said. 'But you can't put what you feel into words. No Merryweather can. We don't wear our hearts on our sleeves.'

'Please, Sir,' said Maria, 'what is the meaning of those words that are carved over the fireplace in the parlour?'

' "The brave soul and the pure spirit shall with a merry and a loving heart inherit the kingdom together",' quoted Sir Benjamin. 'That's our family motto, my dear. It's been our motto since the days of the first Sir Wrolf. It refers, I think, to the two sorts of Merryweathers, the sun and the moon Merryweathers, who are always merry when they love each other. It is also, perhaps, a device for linking together those four qualities that go to make up perfection—courage, purity, love, and joy.' Sir Benjamin paused a moment, and then with intense relief suddenly bellowed, 'Sausages!!!'

For a moment Maria thought that Sausage was another thing that one must have to attain perfection, but then a delicious smell told her that her cousin had descended suddenly from the spiritual plane to the material, where she guessed that he was really happier and more at home.

Almost at the same moment the door from the parlour opened to admit Miss Heliotrope in her rustling bombasine skirts, her black shawl and white mob-cap, happy and smiling after an excellent night, most unusually free from the nightmares of indigestion, and the door from the kitchen opened to admit the old coachman carrying an enormous dish of steaming sausages.

'Good morning, Digweed,' said Sir Benjamin.

'Morning, Sir; morning, ladies,' said Digweed.

Seeing him in daylight, without his hat, Maria immediately loved old Digweed. He had wide innocent blue eyes like a baby's, a high wrinkled forehead and a completely bald head. His patched greatcoat had given place now to a mouse-coloured coat and waistcoat, with a big leather apron tied round his waist. The smile that he bestowed on Maria and Miss Heliotrope was sweet and loving, and he set the sausages on the table with a gesture that seemed imploring them to eat the lot.

But they didn't have only sausages for breakfast. Digweed brought in as well a huge home-cured ham, brown boiled eggs, coffee, tea, new-baked bread, honey, cream with a thick yellow crust on the top of it, freshly churned butter, and milk so new that it was still warm and frothing. So wide and delicious was the choice that Maria excelled herself in the way of appetite; and so did Wiggins, whose green dish had now been unpacked and was set before the hearth and filled with sausages by the generous hand of Sir Benjamin himself. . . . Wrolf, it seemed, always had his meals in the kitchen, because he was partial to raw meat and was not a pretty feeder. . . . Even Miss Heliotrope, encouraged by the freedom from nightmare, ventured on a brown boiled egg. As for Sir Benjamin, it was incredible what he ate, and the sight of the family appetite, combined with the sight of his girth, made Maria hesitate a moment over eating sausage as well as egg.

'You need not fear, my dear,' Sir Benjamin reassured her. 'Only the sun Merryweathers run to fat. The moon Merryweathers can eat what they like and remain as slim and pale as a sickle moon.'

Maria smiled broadly and took the sausage.

'Where did the habit come from, Maria?' demanded Miss Heliotrope suddenly.

'I found it in my room,' said Maria.

'I think it would have been better to put on your gown, as usual, for your morning's instruction,' said Miss Heliotrope reprovingly. 'That little parlour will make an excellent schoolroom, and we will set to work as soon as we have finished breakfast.'

Maria looked up with eyes full of a desperate pleading, and found Sir Benjamin gazing at her habit in profound astonishment. He had not, it seemed, noticed it before. But he recovered himself and answered the pleading in her eyes.

'You are too conscientious, Madam,' he said to Miss Heliotrope. 'You should allow yourself a morning of leisure, to settle into your new home and rest yourself after the fatigue of the journey. For this morning, Madam, I will take over the instruction of your pupil for you.'

He spoke with the utmost courtesy but with the utmost firmness too, and Miss Heliotrope yielded at once. Indeed, she was glad to yield, for a quiet morning putting things to rights in her charming bedroom was exactly what she was longing for.

'Now, Maria,' said Sir Benjamin as soon as breakfast was over, 'put on your hat, take a handful of sugar from the bowl, and come along. . . . Wrolf. . . . Wiggins. . . . Come along.' And then, bowing to Miss Heliotrope, 'Good-bye, Madam, have no fear for your charge. She will be safe with me.'

'I know that, Sir,' said Miss Heliotrope, and actually watched her beloved Maria go out of the hall to she knew not what without a tremor, so great was her faith in Sir Benjamin.

'Oh!' cried Maria on a long note of ecstasy, as she stood with her guardian at the top of the flight of steps outside the front door and looked at what was waiting at the foot of them.

·: 3 :·

Digweed was waiting at the foot of them, holding the bridle of a fine strongly built chestnut cob and the leading-rein of a small, round, fat dapple-grey pony with very short legs, a long tail and mane, and a merry eye.

'Atlas and Periwinkle,' said Sir Benjamin, introducing them. 'They are well named, I think. Atlas because he bears up heroically beneath my weight, and Periwinkle because the flower I named her after grows close to the earth and is called by country people Joy-of-the-ground. Periwinkle's legs are uncommonly short, and she is old, and stout to boot, but she covers the ground with the greatest delight.'

But Maria had not stopped to listen to him. She had raced down the steps and was holding out her handful of sugar to Periwinkle. As she felt the soft warm muzzle in her hand, a thrill of joy went through her. With her free hand she patted the little pony's dappled neck and twined her fingers in the long grey mane that fell so untidily, yet so prettily, over the bright sparkling eyes. 'Periwinkle! Joy-of-the-ground!' she whispered, and then, the sugar being finished, she cocked her charming feathered hat on the side of her head, placed one hand in Digweed's outstretched palm and her foot on the mounting-block that stood beside the steps, and swung herself into the saddle as though she had been doing it all her life. . . . Digweed chuckled appreciatively, and Sir Benjamin, descending the steps, gave a great bellow of delighted laughter.

'No need to teach a Merryweather how to ride, Digweed,' he said. 'I'll not insult the little Mistress with the leading-rein.

Take it away.' And with a heave and a grunt he was up on the mounting-block and then upon Atlas's broad patient back, and with Wrolf and Wiggins behind them they were trotting through the bright sunshine and the early spring loveliness of the formal garden, out through the door in the old battlemented walls, and away into the glory of the park.

Maria never forgot that morning. It was not quite true that she did not need to be taught. Sir Benjamin had to teach her how to adjust herself to the rhythm of Periwinkle's trotting feet, how to manage reins and crop, how to hold on when Periwinkle broke into a joyous canter over the sweet turf. But she learned in two hours what most girls of her age would only have learned in two weeks, for she was without fear, and after each tumble she was up again, dizzy and bruised yet laughing, and back in the saddle almost before Sir Benjamin had time to draw rein.

He was hugely pleased with her. He noted that she had grit and skill, and that sense of oneness with her mount that makes the true horsewoman. Periwinkle was pleased too, co-operating in the riding lesson with all her power, and it was obvious that she had fallen as deeply in love with Maria as Maria with her.

'Listen, my dear,' said Sir Benjamin as they trotted homeward again, 'you may go where you like in the valley, in the company of Wrolf or Periwinkle. You must not ramble about the countryside alone, but with them you may go where you will.'

Maria looked up at her guardian with eyes wide with amazement and delight. At this date it was not considered proper for young ladies to go anywhere without a servant in attendance, a custom which had always irked the independent Maria.

'You mean,' she whispered, scarcely believing it, 'that I may go to the village, to Merryweather Bay, and Paradise Hill, with asking your permission first?'

'Not to Merryweather Bay,' said Sir Benjamin. 'There is just that one exception. I would rather you did not go to Merryweather Bay, and I'll tell you why. The fishermen down there are a very rough lot. They are not on good terms with the village people, or with us at the manor. It's a great nuisance, because they refuse to sell us their fish, and a little fresh fish would be welcome now and then. What fish we do get is bought in the market town beyond the hills, and is never really fresh. So avoid Merryweather Bay, my dear, but go anywhere else you like provided Wrolf or Periwinkle, or both, are with you.'

'I don't know what Miss Heliotrope will say about me going out with only the animals,' said Maria. 'In London I wasn't allowed to walk even to the other end of the street unattended.'

'I will talk to her,' said Sir Benjamin. 'A Princess called to rule a kingdom must know it through and through, if she is to reign worthily. And how can she know it, if she is not given the freedom of it?'

Maria gazed at him. This was the second time that he had spoken of Moonacre as hers. Did he mean that when he died she would be his heiress? But the thought of Sir Benjamin dying was so awful that she put the thought away from her and did not pursue it further. Nor did Sir Benjamin, for they were back in the garden again and riding round to the stables on the east side of the house.

The Moonacre stable-yard was entered by a wide archway in the thick stone wall and was an enchanted place. Just inside the archway, as one entered it, stood a tall dove-cot, and the cooing of the doves and the loveliness of their plumage made up a large part of the enchantment. And then it was cobbled with rounded softly coloured stones that looked like opals, with tufts of bright-green moss growing between them, and in the centre of it was a huge well with a stone wall all round it.

Maria dismounted and ran eagerly to the well. Luxuriant ferns grew inside the wall, right down to the water-level, for a roof of weather-worn tiles supported on stone pillars made it all cool and dark inside. The shadowed water was so inky black that when Maria leaned over and looked down she could see herself reflected with a startling brilliance. It was ice-cold, too, as though the water welled up from unimaginable depths.

'Is it very deep?' she whispered with awe to Sir Benjamin, as he too dismounted and tossed his reins to Digweed, who had appeared to take Atlas and Periwinkle to their breakfast.

'No one knows how deep it is,' he answered. 'The water has never been known to fail, even in the longest drought, and in the height of summer it is as cold as it is in January. On the hottest day we can always keep our milk and butter cool. Push aside the ferns, my dear, and see what is behind them.'

Maria did so, and saw that just above the water-level stones had been removed from the wall to make little cupboards, and in them stood bowls of cream and milk and pats of butter folded in scalded muslin. She cried out in delight at the sight of these dark hidden shelves behind the ferns, and thought to herself what wonderful hiding-places they would make for other things besides butter and milk. If she had been a Merryweather lady living here in the days of wars and tumults she would, she thought, have hidden her jewels here.

The stable-yard was bordered to the west by the house, and here another flight of stone steps led up to the back door, with another mounting-block at its foot, and doors to right and left that Sir Benjamin told Maria led to the store-rooms and Digweed's room.

To the south, the stable-yard was bordered by the wall with the archway leading to the garden, to the north by the stables, and to the east by harness-rooms and coach-houses. A tunnel led through the buildings to the east and, looking through it, Maria saw the kitchen garden beyond. She had never explored a place like this before, and when Sir Benjamin took her into them, she was enchanted by the great coach-houses, where the shabby old carriage that had brought them from the station stood beside Sir Benjamin's gig and a little old pony carriage almost falling to pieces with age. She liked the horse-boxes too, the mangers full of sweet-smelling hay, the harness-room, and the great hay-loft above the stables on the north side. Sir Benjamin showed her how to take off Periwinkle's bridle and saddle and how to put them on again, so that she should not be dependent on Digweed, and he introduced her to the other occupants of the stables, the two fat carriage horses, Darby and Joan, Speedwell, the cream-coloured mare that drew the gig, and his great black hunter Hercules, old too, but still possessed of enormous strength and power; as any horse must needs be, to support the weight of Sir Benjamin.

'Who used to ride and drive Periwinkle?' asked Maria suddenly. The pony carriage had obviously not been used for years, but it must have been got for somebody, and Periwinkle had seemed quite used to having a lady on her back.

'Eh?' ejaculated Sir Benjamin, as though he hadn't heard her, though he was not in the least hard of hearing, and then, abruptly: 'Ah, look at those doves in the sunlight, my dear! Did you ever see such a pretty sight?'

And, looking up at those white wings, gleaming like pure snow in the clear silver light of the West Country, Maria thought that, no, she had never seen anything more lovely; unless it had been those seagulls flying inland in the early morning.

'Just time to take a look at the kitchen garden before we go in to dinner,' said Sir Benjamin, and led the way through the archway.

The kitchen garden was an enchanted place too. It was surrounded by old stone walls, those to north and east the battlemented walls, and against them grew fruit trees, plums and peaches, nectarines and apricots. A mulberry-tree, so old that its branches had had to be fastened up with chains, stood in the centre of the garden, with a bench beneath it, and all about it were the neat vegetable patches, with strawberry beds and raspberry canes, currant and gooseberry bushes, and beds of herbs, and between them all were narrow paved paths, hedged with box. There were rather a lot of weeds, but Sir Benjamin explained apologetically that he had no regular gardener. Digweed worked in the garden when he could, and so did Sir Benjamin himself, and so did the shepherd boy, but there was no one regular.

'The shepherd boy?' thought Maria. 'I haven't seen him yet.' And suddenly she felt unreasonably excited because there was a shepherd boy. A door in the east wall led into an orchard, and Sir Benjamin unlocked it, so that Maria might peep through and see the gnarled old apple-trees covered with silver lichen, pear-trees and cherry-trees and medlars. In the tawny grass beneath the trees there were already a few drifts of snowdrops, and presently, Sir Benjamin told her, when she stood among the trees and looked up, she would scarcely be able to see the blue sky for the canopy of pink and white blossom over her head.

Walking back through the kitchen garden towards the stable-yard again, Maria noticed a water-butt to the left of the tunnel and a little latticed window over it, and in the window were pots of beautiful geraniums, extra-large ones of deep salmon pink. In what window did they stand? The coach-houses to right and left of the tunnel had reached to the roof. There had been no lofts over them. Was there a little room over the tunnel? She would have asked Sir Benjamin, but at this moment he pulled out his great turnip watch and gave an exclamation of surprise.

'God bless my soul!' he cried. 'Time has flown. Scarcely time to change for dinner.'

The rest of the day passed quietly. Miss Heliotrope and Maria dined with Sir Benjamin, and afterwards they sat in the parlour, and Maria played and sang to her guardian, while Miss Heliotrope dozed in the winged armchair. And then Digweed brought in the tea-things, and Maria made tea for them all. And then Sir Benjamin went away on business of his own, and Miss Heliotrope and Maria read aloud and embroidered. And then it was time for supper. And then it was time for bed.

It was not until she was in bed, and just dozing off, that it suddenly occurred to Maria that she had not seen the kitchen. Nor Zachariah the cat, who doubtless lived there.

'In the morning,' she said to herself. 'In the morning, quite early before breakfast. I'll go straight away and see the kitchen. . . . And Zachariah.'

Chapter Three

·: 1 :·

But it so happened that the next morning she overslept herself and was awakened by the sound of the knocker on her little front door. Running to open it, she found Miss Heliotrope outside.

'Maria,' said Miss Heliotrope with some sternness, 'it is the Lord's Day. You will not put on your riding-habit this morning. You will put on your best lavender gown. I have already ascertained from Sir Benjamin that—as I expected—it is his habit to attend divine service upon a Sunday morning. We shall attend it with him.'

'Oh,' said Maria. And then added tentatively, 'Perhaps I shall be able to go riding in the afternoon?'

'Certainly not,' said Miss Heliotrope. 'Tearing about on horseback on the Lord's Day would be most unseemly. Now make haste, Maria, the aroma of sausage is already strong in the house.'

Maria quickly washed herself in the warm water that, as before, had been put ready for her, dressed herself beside the fire that the mysterious good person had lit for her while she slept, and then looked about her for the lavender gown.

But she did not have to look far. Upon the top of the chest, where she had found the habit yesterday, it was lying neatly folded, together with her best Sunday pelisse, and bonnet and muff of purple velvet, all trimmed with white swansdown, and her purple silk mittens. And beside the pile of clothes was a big black prayer-book fastened with a gold clasp, and on top of the prayer-book was a bunch of purple violets with the dew still upon them.

Maria unfastened the gold clasp and peeped inside the prayer-book. It was evidently an old book, because the fly-leaf was yellowed with age. On it was written in delicate handwriting, L. M., and then the family motto. Maria smiled, and then blinked, because again she felt rather as though she wanted to cry. 'I'll say my prayers very nicely, L. M.,' she promised. 'I'll say my prayers as well as I can out of your book.' Then she slipped her Sunday gown over her head and fastened the bunch of violets in the front of it.

Sir Benjamin, already dressed for church, was a sight to behold at breakfast. He wore the beautiful satin waistcoat embroidered with roses and carnations, the great ruby ring and the cravat of Honiton lace that he had worn to welcome her on the evening of her arrival, and his huge white cauliflower wig had evidently had a wash and a fresh dusting of powder the night before, for it was whiter than ever. But instead of riding-coat and breeches he wore a coat of mulberry velvet, and mulberry breeches fastened at the knee with silken tassels, and black shoes with silver buckles.

The coat and breeches were shiny at the seams, and so

much too tight for him that when he seated himself at the breakfast table it had to be very slowly and with ominous creakings, and the shoes were very rubbed at the toes. But there was not a speck of dust upon the velvet, and the polish upon the shoes and buckles was so bright as to be dazzling. As for Sir Benjamin's face, it had been shaved and then scrubbed to such an extent that it was absolutely scarlet, with a shine upon it that almost equalled that upon his shoes.

'Cleanliness,' chuckled Sir Benjamin, noting his great-niece's delighted smile as her eyes rested upon him, 'comes next to godliness, eh, Maria? That's always been the opinion of Merryweathers, anyway.'

Digweed drove them to church in the carriage, open today to the sweet air. It had evidently been given a Sunday scrub-up, for the floor was still wet when Miss Heliotrope, Sir Benjamin and Maria climbed into it and seated themselves in a solemn row upon the back seat, Miss Heliotrope in the middle and Sir Benjamin and Maria protectingly upon either side of her.

They looked perhaps a trifle odd sitting there in a row, a little pressed for space because of Miss Heliotrope's hoop and Sir Benjamin's bulk. Miss Heliotrope also of course had an umbrella and her reticule, and they all had large black prayer-books.

But laden though they were with one thing and another in the way of impedimenta, they were entirely eclipsed by Digweed, who had upon the box beside him the very largest musical instrument Maria had ever seen in her life. . . . It was twice the size of Digweed.

'A double bass,' said Sir Benjamin. 'He plays it in church.

He's the chief man in the choir, you know. He's a good musician, Digweed. Grand.'

Digweed smiled, clucked to Darby and Joan, and they were off, watched from the top of the steps by Wrolf and Wiggins standing side by side in a very stately manner. Wiggins looked very tiny beside Wrolf, and Maria felt a little nervous.

'Wrolf—won't—eat—Wiggins, will he?' she whispered falteringly to Sir Benjamin.

'No! No! No!' her guardian assured her hastily. 'Wrolf took possession of you yesterday morning. Don't you remember? Not only you yourself; all that is yours is now under his particular protection. Even though not personally attracted by Wiggins, he would die rather than let harm come to a hair of his head.'

The park was very lovely this morning under the bright silvery sunshine. The promise of spring was a magic in the air that surrounded each flower and tree and scampering lamb with a sort of halo of wonder, as though it were the first flower or tree or lamb that had ever been created. Each glade looked as though it must lead straight into Paradise, and when they stopped a minute, because Darby had a stone in his hoof, they could hear the carolling of the birds like the music of heaven. . . .

But though she looked this way and that Maria did not catch a glimpse of the little white horse. . . . And then she forgot about him, looking out eagerly for the tunnel through the rock by which they had entered the park on their arrival. But the road forked, they swerved away to the right and she did not see it.

'Don't we drive through the tunnel?' she asked Sir Benjamin.

'No, my dear,' he said. 'Don't you remember the map? Moonacre and the village lie together in a cup in the hills. That tunnel pierces right through the hillside into the outer world. Silverydew is not in the outer world, it's in our world.'

And it was so. They drove only a little farther and the road ended at an old broken gate propped open by a stone, and they drove through into the village street.

'What a lovely village!' cried Maria. 'Oh, Sir, it's the loveliest village that ever was!'

'It's your village,' said Sir Benjamin.

'And the people are smiling at me!' cried Maria. 'Sir, the people are smiling at me as though they knew me!'

'They are your people,' said Sir Benjamin, lifting his absurd great hat in acknowledgement of the smiles and curtsies and touching of foreheads that made their journey along the village street seem almost like a royal progress. 'That's right, Maria. Smile and kiss your hand. They have waited for many a long year to have another Princess at Moonacre.'

Maria was right to cry out in delight at the sight of Silverydew and its people. There was not such another village, and there were not such people, in the whole of the West Country. The whitewashed cob cottages were thatched with golden straw and set in neat gardens bright with spring flowers. A stream ran down one side of the village street, and each cottage had its own little stone bridge, that spanned the stream before each garden gate. Behind the cottages were orchards, where the thickening buds were crowded together on the trees.

The cottages all looked prosperous and well cared for, and besides the flowers the gardens had beehives in them and fruit bushes and herb-beds. And the people looked as happy and prosperous as their homes. The children were sturdy as little ponies, healthy and happy, their mothers and fathers strong-looking and serene, the old people as rosy-cheeked and smiling as the children. And their clothes were gay as their gardens, the dresses sprigged with flowers, the bonnets tied with bright ribbons; the colours of the men's well-worn Sunday coats, bottle-green, hyacinth or plum-colour, rather beautified than dimmed by age.

Remembering some ugly things that she had seen in London—tumbledown houses and ragged children and poor barefoot beggars—Maria said to herself: 'This is how it ought to be. This is how it always *must* be in Silverydew. There's nothing I wouldn't do to keep Silverydew always like this.' And she braced her shoulders and tilted her chin and looked very determined indeed.

'Now we are at the lych-gate,' said Sir Benjamin. 'Miss Heliotrope—Madam—let me give you my hand.'

He helped her out of the carriage and offered one arm to her and the other to Maria, and with slow dignity they passed together under the old carved lych-gate and up the steep path through the churchyard to the church porch. Over their heads the bells were pealing joyously such glorious bell-music as Maria had never heard before.

The bells were actually speaking, though just now she was too confused by happiness to catch the words. She looked up to the tall church tower, bright in the sunlight, and then up to the slopes of Paradise Hill beyond, and then up to the bright blue sky above, and was so happy that she thought she would burst.

•: 2 :•

The church was as lovely inside as it was outside, with beautiful soaring pillars like the trunks of trees and arches that sprang upwards like a shout of joy to meet the grand upward curve of the vaulted roof. The windows glowed with the deep rich colours of very old stained glass, and the sun shining through them painted the flag-stones below with all the colours of the rainbow.

To the left of the chancel steps was a tall pulpit, and to the right was a very old small stone chantry with a small doorway, through which Maria could just make out the figure of a knight in armour lying upon his tomb. At sight of him her heart missed a beat, because she knew, without being told, that the chantry was a Merryweather shrine and that he was her ancestor.

Under the east window there was a simple stone altar, spread with a clean white linen cloth, and upon the altar step below was a great earthenware pitcher, filled with the first catkins and branches of glorious golden gorse. Though, of course, ladylike behaviour forbade the turning of her head to look, Maria was aware from the sounds of the scraping of chairs, the muffled voices, and the soft tunings of strings, that over the western doorway there was a gallery, and that the village choir, with the fiddles and cellos and Digweed's double bass, had already arrived.

And in the tall boxed-in wooden pews many worshippers

were gathered, the bonnets of the women and the bare heads of the men just visible to Maria as she passed. Presently, when the villagers they had seen outside had come in also, the church would be quite full. For the people of Silverydew loved their church.

They were at the door of the Merryweather pew, exactly underneath the pulpit, and Sir Benjamin was motioning to her to follow Miss Heliotrope inside. He followed her and shut the door with a click, and now she couldn't see anything of the church any more, except the roof and the tops of the arches and the upper part of the pulpit, for so high were its walls that the pew was like a little room.

There was space on the cushioned seat that ran along the back wall for quite a family; a father and mother and ten children could have sat upon it in a row quite easily, Maria thought, so long as some of the children were quite tiny. And when she came to count the hassocks that stood in a row in front of the seat, she noted that there were twelve of them in order of size—a great big one for the father of the family, and a tiny one, hardly bigger than a toadstool, for the youngest child. A broad shelf ran the length of the wall opposite the seat, broad enough for the father and the sons to put their hats on and the mother and daughters their reticules and parasols.

It was all, in fact, most comfortable and homelike, and kneeling down upon a medium-sized hassock, letting her muff swing on its chain, and laying her prayer-book upon the shelf in front of her, she covered her face with her mittened hands and was glad, because in this pew, as well as in the manor house, she felt that she had come home.

'All people that on earth do dwell, sing to the Lord with cheerful voice.'

The tremendous voice pealing out over her head, nearly made her jump out of her skin. It sounded like a great trumpet announcing the end of the world, and she scrambled up from her knees in alarm, almost expecting to see the roof of the church splitting open like a peapod and the blue sky above rolling up like a scroll to let the angels down. But it wasn't anything of that sort. It was only the Parson announcing the first hymn.

But what a noise! She had thought Sir Benjamin had a powerful voice, but it was nothing to the Parson's. And at first sight she had thought Sir Benjamin an odd-looking elderly gentleman, but in oddness he couldn't hold a candle to the old man in the pulpit. Standing just below him, quite collected and demure again now, her muff still swinging on its chain, and her mittened hands holding her prayer-book, she looked straight up into his face and he looked straight down into hers with a keen searching look rather like Sir Benjamin's when they had first met. He gave a flashing smile, and she smiled back, and from that moment Maria Merryweather and the Parson of Silverydew were firm friends.

But there was no doubt about it, he was a very extraordinary old man, more like a scarecrow than anything else. He was very tall and very thin, and he had a brown clean-shaven weatherbeaten face, fine and keen and proud, and beautifully shaped brown hands with very long fingers, and snow-white hair that nearly touched his shoulders. He wore a black cassock and white bands beneath his chin.

He must have been very old, yet the dark eyes beneath his

bushy white eyebrows flashed fire, and his voice—well, for power and volume it was enough to waken the dead. It was wonderfully clear-cut and articulate too, with just the faintest trace of some foreign intonation that gave it charm and originality. He gesticulated with his hands when he spoke, so that they seemed speaking too.

'Now then, good people of Silverydew,' he cried, his flashing eyes passing over the packed congregation, 'with all your hearts and souls and voices sing praises.' Then he raised his head and glanced at the choir in the gallery. 'And you up there, keep in tune for the love of God.'

Then he suddenly whisked up a fiddle from somewhere inside the pulpit, tucked it under his chin, raised his right arm with the bow clasped in his thin brown fingers, brought it down upon the strings with superb artistry, and swung his people into the winging splendour of the Old Hundredth, with something of the dash and fire of a cavalry officer leading his men to the charge.

What a row! Up in the gallery the fiddlers and the cellists and Digweed played like men possessed. Though she could not see them, Maria could picture their red perspiring faces, and their arms sawing back and forth, and their shining eyes almost popping out of their heads with eagerness and joy. And every man and woman and child in the congregation was singing at the top of his or her voice.

Maria herself sang till her throat ached, with Sir Benjamin upon one side of her bellowing like a foghorn and Miss Heliotrope upon the other trilling like a nightingale. Miss Heliotrope's trilling astonished Maria. She had never heard Miss Heliotrope trill before. She hadn't even known she could trill.

And it seemed to Maria, her imagination running riot to a shocking extent, that beyond the walls of the church she could hear all the birds in the valley singing, and the flowers singing, and the sheep and deer and rabbits singing in the park and woods and fields, and up on the slopes of the great hills. And somewhere the waves of the sea that she had not seen yet were rolling into Merryweather Bay, and crying Amen as they broke upon the shore.

And up there in the tall pulpit stood the Parson playing the fiddle as Maria had never heard a fiddle played before, and never would again, because no one in all the world ever had, or ever would, play the fiddle as superbly as the Parson of Silverydew.

The hymn ended and, with a soft rustling of Sunday skirts and petticoats and a creaking at the seams of Sunday coats that were a bit too tight, the congregation sank upon its knees, while the Old Parson, laying aside his violin and standing very straight with his lean brown hands clasped upon his chest, closed his eyes, lifted his head and began to pray, his tremendous voice slightly lowered now, but so clear and true that if any members of his congregation missed a word here and there no excuse could be made for them unless they were stone deaf.

Maria had never heard anyone pray like this Old Parson, and the way that he did it made her tremble all over with awe and joy. For he talked to God as if he were not only up in heaven, but standing beside him in the pulpit. And not only standing beside him but beside every man, woman, and child in the church—God came alive for Maria as he prayed, and she was so excited and so happy that she could hardly draw her breath.

And when the Old Parson read the Bible to his people, he did not read it in the sing-song sort of way that the parsons in London had read it, a way that had made one want to go to sleep. He read it as though it were tremendously exciting; dispatches dictated on a battlefield, or a letter written only yesterday and bringing great news. And when he preached, taking as his subject the glorious beauty of the world, and the necessity for praising God for it every moment of the day or else standing convicted of an ingratitude so deep that it was too dreadful even to be spoken of, it was as thrilling as a thunderstorm. In London Maria had always thought about her clothes in the sermon or taken an interest in other members of the congregation, but today she only patted the pleats in her pelisse and stroked her muff a very few times, and only once craned her neck in a futile attempt to see a little something over the top of the pew door.

Maria listened spellbound. And when they sang the last hymn, in a way that almost lifted the roof off, she found that she was not tired at all, but feeling as fresh as when the service had started.

After the last Amen had died away, the Old Parson climbed down from the pulpit, and went striding down the aisle, to stand at the west porch and greet his people as they filed out past him. Maria had never seen a parson do this before. But then she had never seen any parson in the least like this old man, or attended any service in the least like this one. Nothing in this enchanted valley seemed in the least like anything anywhere else.

The Old Parson, it seemed, was one of those people who don't in the least mind what they say, for as she went down the aisle Maria could hear his tremendous voice scolding a farmer for beating his dog, a mother for letting her child go to school with a dirty face, a boy for robbing a bird's nest, and a little girl for drinking the milk that had been put out for the cat.

He seemed to know what each of them had been doing during the past week, and his scoldings were so scorching that Maria thanked heaven that he could not possibly know anything of her own past peccadilloes. . . . If he ever really scolded me, I think I should die, she said to herself. . . .

Yet none of his people seemed to resent either his scoldings, or the fact that they were so loudly spoken that the porch echoed with them. They went as red as beetroots, they hung their heads, and they murmured their apologies with real sorrow. In Silverydew, it seemed, the Old Parson was as privileged as though he were a king.

And he could praise too. Now and then the anger went out of his voice, and a deep note of delight stole into it, like wine poured into water. One little girl had helped her delicate mother with the washing, a young husband had minded the baby while his wife had an outing, and a boy had bound up a puppy's injured paw, and to hear the warmth with which the Old Parson commended their deeds, you'd think that at the very least they'd saved Queen Victoria from drowning.

Then the manor-house party reached the porch and the Old Parson was holding Miss Heliotrope's hand and Miss Heliotrope was all of a twitter. Yet she needn't have been, for at sight of her the Old Parson's smile flashed out over his weatherbeaten face, like sunshine over snow. 'Welcome, Madam,' he said, giving her much the same greeting as Sir Benjamin had given her upon her arrival. 'This countryside is honoured by your presence here.' Then they looked at each other most attentively, and it was obvious to the onlookers that they had taken a great liking for each other. It was with reluctance that the Old Parson relinquished Miss Heliotrope's hand, and took Sir Benjamin's instead.

'Squire,' he bellowed in a sudden wrath, 'on Wednesday last I found a rabbit caught in a trap in your park. I have told you before, and I tell you again, that if you permit traps to be set for God's wild creatures on your land you will spend your eternity caught in a trap yourself!'

Sir Benjamin, whose face was red as a beetroot at the best of times and couldn't go much redder, went a deep purple and loosened his stock. 'It's not my fault, Parson,' he said. 'Those black-hearted fellows from Merryweather Bay set traps on my land without my knowledge.'

'I'll put up with none of your excuses, Squire,' boomed the old man. 'You hold your park in trust from God, and every inch of it should be kept constantly beneath your eyes. You stand convicted, Squire, of gross laziness and neglect of duty. Take the necessary steps to see that the cruelty is not repeated.'

Sir Benjamin did not say, as he very well might, that it was quite impossible to keep his eye upon every inch of a park the size of his. He didn't say anything. He just rubbed his great beak of a nose with his forefinger and looked most terribly worried.

Then it was Maria's turn, and she found that she had been

too optimistic in thinking that the Old Parson knew nothing as yet of her faults and failings. 'Neatness of attire is to be commended in a woman,' he told her, holding her hand in a grip of steel. 'But not vanity. Vanity is of the devil. And excessive female curiosity is not to be commended either. Nip it in the bud, my dear, while there is time.'

So he had seen her patting her pelisse and stroking her muff. . . . So he had noticed her trying to see over the door of the pew. . . . She did not hang her head, for that was not her way, but the eyes that she kept unwaveringly upon the Old Parson's face filled with tears, and she blushed rose-pink from forehead to neck. . . . Because she discovered suddenly that the approval of the Old Parson was something that she wanted terribly badly, and she appeared to have lost it already.

But no. The anger went out of his voice, and that warm note of commendation took its place. 'A true Merryweather,' he said. 'Come here whenever you like, child. This church is especially the home of the young.'

Then once more he gave her the flashing smile that he had given her when he had looked down at her from his pulpit, and she curtsied, and then she and Sir Benjamin and Miss Heliotrope once more made a royal progress from the porch to the lych-gate, with Sir Benjamin stopping every minute to introduce her to first one and then another of the smiling villagers. 'The little lady be a true Merryweather,' they kept saying. And one old man whispered to her very low, so that only she heard what he said: 'Be you the one, my dear?' And an old woman whispered: 'Keep a stout heart, dearie, for maybe 'twill be you.'

To these Maria could only reply with a smile, because she did not know what they were talking about.

·: 3 :·

Driving home again in the carriage, Maria asked Sir Benjamin what the Old Parson had meant by saying that the church was especially the home of the young.

'He likes the children of the parish to use the church as a nursery,' said Sir Benjamin. 'He lets them play with the little statue of the Virgin, and the bell, and he tells them stories. I must tell you, Maria, that out in the world beyond our valley Old Parson is regarded as something of an oddity. He is scarcely approved of in some quarters, though here in the valley we love and revere him. He is, of course, unusual. He says what he likes and does what he likes, and has done since he first came here forty years ago. He is the true king of this small kingdom, an aristocrat to the last drop of blood in his body. I've never known what his ancestry was, but I'll eat my hat if there's not royal blood in him somewhere.'

'You say, Sir, that he came here forty years ago?' said Miss Heliotrope.

'About that,' said Sir Benjamin. 'I don't know anything about his past history. The only thing he ever told me about himself was that he was once an atheist, but riding one day in a thunderstorm his horse took fright and threw him, and the bad blow on the head which he received through the fall knocked sense into him. He saw the error of his thought, was converted, and became a priest.'

Miss Heliotrope sighed deeply and was silent until the

manor-house came in sight. Then she suddenly roused herself.

'Maria,' she said, 'you are sitting carelessly. Put your shoulders back. Sit up. After dinner you must spend an hour upon your backboard, before you read our Sunday sermon to me.'

Maria sighed.

'Another sermon?' asked Sir Benjamin in tones of shocked sympathy that were as balm to Maria. 'Why, the one we had this morning lasted a good hour!'

'Every Sunday afternoon,' said Miss Heliotrope firmly, 'Maria reads aloud to me one of the sermons composed by my excellent father.'

'Even on a fine Sunday afternoon?' asked Sir Benjamin, obeying an appealing glance directed at him by Maria over the top of her muff.

'I have never taken weather into consideration in my training of Maria,' Miss Heliotrope informed him. 'In my opinion, too much attention to weather makes for instability of character.'

She spoke so sternly, and her nose looked so alarming, that Sir Benjamin said no more, and neither did Maria. She straightened her shoulders and smiled at Miss Heliotrope because she did not want her to think that she loved her less because they had come to this wonderful place. Wherever she was, whatever she did, however many new and exciting people she would find to love in this new and exciting life, Miss Heliotrope would always be her dearest and her best. Sir Benjamin meanwhile fell into an anxious reverie, and every now and then Maria heard him muttering, 'That trap! They are up to their tricks again! There's no end to it. Just no end.'

In the parlour after dinner, lying flat on the backboard that had now been placed there together with the globe, the lesson books, the quill pens, the pencils, paint-brushes, and watercolour paints that were the paraphernalia of Maria's education, she wondered what it was of which there was no end. Were those wicked men who would not sell their fish to the village people, and set traps in the park, a really serious threat to the happiness of the valley? The people of Silverydew had looked happy and prosperous, but people often had worries which did not show outside. She did not want her people to be worried.

'They shan't be worried,' she said to herself. 'I'll find out what's wrong and put it right. I'll be—what did that old woman say?—"the one" to put it right.'

Then she laughed at herself, for if Sir Benjamin, who knew what was wrong, could not put it right, how could she, who did not know?

'I'll find out,' she said. And when Miss Heliotrope came in with the book of sermons she was lying on her backboard looking so stonily determined that her governess thought she was going to be rebellious and naughty about the sermon-reading.

But Maria jumped up with a loving smile, took the book, and read aloud more beautifully than she had ever done before.

'Dear child!' thought Miss Heliotrope. 'Moonacre Manor seems to have upon her an influence which is all for good.'

Chapter Four

·: 1 :·

The next morning Maria woke up so early that the only light outside her little room was the faint grey light of dawn's beginning. She lay quiet for a little while, listening to the faint country noises, the rustle of leaves, the twitter of birds, the bleating of the lambs in the park, and the cry of an early seagull flying over the roof. Woven together these noises were the notes of a line of music that moved her strangely, as though her heart itself were the keyboard over which the music stirred. Then Wiggins, stretched at her feet, awoke and snorted, and the rather worldly noise that he made (he had a very worldly snort) brought her instantly to remembrance of what she was going to do this morning—find out what the kitchen was like and endeavour to set eyes upon that elusive creature, Zachariah the cat. In the twinkling of an eye she had flung her bedclothes back and leaped out of bed.

She had awakened early, but not too early for the good person who cared for her comforts; as before, her fire was alight, her hot water was waiting for her, and her riding things put ready.

Maria washed and dressed so quickly that the light was still only grey and dim as she and Wiggins stole down the tower stairs. But the curtains had been drawn back in the parlour, and the fire was already lit in the great hall, with a wakeful Wrolf stretched before it blinking at the flames. He got to his feet when he saw her, and stood looking at her, his tawny eyes shining in the dimness with a light that seemed somehow affectionate and welcoming, slowly swinging his great tail. She had the feeling that he was waiting for her; waiting to take her out.

'In a minute, Wrolf,' she said. 'I just want to look at the kitchen.'

Wrolf's tail stopped waving, and the affectionate shining of his eyes changed all in a moment to a frightening blaze of contemptuous anger. . . . Almost he looked as though he might eat her. . . . She sped past him in terror and laid her hand upon the latch of the kitchen door, anxious now not only to see the kitchen but to get away from Wrolf.

But here, in spite of her fear, she paused, for there suddenly flashed into her mind something that the Old Parson had said to her yesterday.

'Excessive female curiosity is not to be commended. Nip it in the bud, my dear, while there is time.'

Gentlemen, it seemed, did not like females to be curious—though it was difficult to see how one could find out what one wanted to know if one wasn't. Sir Benjamin had not shown her the kitchen yesterday, she remembered suddenly. Perhaps he did not want her to see it yet. It seemed to her that the omission was much the same as marking PRIVATE upon the door. Perhaps she had better wait a little. Bitterly disappointed, she dropped her hand from the latch, and with all the courage that she had forced herself to turn back and face the angry Wrolf. . . .

But he wasn't angry any more. . . . His tail was swinging once again, and his eyes beaming with affection. She ran to him and caressed his great head, and was ashamed of herself that she had thought he was going to eat her. Of course he hadn't even thought of such a thing! Hadn't he completely accepted her only the day before yesterday? He had been merely recalling her to honourable Merryweather behaviour.

'I'm going exploring on Periwinkle, Wrolf,' she said to him. 'Come with me and take care of me.'

Immediately Wrolf stalked to the great front door, lifted the latch with his nose, swung the door open with one of his great paws, and preceded her and Wiggins down the steps and along the path to the stable-yard.

Periwinkle, or Joy-of-the-ground, was wide awake in her stall when Maria and Wrolf and Wiggins went in. She whinnied joyfully, and then stood perfectly still while Maria, slowly and fumblingly, because this was the first time that she had done it, saddled her, and adjusted bit and bridle, and then she ambled of her own accord out of the stable to the mounting-block beside the steps leading to the back door, and stood still for Maria to mount her. And then the little cavalcade, Maria on Periwinkle with Wrolf and Wiggins one on each side of her, trotted gaily out of the stable-yard, through the garden, and out through the door under the great archway into the park. It was not locked. Sir Benjamin had told Maria that it was never locked. He liked to feel that the villagers could get to him at any hour of the day or night if they were in trouble.

Maria knew exactly what she wanted to do when she got into the park. Without a moment's hesitation she swung east. She must not go to Merryweather Bay, but she would explore the park in that direction. . . . She might perhaps see the sea in the distance.

The morning was enough to make anyone feel joyous. The tawny grass was still crisp and sparkling with frost under the pony's flying feet, and overhead the swelling buds on the trees, just catching the rising sun, were ruby red against a sky of sheeted gold. The air was like wine, warm and yet still laced with the sharp tang of the frost.

Maria had no difficulty in keeping her seat today. She rode as though she had been riding all her life, managing her reins and crop quite easily, able now and then to lift a hand to her head when her feathered hat threatened to come off.

There were not so many trees in this part of the park, and as she rode they thinned out more and more, the beeches and oak-trees and bushes of golden gorse giving place to solitary groups of wind-twisted pines, with here and there boulders of grey rock pushing their way through the tussocks of heather. To the cold fresh tang of the frost there was added now the salt tang of the sea. Maria had not met with it before, but she knew at once what it was and sniffed joyously.

The seagulls were with her now in even greater numbers, calling to her, leading her on. She looked up at them and laughed and waved her crop. Soon now she might see the sea.

·: 2 :·

But, as it turned out, she did not see it that morning. In mid-gallop she was halted by a strange and terrible sound, a thin high screaming that came threading through the happy sounds of the wind and the crying gulls and Periwinkle's galloping feet, and pushing into her heart like a sharp needle.

She pulled in her pony and sat listening, her heart beating fast with sudden fear. Away to her right, beyond a sombre belt of pine-trees, was a deep hollow filled with gorse and blackberry bushes, and from it came the frightening sound. Somewhere down there some child or animal was being hurt. She hesitated for only a moment, and then, gulping down the fear that had come up like a hard lump into her throat, she turned Periwinkle away from the longed-for sight of the sea and rode hard for the hollow beyond the pines.

The sides of it were so steep and stony, and so thickly grown with gorse, that she had to dismount and, leaving Periwinkle beneath the pine-trees, climb down by herself. Wiggins, after one glance at the prickly gorse, decided to stay under the pine-trees too, and Wrolf did the same, lying down with nose on paws beside Wiggins.

It surprised and hurt her that Wrolf should not come with her, because somehow she had thought he would want to take care of her. It made her more afraid too. But she went on just the same, pushing her way down through the thick bushes, her face and hands getting scratched and torn, and that horrible screaming sound coming nearer and nearer.

As she neared the bottom of the hollow the bushes thinned out, and she could see that down below there was a clear space of turf carpeted with primroses like a round embroidered green carpet. Maria would have exclaimed in delight at the beauty of the place, only the beauty was spoiled for her because on the centre of the carpet was a trap, and caught in the trap was a screaming hare.

Maria did not know it was a hare, because she had never seen one before. She thought it was an outsize rabbit; and immediately she remembered the little scene between Sir Benjamin and Old Parson yesterday, and Sir Benjamin's worried exclamations as they drove home. . . . Who had set that trap?

In a minute she knew, for as she pushed her way down through the bushes to rescue the poor hare she saw another figure coming quickly down upon the other side of the hollow, a tall man dressed all in black: black trousers pushed into black sea-boots, and a black fisherman's jersey, with a matted black beard, carrying in his hand a cruel-looking cudgel, and with a black cock sitting on his shoulder. She could not see him very clearly, because her fear was now not only a lump in her throat but a mist in her eyes, but she knew quite well that he had set the trap and that he was going to kill the hare with his cudgel. . . . That is, if she did not get there first and save it. . . .

She ran, and he, catching sight of her, ran too; but she got there first, catching her foot in a rabbit hole and falling headlong at his feet just as he raised his cudgel to finish off the hare.

'Let that rabbit alone!' she cried, all her fear suddenly lost in a surge of hot anger and passionate love for the hare. 'Let it alone. It's my rabbit! It's my rabbit, I tell you!'

The Black Man laughed and swung up his cudgel again, and it might have gone ill with the hare, and perhaps with Maria too, had it not been for the sudden appearance upon the scene of Someone Else.

Maria, bewildered by her fear, still all in a fury of love and anger, was aware of a slim brown figure bounding towards her, of a curly head lowered like that of a butting goat, and then over went the Black Man flat on his back, well and truly winded, while there rang through the hollow a laugh as merry and carefree as a cuckoo's cry, a boy's laugh, clear as a bell, a Puck's laugh, full of impish glee.

'Quick! Quick!' cried a joyous voice that was as familiar to Maria as the answering beat of her own heart, in equal joy. 'Hold the hare while I unfasten the trap. Then run! There'll be more of them about. The Black Men never hunt alone. Quick!'

They ran to the trap, and Maria, her slim hands clasped about the panting body of the poor hare, in her bewilderment saw no more of her companion than strong brown fingers skilfully loosing the hideous rings of steel that had closed upon the hare's left hind leg. But those brown fingers were as familiar to her as her own white ones.

'Now run!' said the boy, and they ran, the boy going first with the hare in his arms, leaping nimbly up the slope in the direction from which Maria had come.

Maria following after, panting and stumbling in her efforts to keep him in sight. They reached the top of the hollow, and there was Periwinkle still waiting with Wiggins. Wrolf was there too, but he was not lying down now, he was standing planted firmly on his four feet, lashing his tail and growling like a thunderstorm, his great blazing eyes fixed upon the shadows beneath the pine-trees, where black figures skulked, tall thin nightmare figures that were hardly distinguishable from the pine-trees, yet made one afraid, like the yew-tree men in the garden.

Now Maria knew why Wrolf had not come down with her into the hollow; he had stayed up here to keep those nightmare figures at bay. He had known better than she did how he could best be of service to her.

'Canter for home!' commanded the boy, and Maria scrambled into the saddle and they were off, the boy running on one side of her with the hare in his arms, and Wiggins running on the other. . . . Wrolf stayed behind.

Within sight of the manor, Periwinkle stopped cantering and slipped into a gentle ambling trot, for the danger, it seemed, was left behind now. Maria had got her breath back and her wits about her again and was gazing wonderingly and joyfully at the boy beside her, and he was looking back at her and laughing.

He was just the same, just as he had been in her dream the night before. He had not changed at all since those days when he had come to play with her in the Square garden; except that he had grown, even as she had, so that he was still a head taller than she was.

His dark eyes still sparkled with fun when he looked at her. His thick chestnut hair still curled tightly all over his head, with the final curl making a comic twist in the back of his neck, like a drake's tail. His rough brown coat was still the colour of fallen beech leaves, and the battered old hat that he swung in one hand still flaunted the long green feather.

'Robin!' she cried reproachfully. 'Why did you leave off coming to the Square garden?'

'We were getting too old for those children's games,' he said. 'Soon you would have been bored with them, and as soon as you had begun to be bored you wouldn't have believed in me any more. People only believe when they are interested. It was better to go away before you began to be bored. I knew you'd come to Moonacre. I knew I'd see you again. You won't be bored by what we have to do together here—my word, you won't! You'll be frightened, but you won't be bored.'

'What *are* we going to do together here?' demanded Maria.

'You'll soon know,' said Robin.

Maria choked down her curiosity, for Robin had always hated being asked questions, and if she asked too many would just disappear, and she did not want him to disappear just yet.

·: 3 :·

They went together to the stable-yard, sat on the parapet of the well, and attended to the hare. It was frightened no longer, but nestled up to Robin with complete confidence. He bathed its hurt leg with water from the well and bandaged it with Maria's handkerchief torn into strips. And he did it all so skilfully that the hare did not seem to feel any pain.

'There!' he said when he had finished and put the creature into Maria's arms. 'There you are. She's your hare.'

'Hare!' exclaimed Maria. 'Why, I thought she was an extra-large rabbit!'

Robin laughed. 'Rabbits are all right,' he said. 'Rabbits are jolly little beggars, and they're fun to keep as pets. But a hare, now, is a different thing altogether. A hare is not a pet but a person. Hares are clever and brave and loving, and they have fairy blood in them. It's a grand thing to have a hare for a friend. One doesn't often, because they have a lot of dignity and keep themselves to themselves; not like rabbits, who are always underfoot; but if you *do* win the love of a hare—well—it's a fine thing for you. . . . And you've done it.'

Maria looked down at the beautiful creature lying in her lap, still and tranquil, and very tenderly she stroked the long silky ears. Now that she looked at her hare attentively, she saw that it was almost an insult to compare her with a rabbit. She was of a far more substantial build and had a regal air. Her fur was silver-grey, soft and fine, and her ears were so large that they were more like banners than ears; but though large they were beautiful and graceful, and lined with superfine pink velvet. Her tail was not an absurd little white bobble of a thing, like a rabbit's, but an exquisite fountain of white fur that drew attention to the strength and grandeur of her finely shaped hind legs. Her front legs were fine legs too, but lacked the poise of the hind ones. Her eyes were large and dark and lustrous, and her silver whiskers twice the length of Wiggins's. . . .

Wiggins eyed the hare with profound disfavour. . . . She was slightly larger than he was, and her beauty constituted a challenge to his own that he was not disposed to take lightly. He sat down abruptly and, with his back to the hare, scratched himself. The action was a studied insult, but she seemed not to mind. She was obviously a hare of a serene disposition.

'I shall call her Serena,' said Maria. 'Do you know, Robin, I loved Serena on sight, and when I saw her in the trap I was so angry at the way she had been treated that I wasn't afraid any more.'

There was no answer, and looking up she saw that Robin had disappeared, even though so far as she knew she had not asked a single question. But though annoyed she was not upset, because she knew he would come back again. . . . They had that job of work to do together. . . .

She handed Periwinkle over to Digweed, who appeared at this point, grinning from ear to ear, and went round into the garden, and up the stairs to the front door, with Serena in her arms and Wiggins at her heels. Sir Benjamin was standing at the front door, smoking a long clay pipe. Behind him in the hall the table was laid for breakfast and the fire was burning brightly, and before the fire lay Wrolf, fast asleep.

'I felt a bit anxious when he came in without you,' said Sir Benjamin.

'We came home separately,' explained Maria. 'We fell in with some poachers. Wrolf stayed behind to chase them away while I came on with Serena, my hare, whom we rescued from them.'

Maria did not say a word about Robin. She had made up her mind not to mention him to any of the grown-ups. They would only tell her she had imagined him.

At the mention of the poachers Sir Benjamin looked a bit worried, but he said nothing. Then he gazed at Serena, and Serena gazed at him.

'Serena is not to be put in a pie,' said Maria firmly. 'She is my friend, and is never, never to be eaten. Eating rabbit is bad enough, but eating hare is a crime.'

'My dear,' said Sir Benjamin, 'I seldom eat hare, and when I do I have it not in a pie but jugged in port wine—my best port wine—a royal mode of cookery that befits so regal an animal.'

'You're not to jug Serena,' said Maria.

'My dear, I wouldn't dream of jugging Serena,' said Sir Benjamin very humbly indeed.

And the respect with which he gazed at Serena was only equalled by the respect with which he now gazed at Maria. His young ward, he realized, would not need much managing. She was much more likely to manage him.

Chapter Five

·: 1 :·

Maria had expected to find it dreadfully difficult, that morning, to concentrate upon lessons with Miss Heliotrope in the parlour. The out-of-doors of Moonacre was so wonderful, so full of mystery and adventure, that while she had been eating her breakfast she had felt that every minute that she spent indoors would be a torment.

Yet when she and Miss Heliotrope were seated before the log fire in the cool parlour, the west window wide open to the rose-garden, all feeling of restlessness left her, and a lovely feeling of peace took its place. To please Miss Heliotrope, she had taken off her riding-habit after breakfast and had put on a full-skirted green linen gown that echoed the green of the chair-seats and the carpet, and so she felt in place in this lovely room and a part of it. Wiggins had followed them in and was sleeping upon one side of the hearth, and Serena, accommodated in a rush basket that Sir Benjamin had found for her, was sleeping upon the other. Wrolf, Maria knew, was still asleep before the fire in the hall, though they had left the door ajar so that he could come in if he wanted to. Digweed was at work in the formal garden, and Sir Benjamin had ridden out to visit one of his tenants at an outlying farm. So far as Maria knew, she and Miss Heliotrope were the only people in the house—apart from the animals, who were so deeply asleep that they hardly counted.

Maria looked round the room. The harpsichord, from which she had liberated that lovely tune, looked alive now it had been played upon, but the chessmen and the workbox were still frozen. The workbox in particular drew her like a magnet. She simply must lift the lid and find out what was inside.

'Please, Miss Heliotrope, may I sew this morning?' she asked.

'Certainly not,' said Miss Heliotrope severely. 'You sew on Fridays. Today is Monday. On Mondays you study the art of reading verse aloud—an art in which you are by no means as proficient as you should be.'

Maria opened her mouth to protest and then, glancing up at the strange dim picture over the hearth, shut it again. Patience. Patience. The little white horse and the tawny animal, galloping together along that forest glade, seemed in no hurry to arrive. They had perhaps been galloping for years, yet the happiness that breathed from the picture was untarnished by the least shadow of impatience. One did not hurry in the country. She got up, fetched the poetry books from the pile that had been stacked in the corner of the window-seat, and spread them out on the rosewood table.

First she read aloud from a little book with a worn olive-green cover, a volume of French poetry that belonged to Miss Heliotrope. It had been given to her in her youth, she had told Maria, by a French refugee who had fled to England to escape one of the revolutions France was always having, and had taken rooms in the Cornish village of which Miss Heliotrope's father had at that time been rector.

Miss Heliotrope had taught him English and had given him a book of English poetry, and he in return had taught her French and given her this French poetry book. Her name, Jane Heliotrope, was written on the flyleaf in most beautiful handwriting, and beneath it he had put his own name, Louis de Fontenelle. Today it occurred to Maria to ask Miss Heliotrope what he had been like.

'He was a very handsome young man, tall and dark,' Miss Heliotrope said, 'and very aristocratic—a marquis. Very gifted also, a skilled linguist and musician, a scholar and scientist. And he was a man of action too—in his early youth he had been a cavalry officer. But, alas, like so many Frenchmen, he was that terrible thing, an atheist, a man who did not believe in God. When my father found that out, he would not permit him to come to the Rectory again.'

'What happened to him?' Maria asked.

'He just went away,' Miss Heliotrope replied with a gentle sigh and, though burning to ask a thousand questions, Maria held her tongue between her teeth and said no more, for there was a finality about Miss Heliotrope's sigh that forbade them.

Usually Miss Heliotrope listened intently while her pupil read aloud and corrected her mistakes very severely indeed, but this morning she seemed a little inattentive, as though the revival of old memories had made her want to go away and be by herself.

'That will be enough reading for today, my dear,' she said when Maria reached the end of a poem. 'Now I should like you to compose a little poem yourself. Meanwhile, dear, I'll just slip upstairs and mend the curtains of that four-poster of mine. As we noticed upon the evening of our arrival, no one ever seems to do any patching or darning in this house.'

'I know what I'd like to write,' said Maria. 'There's a tune that I played the other morning. It came out of the harpsichord when I opened it. May I write words for it?'

'You may, dear,' said Miss Heliotrope. 'I can, I know, trust you not to idle, but to remain in that chair in a decorous ladylike position, feet together, back straight, until your composition is completed to the best of your ability.'

Then, picking up her skirts upon either side, she disappeared through the little door to the turret staircase.

Maria fetched pen and paper and settled herself once more in her chair before the fire. But though obedient up to a point, she was perhaps not altogether obedient, her position being hardly decorous. For though she kept her back straight she swung her feet angrily, making a swishing sound among her petticoats. She disliked being thwarted in this way. She had wanted to see the kitchen, the cat, and the sea before breakfast, and she hadn't been allowed to see any of them. And now she wasn't allowed to lift the lid of the workbox. It was too bad of Moonacre.

'Song' she wrote at the top of her paper, the ink spluttering from her angry nib. . . . Ah, but she had seen Robin. The sight of Robin had come like a reward to a good girl, because she had not pushed her way into the kitchen. . . .

Moonacre *was* showing her things, but in its own time and its own way. She must just be patient.

She smiled, threw the blotted piece of paper in the fire, took a fresh sheet, and began again; and to her surprise, in spite of her rebellious mood, the simple little words came easily, fitting themselves to the tune that had come out of the harpsichord. It didn't seem to her that she made them up at all. It seemed to her that they flew in from the rose-garden, through the open window, like a lot of butterflies, poised themselves on the point of her pen, and fell off it on to the paper.

SONG

Like a spear, like a sword
Drawn most slenderly fine,
As bright and as tempered,
This lady of mine.

Like the wind, like the waves,
Like winged arrows in flight,
As merry my love,
And as swift in delight.

Like a sigh, like a song,
That is plucked from the strings,
Like the dawn and the dew
And the stirring of wings.

Like a star, like the moon,
In her glimmering pride,
Like the ghost of a dream
To her love denied.

When she had finished she went to the harpsichord, opened it, and played and sang her song right through. . . . But no, it wasn't her song, it was somebody else's. . . . And again she was sure there was someone listening out in the rose-garden. She ran to the window and looked out, and just for a moment she thought she saw a small figure, more like a fairy than a human being, moving out there. But when she looked again there was nothing to be seen except the tangled briars and all the lovely little birds with their rainbow-coloured wings. They were singing gloriously this morning, twittering and chirping and carolling and shouting and fluting and humming in praise of spring, until it was a wonder they did not burst their throats. What was the bird that hummed like that? Maria had heard of hummingbirds, but she had not thought that they lived in England. The humming, which had been just a small thread of sound at first, grew louder and louder, until it did not sound like humming at all, but like a powerful kettle on the boil. And it did not come from the rose-garden but from the room behind her. She turned round, and there, seated before the fire, between the sleeping Wiggins and Serena in their respective baskets, staring into the flames and purring loudly, was a black cat.

·: 2 :·

Zachariah.

Maria held her breath and stared. Never in all her born days had she seen such a cat. He was enormous, twice the size of any cat she had ever seen in London. His black fur was short, but so exquisitely glossy that it gleamed like satin. His tail stretched out along the floor behind him for a good yard and looked like a fat black snake; the tip of it, slightly lifted, was twitching from side to side, suggesting that in spite of that tremendous booming purr Zachariah's temper was something that had to be reckoned with. He had a noble head, with a great domed forehead, and large but beautifully shaped ears. His chest, as was only to be expected when one considered the volume of sound that came out of it, looked unusually powerful, and so did his broad shoulders and haunches and strong paws.

He was altogether a most imposing-looking animal, and when he turned his head and his great emerald-green eyes blazed out at her, she was almost as scared as she had been when first introduced to Wrolf. He was of a solitary disposition, she remembered Sir Benjamin telling her, and she did not like to approach him without his permission. She just stood where she was and dropped him a curtsy.

This piece of politeness seemed to please him, for he arose and approached her, arranging his tail in the air over his back in three neat coils and stepping forth over the sea-green carpet with a dignity that was almost shattering. When he arrived at Maria, he began walking round her in circles, each circle a little narrower than the one before, until at last he was going round and round against her skirts, pressing so close that she could feel the vibration of his purring against her legs.

Then and then only, did she dare to bend down and touch his head with her fingers. . . . It was exquisitely soft. . . . He did not seem to mind. He circled against her legs once more, then abruptly ceased purring, and led the way towards the half-open parlour door. With a beating heart Maria followed him through into the hall.

Wrolf was awake but did not, this time, express any dissatisfaction with Maria's purpose—though visiting the kitchen this time was not, strictly speaking, Maria's purpose but Zachariah's. . . .

Zachariah stood upon his hind legs and knocked up the latch of the kitchen door with one blow of his powerful right paw. He went in, Maria following, and Wrolf arose and pushed the door shut behind them.

Maria, in the kitchen, once more stood and gazed. The kitchen was glorious, flagged with great stone flags scrubbed to the whiteness of snow, and nearly as big as the hall. Its ceiling was crossed by great oak beams from which hung flitches of bacon and bunches of onions and herbs. It had two open fireplaces, one for boiling stews and cooking pies, and another, with a spit, for roasting. There were two oval bread-ovens set in the thickness of the wall, and hanging from hooks all round the walls were pots and pans, so well polished that they reflected the light like mirrors. There was a large wash-tub in one corner, and against the wall an enormous oak dresser where gay china stood in neat rows; and an oak table stood in the centre of the room. There were several doors which Maria guessed led to the larders and the dairy. The windows looked out over the stable-yard, so that the morning sun filled the room, and the whole place was gay and bright and warm and scrupulously clean. There were no chairs, but a wooden bench against the wall, and several three-legged wooden stools. One of these stools had been pulled up to the table, and standing upon it, facing Maria as she came in, was a little hunchbacked dwarf making pastry. He gave a brief nod and pointed with his rolling-pin to the bench against the wall.

'Marmaduke Scarlet, at your service, young Mistress,' he said in a crisp squeaky voice. 'Seat yourself, but do not articulate. I cannot indulge in conversation while I am engaged in the creation of a veal pie.'

Yet though his manner was abrupt he seemed well-disposed towards her, for there suddenly flashed across his face a smile so broad that the ends of it seemed to run into his ears, and his small round sparkling black eyes twinkled at her very pleasantly. Yet Maria was heartily thankful that Wrolf had prevented her from entering his kitchen uninvited this morning, for there was something about him that told her he was not a person to be taken liberties with. She crossed to the bench, sat down, and folded her hands very humbly in her lap.

Zachariah, meanwhile, mounted upon another stool beside the dwarf, and sat there purring and swinging his tail and occasionally stretching out a huge paw and helping himself very daintily to a piece of pastry. It was obvious that these two were affectionate and inseparable companions, and that he was privileged. And there wasn't much difference in their size, Zachariah being nearly as big as the dwarf.

Sitting humbly on her bench, Maria looked at the dwarf. He wasn't looking at her now, he was absorbed in his pastry, and so she was able to have a real good stare. Never had she seen such a creature, and her lips parted slightly in astonishment.

He must, she thought, be very old, for the fringe of

whisker that encircled his whole face like a ham frill was snow white, and so were his bushy eyebrows. Except for the whisker frill, his face was clean-shaven, brown as an oak-apple, and criss-crossed with hundreds of little wrinkles. His nose was so snub that there seemed very little of it; but what there was of it was evidently sensitive, for it quivered as he worked, like a rabbit's. His sense of smell, like that of all good cooks, was obviously very highly developed indeed. His large mouth was a great half-moon of generosity when he smiled, a rat-trap of determination when he shut it. His brown ears were much too big for the rest of him, but they were beautifully shaped and tapered to a delicate point, like a fawn's. His arms, too, were much too big for the rest of him, and when he let them hang down his big brown hands reached nearly to his ankles. His feet, on the contrary, were small and dainty as a child's, but he was very bow-legged and his hump was as pronounced as that of Mr Punch.

But in spite of being so oddly assorted in the matter of limbs he was, nevertheless, a delight to the eye because of the sparkling cleanliness of his person and the brightness of his clothes. Upon his head he wore a scarlet skull-cap. His coat and breeches were heather-coloured, and were worn with an emerald-green waistcoat, embroidered with scarlet poppies. His worsted stockings were heather-coloured too, and his brown shoes were ornamented with shining silver buckles. He wore a snow-white apron with a bib to it, to protect his finery while he worked.

It was a delight to watch Marmaduke Scarlet making pastry, for if ever a man was a master-craftsman at his work that man was Marmaduke. He wielded his rolling-pin like a king's sceptre, and so light was his pastry that it looked more like sea-foam than dough as he flicked it over on his board. Beside him stood a great dish full of succulent chunks of veal and ham, hard-boiled eggs, parsley, and chopped onion. Maria's mouth watered as she looked at it, and when he swung the great oval of white pastry over it she had to swallow hard. Then he started to make the decorations for the top of it, his skilful fingers pinching out flowers and leaves from the dough with an artistry that any sculptor might have envied.

When it was done he carried it to one of the fireplaces, where a log fire was burning low, cleared a space for it, set it on the hearth, and covered it with an iron cover and then with a mound of hot ashes. Then he went to one of the bread ovens and opened the iron door, and inside Maria saw that a bundle of burning faggots was just dropping to hot ash, and that the bricks that lined the oven were glowing hot. Marmaduke raked the ashes to one side, lifted a white cloth from two great bowls on the floor, where the bread had been set to rise, put the loaves in the oven, and slammed the door.

Then he went through one of the doors in the wall, through which Maria could see a cool stone-vaulted larder, and came back with a big blue bowl full of eggs and a blue jug of cream; and, mounting once more upon his stool, he proceeded to make a syllabub. Twelve eggs went to the making of the syllabub, a pint of cream, and cinnamon for flavouring.

'I wonder now,' thought Maria to herself, 'will Miss Heliotrope be able to eat that syllabub after that pie?'

But she need not have worried, for it appeared that Marmaduke's sensitive quivering nose had scented from afar a box of peppermints in Miss Heliotrope's reticule. For as soon as he had whisked up the syllabub he made a nice plain junket, with a dash of brandy in it, and nutmeg on the top.

'For her first course,' he squeaked, suddenly breaking a silence that had lasted for a very long time, 'there will be a coddled egg.'

It seemed that Marmaduke Scarlet had finished cooking for the moment. He stacked his cooking things neatly together, fetched a big red earthenware bowl, and filled it with warm water from the kettle on the hearth. . . . Maria dared to speak at last.

'If you are going to wash up, may I dry?' she asked humbly.

Marmaduke Scarlet considered the question. 'Are you able to give me your absolute assurance that you are not a smasher?' he demanded.

'I don't think I am,' said Maria. 'Of course I don't really know, because I've not dried up before.'

'Are you accustomed to drop your hairbrush when arranging your coiffure of a morning?' demanded Marmaduke.

'No, never,' Maria assured him.

'Then you may dry,' he said graciously. 'You may take one of those dishcloths from the line, fetch yourself a stool, and give me the benefit of your assistance during those ablutions that necessarily, though unfortunately, invariably follow the exercise of the culinary art.'

Marmaduke Scarlet, it seemed, made up for the shortness of his stature by using very long words in conversation. It struck Maria that if she had much to do with him she would need to keep a dictionary in her pocket.

She fetched the cloth and stool as bidden, and the three of

them, Maria and Marmaduke and Zachariah the cat, grouped themselves in a row at the table, Marmaduke standing on his stool and Maria and Zachariah sitting; and Marmaduke washed and Maria dried and Zachariah just purred. Marmaduke looked quite sunny and good-tempered now that he was no longer cooking, and Maria dared to ask him the question that had been burning on the tip of her tongue ever since she had observed his tiny size.

'Please, Mr Scarlet,' she asked, 'is it you who looks after me in my room, lighting my fire and bringing me warm water and milk and sugar biscuits?'

Marmaduke gave her another of his glorious wide benevolent smiles, the ends of it running right up into his ears. 'Naturally, young Mistress,' he squeaked. 'Who else in this establishment, besides yourself, is of sufficiently delicate stature to get through the aperture that leads to your bed-chamber? And if for any reason I don't wish to be seen passing through the hall, I climb up the cedar-tree from the garden and into your room through the window to do for you those small services that are my duty.'

'Thank you, oh, thank you,' said Maria. 'And do you put those lovely clothes ready for me, and lay the little bunches of flowers on them?'

But now, alas, she had said the wrong thing. Marmaduke's face darkened like a thundercloud, his smile broke abruptly in half, the two ends disappearing into his ears like rabbits bolting into their burrows, his great bushy eyebrows beetled at her, and his eyes shot sparks, and when he spoke his voice ceased to be a squeak and boomed at her like a roll of thunder.

'Does my appearance suggest that of a female lady's maid?' he demanded. 'Does any self-respecting male concern himself with ribbons and laces and female rubbish? Allow me to inform you, young Mistress, that if there is one thing in this universe for which I have not the slightest partiality it is a female. And my master, the Squire, entertains in his bosom the same sensations of distaste for the daughters of Eve as those that lodge in the breast of his humble retainer. Until you and your lady governess arrived upon the steps of this mansion no female had darkened our doors for twenty years.'

This was awful.

'But Miss Heliotrope and I couldn't help being born females,' faltered Maria.

'I am unaware that we have blamed you for it,' said Marmaduke. 'It is my distinct impression that we have received you with our best courtesy and cookery, and made the best of an unfortunate circumstance that admitted of no circumlocution.'

'You've both been very kind,' faltered Maria.

The ends of Marmaduke's smile suddenly came out of his ears and attached themselves to the corners of his mouth again.

'The circumstances might have borne upon the Squire and myself with more heaviness than has actually been the case,' he conceded kindly. 'You, Mistress, are of tender years; and femininity, my dear young lady, grows on a female with the passage of time, like all bad habits, and is less objectionable in the early stages. And as for your lady governess, she is a distinct improvement upon that other duenna, who resided here before with the other young mistress, and never stopped asking questions. Through the keyhole I have perceived her to be a woman of great saintliness of character and weakness of digestion, characteristics which, by concentrating a lady's mind upon her own soul and stomach, do not allow her to indulge in that feminine curiosity about the affairs of others which renders her presence so trying to the males whose domicile she shares.'

Maria flushed rosily and refrained from asking who it was who laid out her clothes for her. She was also afraid to ask about the other young mistress, and that other duenna, though she was dying to ask who they were. Nor did she dare ask Marmaduke Scarlet where his bedroom was, though she was dying to ask that too, because she could not think whereabouts in the house it could possibly be.

'Young Mistress,' said Marmaduke, 'the fact that I am disposed to look upon your presence here with favour does not mean that I desire to have you running in and out of my kitchen all day long. I do not. My kitchen is my private domain, to be entered only on my invitation. That invitation will be conveyed to you from time to time by myself, or by Zachariah the cat.'

And then with a wave of the hand and a courteous bow he signified, as a king might do, that the interview was now at an end. Maria curtsied to him and withdrew humbly, Zachariah attending her as far as the kitchen door and standing on his hind legs to lift the latch for her.

She raced through the hall and the parlour and up the tower stairs to Miss Heliotrope's room.

'Miss Heliotrope,' she gasped, 'there *is* a cook, a funny frightening little dwarf with a white beard and a scarlet cap, who uses dreadfully long words and doesn't like females. . . . But he doesn't mind *us* so much because you're so good and I'm so young. He brings our hot water and lights our fires, but he doesn't see to my clothes. . . . Miss Heliotrope, who *does* see to my clothes?'

Miss Heliotrope, darning needle in hand, turned from the mending of her curtains. 'Some woman,' she said. 'They may say what they like, Maria, about no woman having entered this house for twenty years, but there *is* a woman about the place. . . . Look at this.'

She opened the bottom drawer of her chest of drawers and beckoned to Maria to come and see. Tenderly laid out in the drawer were three lace fichus and three mob-caps trimmed with heliotrope ribbon. And between the folds of the fichus were three little lavender-bags made of white muslin, each embroidered with a different heliotrope flower—a violet, a pansy, and an autumn crocus.

'It is real Honiton,' said Miss Heliotrope in a sort of ecstasy. 'Real Honiton—quite priceless—such as I've always longed for. And those ribbons—my favourite colour—echoing my name—and the flowers on the bags—I never saw such perfect embroidery. Maria, I ask you, could any *man,* any mere *man,* have prepared that drawerful of delight that you see before you?'

'No,' said Maria.

Chapter Six

·: 1 :·

When she woke up the next morning, Maria found to her great surprise that her riding-habit had not been put ready for her. Instead there had been laid out a very decorous dark-blue gown with plain white linen collar and cuffs, a dark-blue cloak, and a dark-blue straw bonnet with delphinium-blue ribbons.

Maria was not very fond of this costume. In spite of the ribbons, it was rather a sombre and serious outfit, and it made her feel as serious as itself. However, she knew better than to put it away and get out her habit, for she realized now that what she did day by day was not left entirely to her own choice. She was more or less under orders. And it seemed that her orders today did not include riding.

She put on the blue gown slowly, her mood in tune with the grey day outside her windows. There was no sun to be seen today, no blue sky. Grey clouds hung low over the world. But it was warm and still, and bird-song rose up to her from the rose-garden under her west window. She hoped it would not rain, for she knew that Digweed had driven off in the gig very early this morning to make some purchases in the market-town beyond the hills that enclosed the valley, and she would not like him to get wet.

With her cloak over her arm and her bonnet swinging from her hand, leaving Wiggins still sleeping on her bed, she went down to the parlour, opened the window, and looked out at the tangled briars where now a few fresh green leaves were unfurling. There seemed more birds than ever this morning, their bright wings like flowers among the branches. They were singing so lustily that she felt that she must sing too. She crossed the room, opened the harpsichord and sang the little song that she had liberated from it.

She went on singing until, once more, there came to her the knowledge that there was a listener in the rose-garden. She got up, went to the open window and looked out. And this time the listener was not the small fairy-like figure who had vanished like a dream, but a tall old man who came out from among the rose-trees and came up to the window and held out his hand to her.

It was Old Parson. Without a word Maria put on her bonnet and cloak, climbed up on the window-sill, stepped out of the window, took his hand, and jumped down beside him; and hand in hand and in silence they walked through the rose-garden and the formal garden and out into the park.

Old Parson walked fast, moving with long strides, like quite a young man. He looked very purposeful indeed this morning, and a little grim, and the lean hand that held Maria's held it hard and possessively. He had some business with her, that Maria knew. But she was not afraid. And when he turned and smiled down at her she was more than not afraid; she was elated. She had the feeling that her introduction to Moonacre was more or less complicated, and that today the purpose of her being here would declare itself.

'Where are we going, please, Sir?' she dared to ask.

'To the church,' said Old Parson. 'I have much to show you there. And after that you will take breakfast with me at the Parsonage. It is early yet, but there is much to say and much to do, and we are well-advised to make an early start.'

'Will they be anxious about me if I am not back to breakfast?' asked Maria.

'No,' said Old Parson. 'I left a message with Zachariah the cat.'

·: 2 :·

They took the way that the coach had taken on Sunday, and came out through the broken gate into the village street, and so to the lych-gate. They walked up through the churchyard to the church, and Old Parson pushed open the heavy door and bowed courteously to Maria as she preceded him inside. 'Why!' she cried in astonishment. 'The church is full of children!'

'Children wake up very early in the mornings,' said Old Parson, 'and are a great nuisance to their parents, getting in their mothers' way while the breakfasts are being prepared, or else following their fathers out to the milking, and irritating the cows by their noise and clatter. I therefore gather them together here and keep them amused until their breakfasts are ready for them.'

They had entered quietly, and Maria had a moment or two

to look about her before the children saw her. There were perhaps about thirty boys and girls in the church, none of them more than about twelve years old, and quite a number of small toddlers of two or three. They looked like flowers in their gay bright clothes, and they were gathered in happy groups all about the church, chattering like starlings and intent upon various mysterious games.

'Children!' called Old Parson, leading Maria up to the clear space by the chancel steps. 'Children. Maria Merryweather is with us.'

He spoke as though this were something very important, and the children evidently thought it was too, for they left their games and came crowding round Maria, smiling at her with shy friendliness.

'Show her the Lady and the Bell,' Old Parson commanded them. 'And then later we will sing her the Bell Song.'

Maria's right hand was taken by a pretty little girl as tall as herself, with curly fair hair and a forget-me-not blue dress, whom later she discovered to be Prudence Honeybun, the innkeeper's daughter, while a little round fat brown boy of four years old or so, whose roundness and brownness and glossiness reminded her of a horse-chestnut, attached himself limpet-like to her left hand. His name, the other children told her, was Peterkin Pepper.

Judged by the standards of today, the children of Silverydew had not a great number of toys in the church; indeed, they only had two, but as they were more than satisfied with what they had they were not to be pitied at all; and looking at these treasures through their eyes, Maria quite understood their satisfaction.

First they showed her the Bell, which stood upon the floor near the pulpit. It was a very old bell, and they told her that once there had been a monastery at the top of Paradise Hill, and that the bell had hung in the tower of the monastery church and seven times a day it had rung the monks to prayer, and the people in the valley below, hearing the Bell, had prayed too. They rang it to show Maria what a sweet tone it had, and they told her Old Parson let them use it when they played at being the monks, and when they played at christenings and weddings, or at being the bell-ringers.

'The Silverydew Church bells are famous,' they told Maria. 'You can hear them miles away. Old Parson has made up a song about them. We'll sing it to you presently. They all have names, you know, and when they were hung in the belfry they were christened just as human beings are. They were signed with the sign of the cross and anointed with oil and salt and wine.'

But Maria could not stay long looking at the Bell because Peterkin Pepper was pulling at her hand, dragging her towards a niche in the wall where there was a statue of a Lady with her Baby in her arms. It was a small wooden statue, not much bigger than a doll, and so worn by age and the caressing hands of many children that the features of Mother and Child had nearly been worn away. But the sweep of the Lady's cloak was lovely and graceful, so was the proud poise of her head, and the Baby had His hand upraised in blessing and a smile upon His face. The children had put two vases of flowers in the niche, one on each side of the statue.

'We always give the Lady something pretty,' said Prudence Honeybun. 'Sometimes in the winter it's only berries or birds' feathers that we've picked up. But it's always something. We love the Lady. We'd like to bring her seashells from the shore, but we're afraid to go down to the shore because of Them.'

Peterkin Pepper now spoke for the first time, giving tongue in a deep bass voice that was most startling, coming from one so young. 'I wish I had a great big stick,' he said. 'I wish I had a great big knobbly stick to chase Them away!'

'Have They been stealing your father's chickens again, Peterkin?' one of the children asked him.

'Four chickens,' said Peterkin briefly. 'Yesterday.'

'It's the Black Men,' Prudence told Maria in a whisper. 'They live in the pine-wood, you know, and they are very wicked. They won't let people go to Merryweather Bay, though it isn't really their bay. And they set cruel traps for the wild animals, and they steal our chickens and ducks and geese. And they steal the honey from the hives, too, and fruit from the orchards. We are happy in Silverydew, but we can't be perfectly happy because of the Black Men. But no one knows how to stop them from being wicked.'

A little shiver went down Maria's spine. So the Black Men lived in the pine-wood, did they? That pine-wood that pressed up so close to the manor-house walls. No wonder she was afraid of it. And no wonder she was afraid of the yew-trees, for they were Black Men too. She would have liked to ask Prudence some questions, but the other children were calling out to her that she must come and see the Merryweather Chantry, and the knight, and the two animals.

'Robin's in the chantry,' said Old Parson. 'Let Robin show

her the chantry. It is his right. The rest of you will stay outside.'

So Robin was here! Maria abruptly forgot her fear of the Black Men for joy that Robin was here too, and in the Merryweather Chantry. And she was delighted, too, to find Old Parson and the children talking about Robin as though he were a flesh-and-blood boy. She had always known that he was, even though in London no one but herself had seemed able to see him. But here it seemed that other people saw him too. The children and Old Parson accompanied her to the two worn steps that led up to the chantry, and there they stopped and she went inside alone.

It was a little low stone chamber, just like a cave, and it was almost entirely filled up by a big stone tomb. Upon the top of the tomb lay a life-size effigy of a knight in full armour, with his helmet on his head, the visor raised to show his grim unsmiling face, and his mailed hands crossed upon his breast. His great cross-handled sword was by his side, and it was not carved out of stone like the rest of the effigy—it was a real sword, bent and rusty with its great age, but real. But even more exciting to Maria than the sight of that great sword was the fact that there were two animals carved at the top and bottom of the tomb. The knight's head was pillowed upon the recumbent figure of a little horse, and his feet were propped against a creature the living image of Wrolf. After that, Maria was not surprised to find the Merryweather motto carved in Latin round the tomb. She was just spelling out the faint almost obliterated lettering when Robin popped up from behind the tomb, brandishing a scrubbing-brush. He grinned at her, and she grinned at him, and it seemed to Maria that suddenly the sun came out.

'Whatever are you doing with that scrubbing-brush?' she asked him.

'Scrubbing Sir Wrolf,' said Robin. 'I scrub him most mornings. And the animals too, and the floor, and as much of the rest of it as I can reach. Looks nice and clean, don't you think?'

It looked beautifully clean, and the little bunches of flowers that were placed here and there about the tomb, one between Sir Wrolf's stone fingers, one stuck jauntily behind the ears of the little horse, had a familiar look.

'Is it you, Robin, who puts my clothes ready for me each morning with a bunch of flowers on top of them?' she asked.

'It is I who pick the flowers,' said Robin.

'But who puts my clothes ready for me? And who put those lovely things in Miss Heliotrope's drawer? And who did my prayer-book and riding-habit belong to?' demanded Maria.

Robin just smiled.

'There must be some other small person about the place,' said Maria. 'For only a very small person could get through my door.'

But Robin only grinned, and fell upon Sir Wrolf's grim face with the scrubbing-brush. He had a pail of water behind the tomb, Maria discovered, and a piece of soap the size of a mangel-wurzel.

'No wonder he looks as he does,' said Maria, as Robin plied the scrubbing-brush with more zeal than tenderness. 'If you were more gentle with him, perhaps he'd smile.'

'They say in the village that on the day They can be persuaded not to be wicked any more Sir Wrolf *will* smile,' said Robin. 'He's the founder of the Merryweather family, you know. The one who was armour-bearer to King Edward I. It was his fault, originally, that They started to behave so badly. He must be awfully bothered about it. No wonder his soul can't get to Paradise.'

'Isn't the poor man in Paradise?' asked Maria pitifully.

'They say in the village,' said Robin, 'that he can't get nearer to Paradise than Paradise Hill because of making Them so wicked. They say he rides round and round Paradise Hill sighing and weeping because of what he did. But they say that he is sorry now, and that he would get into the real Paradise if only he could find a way of stopping Them being such a nuisance in the valley.'

Maria regarded her ancestor with pity and concern. Though riding was lovely fun and Paradise Hill a lovely place, she thought that after riding round and round it for so many centuries Sir Wrolf must be heartily tired both of the saddle and of the hill.

'I suppose if They could be persuaded to behave nicely and he smiled, then it would be a sign to us that he had got into Paradise?' she asked.

'Yes,' said Robin.

'But, Robin, who *are* They and what did Sir Wrolf do?'

'Old Parson tells the story best,' said Robin. 'And listen! The children are singing.'

He put his pail and brush neatly away in the corner, and together they went back to the chancel steps, where Old Parson was standing, his fiddle tucked under his chin, with the children all sitting on the steps round him, singing the

Bell Song to his accompaniment. Robin and Maria sat down with the other children, and in a moment Maria had picked up the words and the tune and was singing too. The words were those she had just failed to catch that first Sunday.

BELL SONG

High in the tall church tower,
Signed with the mystic sign,
Theirs since the days of chrism,
The oil and salt and wine,
The great bells wait in silence
Through the long death of night,
For resurrection triumph
And resurrection light.
When dawn comes out of darkness,
Victory out of pain,
Then music shakes the belfry
And spring is born again.

Chorus

Ring again, sweet Marie,
Ring again, Gabriel,
Ring once more, Douce and John,
Cry aloud, tenor bell.
Grey old heads, lifted high,
Peal your old joyful cry
Of life on earth. Life on earth.
Life.

When man and maid are wedded,
With laughter and with tears,
When babes to God are given
For all their coming years,

When oats and corn have ripened
Through blue and golden days,
When harvest home is gathered
With gladness and with praise;
Then grateful hearts are lifted
Up to God's throne above,
Then music shakes the belfry
And joy is born of love.

Chorus

Ring again, sweet Marie,
Ring again, Gabriel,
Ring once more, Douce and John,
Cry aloud, tenor bell.
Grey old heads, lifted high,
Peal your old joyful cry
Of love on earth. Love on earth.
Love.

Earth in a snowy mantle
Beneath the Christmas star,
The shepherds on the hillside,
The wise men from afar,
Ox and ass in the stable,
The children about the Tree,
The father and the mother,
Neighbours, and you and me;
All of us singing praises,
Loving the new-born King,
While music shakes the belfry,
And makes the welkin ring.

Chorus

Ring again, sweet Marie,
Ring again, Gabriel,

Ring once more, Douce and John,
Cry aloud, tenor bell.
Grey old heads, lifted high,
Peal your old joyful cry
Of peace on earth. Peace on earth.
Peace.

When they had finished singing, Robin said: 'Please, Sir, will you tell Maria the story of Sir Wrolf Merryweather and the Black Men?'

Old Parson turned his bright penetrating eyes upon Maria. 'Are you quite sure that you want to hear it?' he asked. 'Sometimes, Maria, a story that one hears starts one off doing things that one would not have had to do if one had not heard it. Sir Benjamin, I notice, has not told you the story. Perhaps he feared to lay upon you a woman's burden, while you are still a child.'

The last sentence settled it for Maria. In her opinion no girl in her teens is a child. 'Please tell it,' she said a little haughtily.

All the children sighed and stirred, rustling like a flock of birds. Then they were quite still, and in the stillness Old Parson laid aside his fiddle and told the story.

·: 3 :·

'Centuries ago,' said Old Parson, 'a piece of land in this lovely valley was given to Sir Wrolf Merryweather as a reward for courageous deeds well done, and he built the manor house where Sir Benjamin lives now, and came to live there with his men-at-arms, his cooks and scullions, his jester, and his huntsmen, his hawks and hounds and horses; and he lived there hunting and hawking, eating and drinking and making merry to his heart's content. For he was a jovial man, a great ruddy Viking of a man, with a lion's heart of courage, a laugh like a lion's roar, and the appetite of a lion for his meals.

'But though he possessed courage and joviality, and a proper appreciation of good food, he was by no means an entirely virtuous man, for he was possessed of a pride and covetousness that made him something of a trial to the neighbourhood. If anything took his fancy then he must have that thing, and such was his opinion of himself that he believed everything he coveted to be his by right.

'At first his manor did not include the whole of this valley, but only the tract of land now occupied by Moonacre Park and the village of Silverydew, with the fields and woods immediately surrounding it. The monastery upon the summit of Paradise Hill had been there since Norman times, and the monks owned Paradise Hill. They grew their corn upon its lower slopes and pastured their sheep upon the sweet turf of the high ground, and made a good deal of money out of selling the wool. Those holy men were a blessing to the whole valley, for they had built this church, and one of their number served it, they taught the children and tended the sick, and saved many a soul by prayer and example. People liked to look up and see the monastery towering against the sky, where now you see a group of trees growing about the holy well that the monks once used, and they liked to hear the Bell ringing out up there.

'But Sir Wrolf wanted Paradise Hill for himself, for the pasture-land was the best in the valley, and he wanted to keep *his* sheep there. It seemed to Sir Wrolf ridiculous that these men of God, who should have been living in holy poverty, should possess such worldly blessings as pastureland and sheep. He thought it neither suitable nor right. And he said as much to the King, when His Majesty visited him at his newly completed manor-house. And the King, whose life Sir Wrolf had saved no less than three times, agreed with him, and Paradise Hill was taken away from the monks, and they were driven out of the valley, and Sir Wrolf kept his sheep on the hill and turned the monastery into a hunting lodge.'

Old Parson and the children who had heard this tale many times before, sighed and shook their heads sadly over the dreadful behaviour of Sir Wrolf, but did not upset themselves about it too much. But Maria sat frozen with horror. For Sir Wrolf was her own relation, and he was really nothing better than a common thief.

'The possession of Paradise Hill did Sir Wrolf little good,' went on Old Parson. 'He was sleeping at the lodge one night when a violent thunderstorm broke, and lightning struck the building and killed some of the sheep. It nearly struck Sir Wrolf, too, and gave him a bad fright. He never went there again, for he believed that the monks had sent the storm to punish him for turning them out, and gradually the monastery fell into ruins, and now there's nothing left of it but a few fallen stones and the well that for centuries has been regarded as a holy well, and where the country people still go to say their prayers.

'But his narrow escape in the thunderstorm did not cure Sir Wrolf of thinking that what he wanted he must have. As you know, this lovely valley is ringed all round by a circle of hills that protect it from the outside world, and it seemed to Sir Wrolf only right and sensible that he should have the whole of the valley, with the circle of hills as the boundary of his property. He'd got Paradise Hill, but there remained the pine-woods behind his manor-house that ran right down to the sea, to what is now called Merryweather Bay, which were the property of Sir William Cocq de Noir, called Black William because of the black cock that was his family crest, and because of his flashing dark eyes, black hair and beard, and sallow French skin.

'And also because of his black heart. Coeur de Noir, men sometimes called him, instead of Cocq de Noir. For he was a bad man, was Black William, cruel to wild creatures, domineering with his servants, morose and ungenerous. Sir Wrolf, with all his faults, was generous as the sun itself, but Black William, like night, kept all he had close in his own darkness, so that no one might share it with him.

'The first Cocq de Noir had come to England with William the Conqueror, and been given his land by no less a person than the Conqueror himself, and the family had therefore inhabited their Norman castle in the pine-woods for much longer than Sir Wrolf had inhabited his manor-house.

'But that did not weigh with Sir Wrolf at all. He wanted to hunt the wild boar in the pine-woods, and he wanted the timber, and he wanted to keep the fishing in the bay entirely to himself. He offered to buy his land from Black William, but Black William refused. Then he appealed once more to the King, but the King this time sided with Black William. Then he threatened Black William, insulted him at every opportunity, tried to set the countryside against him, did everything he could think of to make life in his Norman castle unpleasant for him; but Black William was a man of spirit and returned threat for threat and insult for insult, until at last the whole valley was seething with discord, the followers of the two knights championing the cause of their masters and fighting each other whenever they met. The men of those days were savage fellows, and fighting was the breath of life to them. And the more these men fought the more savage they became, until at last this lovely valley was little better than a battlefield, with the turf of the green meadows stained red with blood, the harvest fields neglected, and gardens choked with weeds.

'But though Sir Wrolf enjoyed the fighting it brought him no nearer to his heart's desire, the possession of Black William's land. Violence being useless, he decided to try guile. Black William was a man of some fifty years a widower, and he had only one child, a young and beautiful daughter who was his heiress. Sir Wrolf, although at that time he was about forty years old, was also unmarried, owing to the very poor opinion he had of the female sex. He was not a lady's man, and he had always vowed that he would live and die unmarried. But it now occurred to him that if he were to marry Black William's daughter, upon Black William's death, he would become possessed of the pine-wood. Though Black William was not an old man, he was in poor health, while Sir Wrolf had never ailed in his life.

'So Sir Wrolf did violence to his own nature and became, not all at once, for that would have aroused suspicion, but gradually, a changed character. An astonishing gentleness became apparent in him. He announced that he had seen the error of his ways. He tidied up the church, which had been grievously neglected since the departure of the monks, built the Parsonage where now I live, and installed a priest there to say mass and care for the neglected souls of the villagers of Silverydew. He even went to church himself and said amen so loudly that the rafters sang. He attended to his neglected fields, weeded his neglected gardens, and punished severely any of his followers who were guilty of violent behaviour towards the one-time enemy.

'And finally, after a decent interval had elapsed, one autumn day when the leaves were falling he rode alone to the castle in the pine-woods and apologized to Black William; and Black William, heartily tired of the last two years of warfare, accepted his apology, and peace descended once more upon the beautiful valley. And then the following Christmas Sir Wrolf made a great feast and invited Black William and his daughter to it, and treated her like the queen of all the earth. And in the spring he subjected her to a swift passionate wooing, and as spring passed into summer he captured her heart and on midsummer day they were married.

'Black William's daughter was a beautiful girl, tiny and exquisite as a fairy child, slim as the sickle moon; not dark-complexioned like her father, but of an exquisite fairness, with silvery fair hair and silvery grey eyes and a skin like milk. Indeed so silvery fair was she, and so regal was her air, that throughout the valley she was called the Moon Princess.

'Though he had not at first wooed her for love, her beauty was so great that by the time their wedding day came Sir

Wrolf was as enamoured of her as a man can be of a woman, and she of him.

'He made the manor-house as beautiful as he could for her, hanging rare tapestries upon the walls and furnishing the chairs with silken cushions. And at the top of one of the towers he made for her a lovely little boudoir, with windows looking north and south and west over the kingdom of Moonacre. He caused the sickle moon to be carved in the stone ceiling, with the stars circling around it like courtiers round their queen, and he made the door to the room so small that only someone of fairy stature could enter the room; for she was not so talkative by nature as he was himself, and he knew she would value this assurance of privacy.

'Sir Wrolf's wedding gift to the Moon Princess was an exquisite little milk-white horse, a little wild mare that he had found the week before his wedding entangled in a thorn-tree on Paradise Hill. They say in the valley that every morning at dawn the white horses from the sea sweep inland in a joyous wild gallop that nobody sees because they are so quickly gone again, and legend has it that this little white horse was one of them. He could not go back to the sea with the others because the thorn-tree had caught him. He was a fairy horse, but different from other sea-horses because he had a horn sticking out of his forehead, and this horn, catching in the thorn-tree, was his undoing; but, of course, I cannot vouch for the truth of that. . . . Though I do know that to this day our villagers believe that old thorn-tree on Paradise Hill to be much frequented by the Little People, and they go there always on high days and holidays and stand beneath its branches and have three wishes.

'The Moon Princess's wedding gift to Sir Wrolf was a great ruby set in a ring and a huge tawny animal, a sort of dog that had been hers since puppyhood. She had no dowry to bring him, for Black William was a poor man, but she did bring with her a lovely string of moony pearls that had been her mother's.

'It was at the time of his wedding that Sir Wrolf adopted as his family crest the two animals, the dog and the horse, and as his family motto: "The brave soul and the pure spirit shall with a merry and a loving heart inherit the kingdom together." '

At this point Old Parson paused for such a long time that Maria wondered if this was the end of his story. But it wasn't. He sighed deeply and sadly and then went on again.

'I should have liked to stop there,' he said. 'I should like this story to be like all the best stories and to end in "Happy ever after". But it did not, and I must tell it as it has been handed down to us through the generations. . . . Well, children, at first all went well with Sir Wrolf and the Moon Princess, for they remained most deeply in love with each other, and they had riches and good health, while the health of Black William rapidly grew worse, and Sir Wrolf saw himself in a fair way to gain possession of the pine-woods and the fishing in the bay. There was only one thing wanting to their happiness, a child; but Sir Wrolf had wrested so much that he wanted from life already that he did not doubt he would have a son, too, all in good time. And then, quite suddenly, Black William got married; not to a great lady but to a farmer's daughter from over the hills, and a lusty little dark-skinned black-browed son was born to him; and Sir Wrolf's cup of bitterness was full.

'That was the beginning of the estrangement from his wife. The little Moon Princess, possessed of a truthful and a pure spirit, had not before realized the depth of her husband's guile. She had believed his conversion from his evil ways to be a genuine one, and she had believed he had wooed her from love alone. Now, as he raged and stormed against her father and his child, unconsciously revealing in his rage every thought of his mind for years past, she understood the truth, and her pride—and she had a very great pride—was wounded to the quick. She would not believe him when he told her that he did now most truly love her. His utterly true protestations of love she took to be lies; and her love for him turned slowly to hatred.

'Then to her, too, there was born a child, the longed-for son. But it was too late for husband and wife to come together again. The babe was like his father who had deceived her, and for that reason his mother could not love him. She left him to the care of nurses and his doting father, and spent most of her time shut up in her tower room or working in the manor-house garden. They say it was she who planted those yew-trees and had them cut into the shapes of black knights or black cocks, just to annoy her husband.

'And then the garden, as well as the house, became hateful to her, and she took to spending more and more time riding her beautiful little milk-white horse through the glades of the park, and up and down Paradise Hill, and down through the heather to the sea. Especially did she like to ride on Paradise Hill, and she would dismount and sit for hours at a time beside the monks' well, and beside the thorn-tree where the little white horse had been found, and it seemed that on Paradise Hill she and her little horse found some happiness and peace. Yet she lived a life of loneliness and sorrow, for as her pride cut her off from her husband and child, so did it separate her from her father and stepmother and their child and the castle in the pine-woods. For her stepmother was only a farmer's daughter and she would not consort with such. And she had, too, though she hated him now, a loyalty to her husband, and would not make friends with his enemies.

'For the old feud had broken out again, and Sir Wrolf and Black William were once more enemies, with their servants fighting each other whenever they met, and the whole countryside groaning beneath the burden of their rage. And then, in quick succession, there occurred two startling events. Black William suddenly disappeared and, as no trace at all could be found of him, he was given up for dead. And only a month later word came to Sir Wrolf that the little black-browed baby had been found dead in his cradle, and that his mother, overwhelmed by her grief, had gone back to her own people beyond the hills, taking with her the body of her son. So now the pine-woods leading down to the sea were the property of Sir Wrolf, through his wife the Moon Princess, and he had won his heart's desire.

'But it did him no good. Though there was no evidence that Sir Wrolf had had anything to do with Black William's disappearance, and no evidence that the little black-browed baby had died of anything worse than one of the usual childish ailments, the Moon Princess, her mind warped by loneliness and wounded pride, was convinced that her husband was responsible for both deaths. She believed him to be no better than a murderer, and she could no longer endure to live under his roof. So, one cool, starry night, when all the household was carousing after the evening meal, she dressed herself in her riding-habit and, taking with her nothing except her string of moony pearls, she stole down to the stable-yard and harnessed her little white horse and rode away into the park, and was never seen again.'

Once more there was a long pause, and Maria found that her heart was beating very fast indeed.

'Did no one ever know what happened to her?' she asked.

'No,' said Old Parson. 'No one ever knew what happened either to her or to the little white horse.'

'What happened to Sir Wrolf?' asked Maria.

'He was heartbroken, and he never ceased to mourn for the little Moon Princess,' said Old Parson. 'And scarcely a day passed that he did not ride his great chestnut horse, with his tawny dog following behind, through the park and the woods and the fields, and round and round Paradise Hill, looking for her. But he never found her. And ten years after she left him he died, a bitter and unhappy man, who got little joy from the fact that he left to his son John the whole of this lovely valley, from hill to hill, as his inheritance, and that of his heirs, for ever.'

'And what happened to the great tawny dog?' asked Maria.

'Throughout Sir Wrolf's life he remained faithful to the master to whom he had been given,' said Old Parson, 'but when Sir Wrolf died he went back to the pine-woods from which he had originally come; and he too was never seen again.'

'But the Black Men?' asked Maria. 'You have not said anything about them. That can't be all the story.'

'It is time that all these children went home to their breakfasts,' said Old Parson. 'And time that you and I took ours in the Parsonage.'

Maria understood. The part of the story the Old Parson had just told her was known to all the world, but there was some more of it that was the private property of the Merryweathers, and this he would only tell her privately. She got up and smoothed her dark-blue gown, and said smiling good-byes to the children as they trooped away to their breakfasts, Robin with them. She was sorry to see Robin go. She had hoped he would have come to breakfast at the Parsonage too. But he didn't. He gave her a beaming smile, tossed her the little bunch of primroses that he was wearing in his jerkin, and went away with the rest.

Chapter Seven

∙: 1 :∙

Maria and Old Parson went out into the churchyard, turned along a path to the right, and so came to a wooden gate leading into a small, sweet, tangled garden where currant bushes and rose bushes and square plots of gay spring flowers spread themselves fragrantly before the Parsonage front door.

The little, grey, squat Parsonage was so old that it looked more like an outcrop of rock than a house. It was overgrown with creepers and clematis and roses and honeysuckle, through which its small diamond-paned windows and old oak front door peeped shyly. Old Parson opened the door, and they were in the living-room of the Parsonage, a place of such attraction that Maria's eyes opened wide in delight.

It was a large room, for apart from the little kitchen leading out of it there was no other room on the ground floor. There was a wide stone hearth at one end, with a bright log fire burning in it, and beside the hearth a fascinating little twisting stone staircase led up to bedrooms in the roof. The floor was of smooth flagstones, scrubbed to snowy cleanliness.

Wooden bookshelves full of books lined the walls, and there were gay check curtains of white and red at the windows, whose panes had been cleaned and polished till they winked and gleamed like crystal. The walls were very thick, and in each deep window recess there stood a pot of salmon-pink geraniums.

There was an oak table in the middle of the room spread with a white cloth and red-and-white breakfast china, and there was a settle by the fire and a couple of hard oak chairs, but no other furniture and no pictures or ornaments. But the room did not need them because of the books, which stood there upon the shelves breathing out a friendliness that seemed to furnish and ornament the room, as did its spotless neatness and cleanliness. Maria had no doubt that the loving usage that had turned the books into living creatures was Old Parson's, but she could not believe that the cleanliness was the work of any mere male.

'Do you live here alone, Sir?' she asked.

'I live alone,' said Old Parson. 'But I have a housekeeper, who lives in the village and comes in each morning for an hour or so to cook and clean. Her name is Loveday Minette.'

Then Old Parson looked out of the window and sighed a little. 'There are times when I wish I did not live alone,' he said. 'Even with the company of my violin, the snowbound winter evenings can be very long. Now take off your bonnet and cloak, my dear, and Loveday will bring breakfast.'

But Maria had done no more than loosen the strings of her bonnet when the door leading to the kitchen opened and a woman came in carrying a tray with brown boiled eggs upon it, and coffee, and milk and honey and butter, and crusty home-made bread.

But for once Maria was oblivious of good food, and with her hands arrested at her bonnet strings she stood and gazed at Loveday Minette as those gaze who look upon a dream come true and wonder if they sleep or wake. For when in lonely moments the motherless Maria had imagined for herself the mother she would like to have, that mother had been exactly like Loveday Minette.

She was slim and graceful as a willow wand, tiny as a fairy's child, with a beautiful milk-white skin faintly tinged with rose. Her smooth straight hair was pale gold, and was wound round her head in a great plait like a crown, which gave her a regal air that was in keeping with the proud erectness of her bearing. Her eyes were grey and direct in their glance as Maria's own, and though her sweet smiling lips were delicately moulded they were strong, too, and there was just a hint of obstinacy in the clear-cut line of her jaw. So great was her beauty that at a first glance she looked young, but at a second glance one saw that she was not young. There was grey in her pale-gold hair and a faint pencilling of lines about her eyes, and her hands, though beautifully shaped, were roughened by many years of toil. She wore a grey linen gown, sprigged with small pink roses, with a plain white kerchief folded across the breast and a white apron. She set the food upon the table, smiled at Maria as though she had known her always, then came to her and unfastened her bonnet strings, lifted her bonnet off her head, and set her hair to rights with a few deft touches. Then she caressed Maria's cheek with her forefinger, smiled at her again, put her bonnet and cloak on the settle, and went away.

Old Parson meanwhile had brought the two chairs to the table and stood holding Maria's very ceremoniously. Feeling like a queen, she seated herself, and he pushed it in, then sat down in front of her and helped her to eggs and coffee.

For a little while Maria ate speechlessly, partly because the food was so good, and partly because the lovely familiarity of Loveday Minette had deprived her of the power of speech. Yet when at last she did speak to Old Parson it was not of Loveday, for somehow Loveday seemed too wonderful, too much of her own, to be spoken of, but of the story Old Parson had told them in the church.

'You did not finish the story,' she said to him. 'There is another part of it, a private part of it, that you could not tell to the other children.'

'That's so,' said Old Parson. 'Sir Benjamin did me the honour of telling me the private part of it not long after I came here. We've always been friends. I have a great regard for Sir Benjamin, and he for me. He takes my outspokenness of speech in good part; and I am, I believe, the only creature to whom he has spoken of that queer mixture of legend and fact that I will relate to you. The old folk among the villagers know the story, but to them he does not speak of it.'

Old Parson stirred his coffee silently for a moment or two, and then began to tell the story with a queer sort of remoteness, as though it were just some tale out of a book. He did this on purpose, Maria thought later, so that all that the story meant to her and for her should not startle her too much.

•: 2 :•

'Nothing is ever finished and done with in this world,' said Old Parson. 'You might think a seed was finished and done with when it falls like a dead thing into the earth; but when it puts forth leaves and flowers next spring you see your mistake. Sir Wrolf, when he was told of the death of Black William's child and when the mother went back to her own people, no doubt thought the Merryweathers had seen the last of that family. His son John, who could not remember his mother, doubtless thought of the Moon Princess and her little white horse as lost for ever out of this world. And doubtless he thought, too, that his father's original deception of his mother was a sin that would not affect succeeding generations.

'Yet all attempts to cut those yew-trees into any shapes but those of black knights and black cocks is doomed to failure; always they go back to their original shapes. And the Black Men live in the pine-woods today. And once in every generation the Moon Princess comes back to the manor; and for a short while there is great joy, for always the sun Merryweathers and the moon Merryweathers consort well together; but then, as if in punishment for the original sin, there is a quarrel, and the Moon Princess once more goes away.'

'Must she always go away?' whispered Maria anxiously. For she herself, she guessed, was the Moon Princess in this generation. And she did not want to go away.

'She always *has* gone away,' said Old Parson. 'Not necessarily from the valley, but from the manor. Yet the old folks in the village vow and declare that one day there will come a Moon Princess who will have the courage to deliver the valley from the wickedness of the Black Men. But like the princesses in all the nicest fairy-tales, she will have to humble her pride to love not a prince but a poor man, a shepherd or ploughman or some such country lad, and to effect the deliverance with his help, and that's a thing which no Moon Princess has yet done, so proud are they one and all, so loath to accept assistance from another.' Old Parson sighed and poured himself a cup of coffee. 'And so it goes on, and the wickedness of the Black Men is still with us.'

'But who are They?' asked Maria. 'If Black William's only son died, they can't be his descendants.'

'Word was brought to Sir Wrolf that the child had died,' Old Parson corrected her, 'but no one was ever found who had actually seen the child dead. There are those who say that his mother, fearing Sir Wrolf might harm her child, said that he was dead and then fled with him to her own people. Be that as it may, fifty years later the black cock was once more heard crowing in the woods, and it was discovered that four Black Men, who might have been the sons of that child, had come from over the hills and established themselves in the castle.

'And their descendants have been there ever since, a curse to the whole neighbourhood. The Merryweathers may say they own those pine-woods running down to the sea and Merryweather Bay, but they no more own that bit of country than they own London Town. The Black Men own it. In the past there have been Merryweathers who have attempted to dislodge them by force or guile, but if driven away for a short while they always come back again. Your uncle wisely makes no such attempt. He endures them, and does what he can to protect animals from their cruelty and to make up to his people for all they suffer at their hands. . . . And waits.'

'For the Moon Princess?' whispered Maria.

Old Parson smiled. 'I don't know,' he said. 'Possibly Sir Benjamin looks upon the old prophecy as just a fairy story.'

'Do you believe in it?' asked Maria.

'In every fairy-tale there is a kernel of truth,' said Old Parson. 'I think it likely that only a Moon Princess can deal with the wickedness of the Black Men, because it is a fact that only the moon can banish the blackness of night. And I think it probable that only when she humbles herself to love a poor man will she do it, because it is a fact that nothing worth while in this world is achieved without love and humility. And as for the fact that though they consort so well together, the union of sun and moon Merryweathers has so far always ended in a quarrel—well—Sir Wrolf was a sinner, and it is a fact that the sins of the fathers are visited upon the children —until the children undo what their fathers did.'

'Do you think that Sir Wrolf killed Black William?' asked Maria.

'I do not,' said Old Parson decidedly. 'That is a crime to which he would not have stooped. The Merryweathers have never been murderers.'

'Then what do you think happened to Black William?' asked Maria.

'I have no idea,' said Old Parson. 'Perhaps he suddenly became fatigued with everything and took himself off to some hermitage, to brood over his wrongs in private. Wicked men do suffer from fatigue a good deal, for wickedness is a very fatiguing thing.'

'And then, perhaps,' said Maria, 'he just got into a boat and sailed away into the sunset and was never seen again. Oh, I'm glad Sir Wrolf was not a murderer!'

'But though not a murderer, Sir Wrolf was covetous, a thief, and a deceiver, and so a great sinner,' said Old Parson sternly. 'You have no cause to congratulate yourself upon your ancestry.'

'I think that Paradise Hill ought to be given back to God again,' said Maria. 'The Merryweathers have no right to it. Things will keep on going wrong between the sun and moon Merryweathers, until they aren't thieves any more.'

'Maria,' said Old Parson approvingly, 'you are a credit to your hitherto not very creditable family.'

'I wonder,' said Maria, 'if Wrolf is a descendant of the first Sir Wrolf's tawny dog, the one which went back to the pine-woods after he died?'

'Possibly,' said Old Parson. 'It is said that a year or so before it is time for another Moon Princess to come to Moonacre a tawny dog comes out of the pine-woods on Christmas Eve and takes up his residence at the manor. And then, when the Moon Princess comes, he has her in his special protection.'

Maria's eyes opened wide. 'Sir Benjamin told me,' she said, 'that Wrolf came out of the pine-woods a year ago.'

'Yes,' said Old Parson.

Maria's eyes opened wider still. 'Perhaps,' she said, 'Wrolf isn't a descendant of the first dog but the first dog himself.'

'Dogs don't usually live for hundreds of years,' said Old Parson.

'But then Wrolf isn't a usual sort of dog, is he?' said Maria.

'No,' Old Parson agreed, 'he certainly is not.'

·: 3 :·

They had finished breakfast now, and, opening a cupboard beside the fireplace, Old Parson took out his fiddle and seated himself on the settle to fit a new string into it. Maria did not feel like a stranger in this room, she felt utterly at home in it, and as though she were at home she crossed to the book-shelves and began looking at the books.

'Borrow what you like,' said Old Parson. 'My books, like myself, are always at the service of my friends.'

'But they are nearly all in foreign languages,' said Maria.

'If you want an English book,' said Old Parson, 'there is a book of English verse at the far end of the top shelf. . . . Though to my mind the French language is the loveliest and the best.'

His slightly foreign intonation seemed accentuated as he spoke, and Maria turned round and looked at him. 'Please, Sir,' she asked shyly, 'are you—French?'

'I am,' said Old Parson, and tucking his fiddle under his chin he began to play, very softly, the air Maria had been playing at the harpsichord before she had joined him in the rose-garden.

'Who taught it to you?' he asked her.

'No one,' said Maria. 'It came out of the harpsichord the very first time I opened it.'

'I guessed as much,' said Old Parson, half to himself. 'It must have been the last one she played before she shut the harpsichord. Yes, I remember that she played it that night. It was her last night at the manor. That was twenty years ago.'

And then he let the soft air he had been playing merge into a gay country dance, so that Maria had no chance to ask any questions, though quite a hundred of them were burning on the tip of her tongue. She swallowed them down and took from the shelf the book that Old Parson had pointed out. It had a faded heliotrope cover, and was small enough to slip quite easily into her hanging pocket. But before she put it there she peeped inside, and saw written on the flyleaf a name that was familiar to her, written in a handwriting that was also familiar to her.

The name was Louis de Fontenelle and the handwriting was that of her governess Miss Heliotrope. . . . The room turned upside-down with Maria. . . . Then it righted itself again, and she stood there silently, her hand holding the book inside her pocket, wondering what she should do. Nothing as yet, she thought. Just wait.

Old Parson was standing up now, and the dance had passed into a great soaring piece of music like a flock of white birds in flight. She did not think he had noticed how the room had turned upside-down with her; indeed, he seemed now to have forgotten all about her. He had been caught away on the wings of his music to the place where the white birds were flying. She dropped him an unnoticed curtsy, put on her bonnet and cloak, lifted the latch of the door, and went quickly out into the small, sweet, tangled garden.

·: 4 :·

But at the wooden gate she paused and waited, and she did not have to wait long, for in a moment or two Loveday Minette came round the corner of the Parsonage, wearing a grey shawl flung round her shoulders, but with her beautiful head bare.

'I knew you would wait for me,' she said in her deep sweet voice. 'Shall we walk to my home together? It is not very much out of your way.'

'Thank you,' said Maria humbly, and when Loveday held out her hand to her she took it shyly, as she would have taken the hand of a queen. For though Loveday's hands were toilworn and she worked for Old Parson as though she were a servant, yet she bore herself with the air of a very great lady indeed, and as such Maria accepted her.

'My name, too, is Maria,' she said as they walked through the churchyard together, 'but when I was a little girl they called me Minette because I was so small, and the name has stuck because I am still so small.'

'My father's mother was called Loveday,' said Maria.

'Loveday and Maria are both Merryweather names,' said Loveday Minette. 'Merryweather women are called Maria, or Mary, because the church is dedicated to Saint Mary. And Loveday—well—moon people love the day and the bright sun.'

They walked hand in hand together along the village street, turned in through the broken gate into the park, and then turned to their right along a narrow footpath.

Upon their left the trees grew thickly as in a wood, but

upon their right was a green hillside with grey granite rocks breaking through the turf and rising up beside them like a wall.

'This is one of the lower spurs of Paradise Hill,' said Loveday as they walked along. 'But it is too steep to climb up it just here. The best way is to take the lane leading up from the village.' Then she stopped, laying her hand on a great grey rock that jutted out from the steep hillside beside her. 'Will you come in for a little while?' she asked. 'I would like to show you my home.'

'Thank you,' said Maria, but she looked about her in bewilderment, for she saw no sign of a house.

'This way,' said Loveday, and walked round the rock and disappeared.

More astonished than ever, Maria too walked round the rock, and there behind it, almost hidden by a rowan-tree that drooped over it from the hillside above, was a door in the hill. Loveday stood just inside it, holding it hospitably open and smiling as though this were a perfectly ordinary door to a perfectly ordinary house. 'Come in,' she said. 'This is the back door. I'm afraid it's a bit dark in the passage. Give me your hand and I'll shut the door.'

When the door was shut it was pitch dark, but with her hand held firmly in Loveday's warm strong clasp Maria felt no fear. They walked together down a narrow tunnel, and then Loveday lifted a latch and opened a door, and a lovely green light, the sort of light that Maria imagined lit the world beneath the sea, flowed over them.

'This is my living-room,' said Loveday.

It was a large cave, but it had windows just like an ordinary room. There were two in the east wall and one in the west wall, diamond-paned windows set deeply in the rock. Outside, they were shrouded by green curtains of ferns and creepers, so that Maria guessed no passer-by could ever have known that the windows were there. The door by which they had entered was in the north wall, and beside it a stone staircase, so steep and narrow that it was more like a ladder than a staircase, was built against the wall and led to an upper room. In the south wall there was another door, with a bell hanging beside it. Hanging on a peg beside the bell was a long black hooded cloak, and upon the other side of the door was a fireplace with a log fire burning merrily upon the hearth, with a white kitten asleep before it. The room was furnished with a settle and table and chairs, made of oak; but in addition there was a dresser against the south wall with gay flowered china upon it and bright copper pots and pans. Pale-pink chintz patterned with roses of a deeper pink hung in the windows, and there were gay rag rugs on the stone floor. There were pots of salmon-pink geraniums on the window-sills and on the table, and bunches of herbs hung from the roof. In its simplicity and fresh cleanliness the room was so like Old Parson's, though it was three times the size of his, that Maria guessed Loveday had arranged them both. She admired Loveday's taste in arrangement, but not her passion for pink. There was too much pink in this room, she considered. She preferred the colour scheme in the manor-house parlour.

'But what fun to live in a cave!' she cried, looking about her delightedly.

'There's something about pink that makes even a cave look

homelike,' said Loveday. 'I love pink. Now come upstairs, my dear, and see where we sleep.'

'We?' wondered Maria, as she followed her beautiful hostess up the narrow staircase. Had Loveday got a husband? There were none of the usual signs of a husband, no muddy boots about or tobacco ash upon the floor. He must be a very tidy husband.

The stone staircase brought them out into Loveday's beautiful bedroom. Here again there were fern-shaded windows to west and east, gay with curtains patterned this time with pink convolvulus. Loveday's four-poster stood against the south wall. It had curtains of the same convolvulus chintz, and a lovely gay patchwork quilt, with pink predominating in the colour scheme. The furniture here looked very old. Besides the bed there was a press for clothes and an oak chest black with age, with a mirror hanging over it. This mirror was not made of glass but of burnished silver, and forming a panel across the top of it was the figure of a little horse in full gallop.

'Hundreds of years ago, when that mirror was made, there was no such thing as glass,' said Loveday, seeing Maria's astonished eyes resting upon the mirror. 'They had to use burnished metal instead.' She laughed softly. 'But it gives back a softened and becoming reflection. Look at yourself in my mirror and you'll find you are prettier than you thought you were.'

With a beating heart Maria went to the mirror and looked, and it was indeed a very lovely face that looked back at her. Her freckles seemed to have disappeared, and her hair, instead of having a reddish tinge, was pure silvery gold. And behind her head there shone a soft moony radiance.

'But it's not *me* in the mirror,' she whispered to Loveday.

'Yes it is,' said Loveday softly, taking her hand. 'Do not be afraid.' Then she pulled Maria away from the mirror. 'Look! That little staircase leads to his room.'

Beside the door another ladder-like staircase led up against the wall, but so much steeper and narrower than the other one that Maria thought one would have to be very small and agile to get up it. Loveday must have, surely, a fairy sort of husband, so small and tidy and surefooted as he evidently was. She longed to see what his room was like, but just as Loveday was moving towards the staircase a bell rang.

'That's Digweed back,' said Loveday, and sped down the stairs to the living-room again; and Maria was obliged to follow her, for well-brought-up people do not in another person's house enter their rooms without permission. Also she was puzzled to know what the bell had to do with Digweed being back.

When she reached the living-room again the bell that hung beside the door in the south wall was still vibrating, and Loveday had put on her long black hooded cloak and was unlatching the door. 'Come, child,' she said to Maria. 'Digweed will be able to give you a lift back to the manor, and that will save your legs, for by this time they are surely weary.'

Maria followed her out into a dark damp tunnel, lit only by the light that came from the living-room. They turned to the right, and there before them was a great oak door, securely barred by the slender trunk of a tree laid across it on supports like a bolt.

Now Maria knew where she was; this was the same tunnel through which they had driven on the evening of their arrival. And that shadowy figure that she had seen there had been Loveday in her black cloak, opening the door to them, as she was doing now, pulling the hood of her cloak forward with one hand, so that her face was hidden before she lifted the tree-trunk away from the door. She must be very strong, thought Maria, even though she is so tiny; as strong as a fairy woman.

The great door swung open, and Digweed in the gig, with Darby between the shafts, drove through.

'I'm alone, Ma'am,' he called to Loveday, and she let the hood fall back from her face again.

'Stop and pick up our little lady,' she said, and he stopped and waited, smiling broadly at Maria while Loveday shut and barred the great door again. When she had done it she helped Maria climb up into the gig beside Digweed. Then she stood beside it, looking earnestly up at Maria, the green light from the open doorway behind her making her beautiful face look strangely unearthly.

'Maria,' she said, 'do not tell Sir Benjamin that you have seen me. Because, you see, he does not know that I live here. Old Parson knows, the whole village knows, Digweed knows that I am Porteress of the Moonacre Gate, but Sir Benjamin does not know.'

Maria was by this time getting used to living in a perpetual state of astonishment and used to curbing her curiosity, so that at this startling piece of information she just nodded, and one question only escaped her.

'But if he doesn't know you are Porteress, who does he think *is*?' she demanded.

'There was an old woman who used to be Porteress,' said Loveday. 'She lived at the manor-house once, but she asked so many questions that Marmaduke Scarlet got annoyed and was rude to her, and so she wouldn't live there any longer, and Sir Benjamin made her Porteress so that she should have a comfortable home. But she quarrelled with him too, for I am afraid she was rather a bad-tempered old woman as well as a curious one; and she would not speak to him or let him set foot in the gatehouse. Then she died and I took her place. But Sir Benjamin does not know that she has died and does not know that I have taken her place. This is her cloak that I wear, and she was a little woman, so that if Sir Benjamin catches sight of me as he drives through he only thinks that he sees old Elspeth. I know that I can trust you, Maria. I know that you will keep my secret, as all the village people do.'

'You can trust me,' said Maria, and she bent down from the gig and she and Loveday kissed each other, and then she and Digweed drove on through the tunnel and out into the warm still loveliness of the park.

·: 5 :·

Maria had not driven this way since the night of her arrival, and she looked about her eagerly. It looked very different in daylight; but the glades that wound away between the trees were just as mysterious, and it would not have surprised her if she had seen the little white horse galloping up one of them. But she didn't, and presently she left off looking and attended to Digweed's conversation, for he had enjoyed himself at the market-town and wanted to tell her all about it. He had bought a new spade and a new scythe, ten new mousetraps, a bottle of cough mixture for his own use, a pig, a canary in a cage, an enormous meatbone, a bag of biscuits, a bunch of radishes, a paper bag full of bull's-eyes and another full of bright pink boiled sweets, a cod's head, and a large packet of tobacco. It was rather a noisy journey, for the pig was squeaking, the canary was singing at the top of its voice, the mousetraps leaped and rattled at every bump in the road, and the cod's head had the sort of smell that one could almost hear. But Maria enjoyed the drive, in spite of the cod's head, for Digweed was so kind and companionable and she loved him very much.

Sir Benjamin and Miss Heliotrope were walking together in the formal garden, and Digweed stopped the gig, so that Maria could get down and join them. When she was down he handed her the pink boiled sweets.

'For you, little Mistress,' he said very shyly.

And then, getting purple in the face, he handed the bull's-eyes to Miss Heliotrope. 'For you, Ma'am,' he said. 'I knows you be partial to peppermint.'

And then he handed the tobacco to Sir Benjamin, and drove quickly off before any of them had time to say thank you properly.

'Always brings us presents from town,' chuckled Sir Benjamin as the three of them strolled back towards the manor. 'That canary, I think, is for Marmaduke Scarlet. Marmaduke is fond of birds, but his pets are apt to be rather short-lived, owing to Zachariah.'

Miss Heliotrope, Maria thought, was looking a little agitated, and Sir Benjamin now explained why.

'I am taking Miss Heliotrope for a little walk in order to calm her nerves,' he said. 'For this morning Marmaduke decided to make himself known to her. Instead of drawing her curtains, and placing her jug of hot water in her basin in his usual noiseless fashion, which does not awaken the lightest sleeper, he did it so noisily that she woke up and saw him.'

'It was a shock,' quavered poor Miss Heliotrope. 'A great shock. No man, except of course my father, has ever set foot in my bedchamber.'

'Marmaduke Scarlet is scarcely a man, Miss Heliotrope,' comforted Sir Benjamin. 'He is—well—Marmaduke Scarlet. And his revealing himself to you is an enormous compliment, for as a general rule his dislike of the female sex causes him to avoid women like the plague.'

'So now you know, Miss Heliotrope, who does the work of the house so beautifully,' said Maria.

'So now I know,' said Miss Heliotrope, beginning to smile a little. 'And I could not have believed that so small and aged —well—I must say gentleman, for lack of a better term—could have been so expert a housewife!'

'Nevertheless, you have had a shock,' said Sir Benjamin sympathetically. 'Would a little carriage exercise this afternoon be beneficial, do you think? I do not believe it will rain before nightfall. You and Maria could go for a drive in the pony carriage. It is a lady's pony carriage, though no lady has used it for twenty years. But Digweed can soon clean it up again.'

'I should like it of all things,' said Miss Heliotrope graciously.

'Oh, Sir,' cried Maria delightedly. 'Could we drive to Paradise Hill?'

'Certainly,' said Sir Benjamin.

They were at the house now, and while Sir Benjamin and Miss Heliotrope paused for a last look at the garden Maria ran up to the hall. All four animals—Wrolf, Zachariah, Wiggins, and Serena the hare—were grouped amiably about the fire, each happily engrossed with the gift Digweed had brought from the town; Wrolf with the huge bone, Zachariah with the cod's head, Wiggins with the biscuits, and Serena with the radishes. They looked round at her with champing jaws and moved their tails and ears in friendly welcome, and she moved from one to the other caressing their soft heads. It all seemed very friendly and homely, and she felt more than ever that her period of introduction to Moonacre was over, and that she was firmly embedded here now, like a jewel in its setting. She felt this more than ever when the kitchen door opened and Marmaduke Scarlet's rosy bearded face was inserted into the aperture, with the very broadest grin running right up into its ears.

'I beg that you will do me the favour, Mistress, of entering the scene of my culinary labours,' he said in his squeaking voice. 'We were informed by Zachariah the cat that you would partake of breakfast at the establishment of the Reverend the Vicar of Silverydew, but having from past experience formed an unfavourable opinion of the sustenance provided in clerical establishments, I have taken the liberty of augmenting the repast of which you have already partaken with a small cold collation. Will you do me the favour of stepping inside?'

Maria stepped inside and found the kitchen table spread with a fair white cloth, and upon it was a plate of pink-iced fairy cakes, a foaming mug of milk, and a small silver dish full of candied cherries. While she munched the sugar cakes and nibbled at the cherries and took long satisfying draughts of the lovely new milk, Marmaduke Scarlet stood upon a stool and hung his canary in the window, and all the while he was adjusting the cage he never ceased smiling at her, and once he even tipped her a wink with his left eye. He was, she could see, very, very pleased with her; almost as though he knew and highly approved the decision to which she had come in Old Parson's parlour while he was telling her the past history of her family.

'Marmaduke Scarlet,' she said, actually daring to ask a question because he was so extraordinarily sunny and friendly, 'how *did* Zachariah deliver Old Parson's message?'

Marmaduke Scarlet nodded towards the great hearth.

'Any communication which Zachariah is called upon to deliver he inscribes with his right forepaw in the ashes,' he said. 'Zachariah is an exceptionally gifted cat. His ancestors were worshipped as gods by the Pharaohs of ancient Egypt, so he tells me, and the blood in his veins is blue, so he tells me. That latter statement I can corroborate, for upon one occasion he had the misfortune to insinuate his nose too near the meat hatchet, while his Sunday meal of beef and liver and bacon was in preparation, and the blood that flowed from the resultant slight wound was deep blue-bell blue.'

Maria set down her mug of milk, ran to the hearth and

looked at the ashes. They had been spread smoothly, as though with the swish of a long tail, and little pictures bearing a marked resemblance to Egyptian hieroglyphics had been traced on them. First came the outline of a fiddle, then the outline of a sickle moon, and these two were joined together by a circle. Next came a little picture of a church and then of a coffee-pot. Maria laughed in delight. The fiddle, she saw, was Old Parson, and the moon was herself, and they were together, and had gone together to church and breakfast.

'Zachariah deserves his cod's head,' said Maria.

'And you, little Mistress,' said Marmaduke Scarlet, motioning her back to the table, 'deserve your sugar cakes, your cherries, and your milk.'

Chapter Eight

·: 1 :·

After dinner, Digweed brought round the pony carriage. He had furbished it up, so that it looked quite bright and shining, though very peculiar. . . . It was of basket-work, and shaped like a very large, almost circular, baby's cradle, set very low to the ground on four large substantial wheels. It had a basket-work hood lined with quilted red twill, and beneath it a wooden seat with red cushions. Digweed had spread fresh clean straw on the floor, and ornamented the whip with a scarlet bow, and Periwinkle had a scarlet bow on the top of her head.

Attended by Sir Benjamin, Miss Heliotrope and Maria and Wiggins descended the steps with considerable pomp, feeling that this first drive in a pony carriage that had not been used for twenty years was something of an occasion. Miss Heliotrope was wearing one of her beautiful new fichus on her purple bombasine dress, her black cloak, and her poke bonnet. She carried her reticule with her book of essays in it, and her beautiful blue eyes were very bright and shining. Maria had put on her green linen dress, beneath a green cloak lined with yellow, and a green bonnet with a yellow feather in it. Wiggins, in his green leather collar, had had an extra good brushing in honour of the occasion, and looked particularly beautiful. Serena, who was now so much better that she could get about quite easily on three legs, followed them down the steps looking very smart in the collar of plaited silver cord that Maria had made for her, with her long ears cocked in happy anticipation.

When Maria and Miss Heliotrope had seated themselves in the pony carriage, and Digweed had spread a plaid rug over their knees, Wiggins jumped in and sat himself at their feet, and then indicated to Serena that she might sit beside him with a graciousness that made Wrolf smile into his whiskers. Wrolf, of course, was coming with them, though on foot, there being no room for his bulk inside the carriage. Zachariah watched them go from the front door, purring benevolently, his tail arranged in three neat coils over his back. He did not offer to accompany them, for unless his presence was actually necessary he liked best to stay at home. Sir Benjamin and Digweed did not offer to accompany them either, for the little pony carriage was altogether too feminine a turn-out for their masculine dignity. But they gave Maria clear instructions as to how to handle the reins and which way to take when they got to the village, and they waved them away with much enthusiasm.

'The sheep you will see on Paradise Hill are mine, Maria, and therefore yours too,' said Sir Benjamin. 'And perhaps you will see my shepherd boy up there. The best shepherd boy in the countryside.'

'I'll look out for them, Sir,' Maria called back as they drove off.

She found that driving did not compare with riding, it was not nearly so exciting. Yet Periwinkle went at a good pace, and the funny little carriage bumped along very merrily. It had turned rather sultry and hot, and they were glad of the breeze of their movement blowing in their faces.

'You're sure you can manage, dear?' twittered Miss Heliotrope. 'You won't upset us, will you?'

'I don't think I could if I tried,' said Maria. 'It is such a very round solid little carriage, and it's so near the ground.'

'Yes, that's true,' said Miss Heliotrope, peering out from beneath the hood. 'If we *did* fall, we shouldn't fall far. You don't think it's going to thunder, dear, do you?'

'It isn't usual to have a thunderstorm so early in the year,' said Maria.

'I do hope we shan't meet any gipsies or poachers, or anything unpleasant of that kind,' said Miss Heliotrope. 'There must be some about, because of that trap being set.'

With her whip Maria indicated the great tawny figure of Wrolf leaping along beside them.

'Ah, yes,' said Miss Heliotrope. 'He's certainly a great protection. Though sometimes, you know, Maria, one's protector can be almost as alarming as what he protects one from.'

'Wrolf would die for those I love,' said Maria with conviction.

But Miss Heliotrope remained in a slightly uneasy mood.

'You're sure you understand which way to take?' she asked.

'Yes,' said Maria. 'And even if I didn't, Periwinkle knows.'

And Periwinkle knew. Without any guidance from Maria she took them through the broken gate into the village, down the village street, and past the church. Trotting past the church, they got a good view of the Parsonage, and Miss Heliotrope exclaimed in delight at the sight of it. 'That's the little house of my dreams,' she said. 'That's the house where I would like to live.'

'But you can't,' said Maria. 'That's where Old Parson lives.'

'I meant, dear,' said Miss Heliotrope with dignity, 'that that is where I would like to live *if* Old Parson were not already in occupation.'

Periwinkle swung round to the left, and they were in a narrow rutted lane, winding uphill between deep banks, where ferns and periwinkles and primroses were growing thickly, banks so high that they could not see what was above them. A gay tinkling little stream ran down one side of it, the same stream that ran along the village street.

'This must be a very old lane,' said Miss Heliotrope. 'I remember my father telling me once that roads sink deeper and deeper into the earth with the passing of the years and the passage of more and more feet over them.'

'The monks would have passed backwards and forwards this way,' said Maria. 'Their shepherds would have driven their sheep down this lane. And Sir Wrolf and his friends would have ridden up here to his hunting lodge. And the Moon Princess on her little white horse would have ridden this way. And all the country people coming through the centuries to pray at the holy well, and to have three wishes beneath the fairy thorn-tree where Sir Wrolf found the little white horse from the sea, will have come this way. They come this way now. No wonder the lane is sunk so deep.'

'What *are* you talking about, child?' demanded Miss Heliotrope.

'Old Parson has been telling me fairy-tales,' said Maria.

'I beg that you will not permit your head to be turned by them,' said Miss Heliotrope.

'No,' said Maria.

The lane was not a long one, but it was so steep that Periwinkle could only go at a foot's pace, and Wiggins and Serena hopped out of the carriage and joined Wrolf. Wiggins picked his way very daintily over the ruts, Serena advanced with long three-legged leaps, and Wrolf strolled amiably upwards, looking immensely strong and purposeful. But it ended at last, and they were out upon Paradise Hill, and Periwinkle stopped of her own accord, so that Miss Heliotrope and Maria might look about them.

Paradise Hill was well named, for it really seemed too lovely to belong to this world.

' "I will lift up mine eyes unto the hills," ' quoted Miss Heliotrope, ' "from whence cometh my help." '

Maria said nothing, but she jumped out of the pony carriage, went a little way over the sweet turf, and stood by herself to look about her. They were so high up that she could look right down upon the valley of Moonacre lying below her. There were the village and the church and the Parsonage, looking at this distance like wooden toys set among the budding trees and the gay gardens. And there to the right was the spur of rocky hillside running out from Paradise Hill into Moonacre Park, within which was hidden the tunnel and Loveday Minette's house. And there was the lovely expanse of the park and the manor-house in the distance. And on her left was the great sombre mass of the pine-woods, clothing the northern hills.

The hills stood all round the valley like a great wall. They were broken only in one place far away to the east, where they fell away like parting curtains to show a shining slab of mother-of-pearl that looked like the doorstep to heaven. What was it? Oh, what was it?

It was the sea! For the first time in her life Maria was looking at the sea. Her heart beat fast and the colour flamed into her cheeks. She was glad, now, that she had not seen the sea that day when she had found Serena. It was best to see it first of all like this, at a far distance. All the best things are seen first of all at a far distance.

When she had gazed her fill at the valley and at that shining doorstep of the sea, she turned and looked at Paradise Hill itself. The grass was bright green, and sprinkled with pale purple dog-violets and the white stars of strawberry flowers. Above her, sheep were feeding on the lovely slopes, and small lambs like bits of fluffy white cloud were gambolling about over the grass and flowers. The group of trees on the summit of the hill seemed quite near now and Maria could see that they were beeches, and beneath them she could see the fallen grey stones that were the ruins of the monastery. The stream came out of the earth somewhere at the top of the hill and wound its way down the hillside between moss-covered stones and clumps of fragrant bog-myrtle. At one point a grey old thorn-tree bent above it, and when she saw the thorn-tree Maria ran towards it.

It was a blackthorn-tree and it was in bloom already, the blossom white as the little horse that Sir Wrolf had found here entangled in the grey branches; captured by them, as he came to the stream to drink, thirsty after galloping up from the sea. Rooted sturdily among the stones, it stretched protectingly right over the stream, so that the petals fell into the bright clear water. At this very moment, Maria guessed, white petals were floating on the stream beneath the little bridges before each garden gate, perhaps carrying with them the fulfilment of the wishes that the village folk wished here upon high days and holidays.

'I'll wish too,' said Maria to herself, and standing with her hand on the old gnarled trunk she wished three things.

That she might rid the valley of the wickedness of the Black Men.

That she might meet that poor shepherd boy and love him.

That she might be the first Moon Princess to live for always in her home.

When she had had her wishes she found that her heart was beating fast. They would be granted, she felt sure, and she was committed to all the adventures that the fulfilment of exciting wishes is bound to bring with it.

'Maria!' called Miss Heliotrope. 'Don't go too far, dear. Don't go where I can't see you.'

Maria ran back to Miss Heliotrope and the animals. 'But I *must* go to the top of the hill,' she pleaded. 'I *must* look at those beech-trees, and the old grey stones.'

'The hill is too steep for the pony carriage,' objected Miss Heliotrope. 'And it is too steep for me to climb. You must stay here, dear, for I can't permit you to go alone.'

'Sir Benjamin doesn't mind where I go so long as Wrolf is with me,' said Maria. 'You stay here in the pony carriage, with Periwinkle and Wiggins to look after you, and I'll go to the top of the hill with Wrolf and Serena to look after me. That will be quite all right, Miss Heliotrope.'

The day was turning stuffy and hot, too hot to argue, and Miss Heliotrope gave in. She permitted herself to be settled comfortably in the pony carriage with her book of essays, Wiggins in attendance, and Periwinkle peacefully cropping the sweet turf.

'Look after Miss Heliotrope, Periwinkle,' commanded Maria. 'Whatever happens, look after Miss Heliotrope.'

Periwinkle stopped munching for a moment, lifted her head and gave her mistress a steady glance. Then she dropped her head and munched again. Reassured, Maria, Wrolf, and Serena started off together for the top of the hill. It was a steep hot climb, and took much longer than Maria had expected. Town-bred girl that she was, she panted a little and got hot, and envied Serena advancing with her long leaps and Wrolf with his tireless strength. And Wrolf did not make things easier by perpetually pushing himself against her, and fixing her with a tawny eye full of annoyance. 'What *is* it, Wrolf?' she demanded. 'What am I doing wrong?'

Wrolf, with a subdued roar at her stupidity, turned himself right across her path so that she came to a standstill, looking down upon his broad back. Then she saw what he wanted and mounted thankfully, as though he had been Periwinkle.

After that everything was easy. Wrolf's beautiful thick fur was soft to sit upon, and with her fingers entwined in his ruff she was able to hold herself steady. She could look about her now, and as they mounted higher see the beautiful countryside unrolling about them like a map, and the line of the sea creeping round the horizon like a silver ribbon. But the sky was very dark and lowering, almost purple in colour, and she thought she heard a mutter of thunder in the distance. . . . And she had told Miss Heliotrope it was too early in the year for thunder. . . . Well, she would be all right, for Periwinkle would look after her.

They were nearly at the top of the hill now, and looking up she could see the old storm-twisted beech-trees, their new leaves burning like tongues of green fire against the violet sky, with the old grey fallen stones beneath them. She was among the sheep now. The mothers lifted their heads to look at her, and baaed in welcome, and the little lambs came gambolling all about her. It was strange to her that they did not seem in the least afraid of Wrolf. One or two came butting into him, and he sent them flying with a playful blow of a great paw that did not hurt them at all but just sent them tumbling head over heels in delight. As for Serena, she lolloped in and out among the sheep and seemed to be telling them something, for they all looked at Maria and were very pleased, and baaed again.

What was that music? Somewhere up there beneath the beech-trees someone was playing a shepherd's pipe, and the gay little tune came floating down to Maria like a voice calling her. She remembered the wish that she had had, standing beneath the thorn-tree. It was the shepherd boy!

They got to the top of the hill at last, and Wrolf stopped and she slipped off his back.

'Stay there,' she said to him and to Serena, and then ran

eagerly forward beneath the beech-trees, climbing over the old grey stones. 'Are you there?' she cried. 'Shepherd boy, are you there?'

But there was no answer, and the music now was still. There was nothing to be heard except the trickle of hidden water. She stood still, and looked this way and that, and listened, but there was nothing. 'I must have imagined it,' she said to herself. 'It must just have been the water.' And for a moment she could have cried with disappointment.

But only for a moment, for Maria had too much sense to let her spirits be damped by minor disappointments, and there was so much to look at that she soon forgot about that fancied tune. The beech-trees, with their smooth grey trunks and branches stretched this way and that, were more like people than trees; like old grey monks with arms held wide in blessing. And deep within the circle of the beech-trees part of the walls of the monastery was still standing, overgrown with ivy and brambles.

Maria found herself standing before a beautiful carved doorway in the broken wall, half hidden by a falling curtain of ivy. She pushed the curtain aside and stepped in, and found herself in what must once have been a small paved court. The paving-stones were still there, littered with fallen stones, covered with weeds and brambles. In the centre of the court was a beautiful clump of ferns, and from deep within it came that tinkle of water. 'Inside there,' she said to herself, 'is the holy well.'

She pulled aside the ferns and found not a well such as they had in the stable-yard at home but a beautiful clear stream bubbling up out of the ground, forcing its way through a choking mass of fallen dead beech leaves, and then along a channel through the paving-stones, and out beneath a low arch in the wall opposite, and so to the hillside beyond. Maria guessed that out upon the hillside it would curve itself around until it became the stream that ran beneath the fairy thorn-tree and then down the hill to the village. Upon one side of the low arch grew a rowan-tree bright with scarlet berries, and upon the other side a holly-tree with glossy shining leaves, and over it was an empty niche in the wall.

Maria gathered her green cloak about her, knelt down upon the paving-stones, folded her hands and shut her eyes, and said a prayer. For this, she remembered, had been a holy place, and her wicked ancestor Sir Wrolf had taken it away from God to have it for himself. And now, they said, his ghost haunted this place and could not enter Paradise because of his sins.

'O God,' she prayed, 'please forgive Sir Wrolf for being so greedy. And please show me how to give this place back to You. And then please let him go to Paradise.'

There was a queer clanging sound, almost like a horse's iron hoofs slipping on stones, and she opened her eyes suddenly. But there was nothing unusual to be seen; only a curtain of ivy hanging on the wall opposite her was swaying a little, as though someone had just passed by. She got up and went to it and pulled it aside, and there behind it was another low stone archway in the wall. But beyond this archway was not the hillside, but darkness, and a flight of steps leading down into the earth.

'There must be a cellar or something down there,' said Maria, and she would have gone in and explored had not her attention been caught by something else; a shepherd's pipe lying on a flat stone beside the doorway. . . . So she *had* heard someone playing a pipe, after all. . . . With a beating heart she knelt down beside the pipe, and she would have picked it up, only quite suddenly the most alarming things began to happen.

The first thing that happened was that the baaing of the sheep outside on the hill changed its note, ceased to be contented and happy, and became a bleating of terror. And then there came a flash of lightning and a crash of thunder overhead.

'Miss Heliotrope!' thought Maria at once. 'Miss Heliotrope! She's terrified of a storm.'

She jumped up and ran back the way she had come, out on to the hillside, and there away in the distance she saw Periwinkle making for home as fast as she could, with the pony carriage leaping and jolting over the rough ground. 'Good Periwinkle! Good Joy-of-the-ground!' cried Maria. 'She is looking after Miss Heliotrope, just as I told her.'

And then, looking about her, she saw the reason for the frightened baaing of the sheep, and saw also that Periwinkle was taking Miss Heliotrope away from something much worse than a thunderstorm. For scattered over the hillside were the figures of some half-dozen men dressed in black, shadowy, frightening figures that looked as though they might have dropped from the storm-clouds overhead. And they were stealing the lambs! Two of them were already making off down the hill with pathetic white woolly forms flung over their shoulders.

'Wrolf! Wrolf!' shouted Maria, but a deep roaring sound

from the other side of the hill told her that Wrolf was engaged with other Black Men whom she could not see. If she were going to rescue those lambs, Merryweather lambs, *her* lambs, she must do it herself.

Though she was absolutely terrified she did not hesitate. Gathering up her skirts in both hands she went dashing off down the hill, shouting as she had shouted when she rescued Serena: 'Put those lambs down, I tell you! They're *my* lambs. Put them down!'

But the men with the lambs went on while the other four came running towards Maria, brandishing their sticks and laughing; though their eyes were flashing in their dark faces in a very nasty way, a way that boded ill for Maria.

'I'm not afraid of you,' she called to them, though she was so afraid that her tongue almost stuck to the roof of her mouth. 'You dare hurt my lambs! You dare!'

After that it became most confusing. The thunder pealed and the lightning flashed and the rain came down like silver spears; and the Black Men were closing in upon her. To her right, through the rain, she dimly saw a slim figure dressed in brown, with a shepherd's crook in his hand, running towards her, and on her left Wrolf was bounding to the rescue with Serena leaping along behind him. . . . But they were not nearly as close as the Black Men were. . . .

And then, through the noise of the thunder and the rain, she distinctly heard the hoofs of a galloping horse pounding upon the turf. As the horseman was behind her she could not herself see anything, but whoever he was the Black Men seemed to see him, for with faces blanched by terror they turned and fled. And then the two men carrying the lambs turned round, looked up, saw whatever it was the others had seen, dropped the lambs, and fled also. And the slim brown running figure came to her and took her hand. . . . And he was Robin.

'Quick!' he cried. 'There are lots more of Them about. Quick! Run to the monastery and take shelter. Wrolf and I will round up the sheep. Run!'

And Maria ran, and as she ran she looked about her for the horseman on the galloping horse. But there was nothing to be seen; only the rain and the old beeches up above her on the top of the hill. She made for these as for the shelter of home, ran beneath them, and did not stop running until she reached the little paved court and the holy well. There it was still and quiet, and the interlaced branches overhead kept off most of the rain. She dropped down panting beside the spring and knew that she was safe. She could hear Wrolf roaring as he herded the sheep, and Robin's clear voice calling to them in comfort and reassurance.

And soon, led by Serena, they all came trooping in around her, the big woolly mothers and the little lambs with their black faces and wagging tails and long ungainly legs. Merryweather lambs. Her lambs. She held out her hands to them and made comforting noises, and they and their mothers crowded round her. They bent their heads to drink from the cool spring, and she stroked their heads and talked to them as though they were her children. The rain stopped, and a shaft of pale sunlight shone down into the little court and turned the bubbling water to silver and the sheep's wool to cloth of gold. Then she looked up and Robin was standing by her, and Wrolf was there too, shaking himself vigorously to get the wet off his fur.

'We are safe here,' said Robin. 'This is a holy place, and the Black Men are wicked and They never come here. They are afraid of it.'

Maria looked up at him. He was looking unusually serious and very wet, and the raindrops were dripping off the end of the feather in his hat.

'So you are the shepherd boy,' said Maria.

'I am Sir Benjamin's shepherd boy and garden boy and general odd-jobber,' said Robin. 'Didn't you know? I was playing my pipe here when suddenly I felt that something was wrong. And I went out and saw Them coming up the other side of the hill. But I could never have chased Them off if it hadn't been for you and Wrolf helping me.'

'And that man on horseback,' said Maria.

'What man on horseback?' asked Robin.

'I heard a man on horseback galloping behind me,' said Maria. 'It was just after I had called "Wrolf! Wrolf!" that I heard him. I didn't see him, but the Black Men did. It's funny that you didn't see him.'

'No, I didn't see him,' said Robin, and he spoke very soberly indeed, and the water went drip drip off the end of his draggled feather.

'You *are* wet, Robin,' said Maria.

'So are you,' said Robin.

Wrolf, who had shaken all the water off himself and wasn't wet any more, now walked to the low archway behind the ivy, where Robin's pipe still lay upon the stone, and then walked back again, giving utterance to a low deep rumble in the throat as he came.

'He's right,' said Robin to Maria. 'You'll catch cold if you don't get your wet clothes off.'

He held out his hand to her and helped her up. 'Come back with me to my house, and my mother will give you dry things. Wrolf will stay here with the sheep until he's quite certain there are no more Black Men stalking around. Once the sun sets, the sheep will be quite safe. The Black Men don't dare even to come to the hill after sunset. No one does. They are afraid.'

'Of the ghost of Sir Wrolf?' asked Maria.

'So they say,' said Robin.

'Is your home far, Robin?' asked Maria. She was, she suddenly discovered, very tired as well as very wet. She felt she could scarcely walk another step. And if Wrolf was staying here with the sheep, she would not be able to ride upon his back as she had done when she came up the hill.

'My home is just here,' said Robin. 'There are rather a lot of steps, but it's downhill all the way. Good-bye, Wrolf.'

'Good-bye, Wrolf,' said Maria, caressing the great shaggy head. 'Good-bye, sheep.' Then she looked about her. 'But where is Serena?' she asked anxiously. 'She was here a minute ago.'

'Don't worry about Serena,' said Robin. 'She must have gone off somewhere to do something. I don't know what, but whatever it is it's sure to be something useful. Hares are very wise.' Then he took Maria's hand and led her across the court to the archway in the wall behind the ivy.

'Is *this* your house?' she asked in surprise.

'Yes,' said Robin. 'This is Paradise Door. We have three doors—Front Door, Back Door, and Paradise Door.'

'And you keep a mother down there?' asked Maria, peering rather apprehensively down into the darkness.

'The nicest mother in the world,' said Robin, and then putting his hand into an alcove in the wall he took out a lantern, took flint and tinder from his pocket, and lit it. 'I'll go first, and you follow, with your dress held well up because it's dusty.'

Maria had thought she was tired, but curiosity soon made her forget all about that, as Robin led her down a stone staircase, right down into the depths of the earth. At least it could be called a staircase only by courtesy, for the steps had been cut very roughly out of what seemed a natural tunnel in the rock.

'My mother says that once upon a time there must have been a stream running down here,' said Robin. 'And the stream made the tunnel. And then the monks made the steps, so as to have a quick way of getting down to the village in bad weather. These hills are full of tunnels and caves, you know. Our house must once have been a cave. Or at least several caves. Our house is great fun. Mother thinks that the monks must have made it for a school or hospital for the village people.'

They went on and on, and quite suddenly the tunnel came to an end, before a small, low, rounded archway fitted with an oak door just big enough to admit a child or someone very small and slim. There was a knocker on the door and it was a little silver horseshoe.

'Robin,' whispered Maria, 'the door is small like my door, and the horseshoe knocker is just like mine.'

'They say,' said Robin, 'that the people who lived centuries ago were most of them smaller than we are now. So that must be why the monks made such a small door. I don't know who put the knocker here. It was here when Mother and I discovered this door, and we believe that no one knows about this passage and door except us. They say *your* knocker was put there by the first Moon Princess.'

He pushed open the door, blew out his lantern, and then stood aside courteously for Maria to go in first.

Inside was a funny little cave, very much the shape of Maria's room at the manor, only smaller. It had only one window, high up in the wall, and through it there was nothing to be seen except a patch of sky. The little room was very bare. There was just a low wooden bed covered by a patchwork quilt, a carved chest and a shelf for books. Upon the farther side of the room was another little archway, with no door this time. Maria would have liked to linger here a little and see what books Robin had on his shelf, but he wouldn't let her.

'Come straight to Mother and get dry,' he commanded, and led the way to the second little archway. Maria followed him and found herself on a very narrow flight of steps, leading downward into Loveday Minette's bedroom.

'Robin!' she cried in delight and astonishment. 'Robin! Is Loveday Minette your mother?'

'Of course,' said Robin matter-of-factly.

'And I thought Loveday must have a fairy husband,' said

Maria, 'because of these narrow steps. But it's *you* she must have been talking about when she said "he".'

'My father wasn't a fairy,' said Robin. 'He was a mortal man, a lawyer. He wasn't a valley man. He and my mother lived in the market-town right away on the other side of Paradise Hill. He died when I was only four years old, and then my mother came back to live in the Moonacre Valley. Because, you see, she had lived in this valley before she married, and people who have once lived here can never be happy anywhere else.'

They had reached Loveday's bedroom now, and he called down the stairs to the room below, 'Mother, are you there? Maria is here, and she's very wet.'

'Coming,' called Loveday's silvery voice, and in a moment she was with them, trim and lovely and looking ridiculously young to be Robin's mother.

'Go downstairs, Robin,' she said, 'and put on the dry clothes that are airing for you in front of the fire.'

Robin obeyed, and Loveday and Maria were left alone in Loveday's lovely bedroom.

'Take off your wet things at once, Maria,' Loveday commanded in bustling motherly tones. 'I have a dress that will fit you exactly. It has never been worn. It is not shabby like that old riding-habit of mine that you wear.'

Maria, in the middle of taking off her wet green dress, stopped and peeped through its folds at Loveday on her knees before the oak chest, rummaging in its depths for the dress that had never been worn.

'*Now* I know,' she said. 'You come to the manor-house in the mornings, don't you, Loveday, while I am still asleep, and lay out my clothes for me? And my prayer-book is yours. And you made those lovely things for my dear Miss Heliotrope. Oh, Loveday, what makes you so good to me?'

'That night you arrived,' said Loveday, 'I opened the big door under the stone archway and let you in. You didn't see me but I saw you, and I loved you as though you were my own daughter.'

'And the moment I saw *you,*' said Maria, 'I loved you as though you were my mother. Oh, Loveday, why don't you wake me up and kiss me when you come to my room in the early mornings?'

'I will, now,' said Loveday. 'You see, I came secretly. I wanted no one to know that I came. Sir Benjamin and Marmaduke Scarlet cannot bear a woman about the place. Until you arrived it was their boast that no female had ever set foot in the manor-house for twenty years. You must not tell them that I come, Maria.'

'I won't tell,' Maria promised. 'But, Loveday, who lets you in?'

'Zachariah the cat,' said Loveday.

'Oh,' said Maria, and pulled off her green dress, and her wet shoes and stockings and stood before Loveday with her shapely little white feet peeping out from beneath her white muslin petticoat.

Loveday rose from her knees and came towards Maria, with something white and shimmering in her arms. She put it over her head and pulled it down around her, and Maria saw that it was an exquisite dress of moony white satin. It was the loveliest dress she had ever seen, and she gasped with delight as Loveday hooked it up. . . . It was a perfect fit.

'It is a wedding dress,' said Loveday. 'But I never wore it.'

'But why not?' asked the puzzled Maria. 'Fancy having a lovely dress like this, and then not wearing it at your wedding after all.'

'The man I was going to marry when I made this dress was not the man I did marry,' explained Loveday. 'I was betrothed to a rich gentleman once, and I made this dress for my wedding with him. Then we quarrelled, and I did not marry him, after all. I married a poor gentleman in a dress of sprigged muslin that was more suited to my bridegroom's lot in life. . . . You look lovely, my darling. Look at yourself in the glass.'

Maria went towards the old mirror of polished silver, not frightened this time because Loveday was standing just behind her, looking over her shoulder and laughing, and she saw their two happy faces side by side. That moony radiance, which was the gift of the glass to the faces it mirrored, gave them a sisterly likeness that rejoiced their hearts.

'Don't we look alike?' cried Maria. 'I'm plain and you are beautiful, but yet in this glass we look alike.'

'We *are* alike,' said Loveday. 'But don't make my mistakes, Maria, whatever you do.'

'What were your mistakes?' asked Maria.

'Too many to tell you,' said Loveday, 'but they all grew out of being aggravating and losing my temper. Never be aggravating, Maria, and never get in a rage.'

'I'll do my best not to,' promised Maria. 'And when I'm married, may I wear this dress?'

'Of course,' said Loveday. 'It will need no alteration. It's a perfect fit.'

They went downstairs and found that Robin had already changed into dry clothes and set the table for tea with bread and butter, honey and cream, and golden-brown parkin. The kettle was singing on the hob, the white kitten was purring loudly, and the strange cave-room looked glowing and cosy, lit by the leaping flames of the log fire. When she had put the children's wet things to dry, Loveday made the tea in a big brown pot like a beehive, and they sat down and fell hungrily upon the lovely food. Robin, sitting opposite Maria at the oak table spread with its snowy cloth, gazed at her in astounded appreciation of her appearance, but was at first too much occupied in eating to say anything about it. However, when he had devoured half a loaf and a lot of parkin he at last gave tongue.

'That's a pretty dress,' he said with his mouth full. 'I've not seen it before. It looks like a wedding dress.'

'It is a wedding dress,' said Maria thickly, for she too was ravenous and was devouring bread and honey at the rate of two bites a slice. 'It's my wedding dress. I'm trying it on to see if it fits.'

'Are you going to be married?' asked Robin sharply, his munching jaws suddenly still.

'Of course,' said Maria, reaching for the cream. 'You didn't expect me to be an old maid, did you?'

'Are you being married today?' demanded Robin.

But this time Maria's mouth was so full that she couldn't answer, and Loveday, who hadn't had her hunger sharpened by fresh air, danger, and exercise, and was nibbling very daintily at a very thin slice of bread and butter, answered for her.

'Of course she isn't being married today, Robin. She isn't

old enough to be married yet. But when she *is* married she will wear that dress.'

'When you *do* marry, *who* will you marry?' Robin asked Maria.

Maria swallowed the last of her bread and cream and honey, put her head on one side and stirred her tea thoughtfully. 'I have not quite decided yet,' she said demurely, 'but I *think* I shall marry a boy I knew in London.'

'What?' yelled Robin. 'Marry some mincing nincompoop of a Londoner with silk stockings and pomade in his hair and a face like a Cheshire cheese?'

The parkin stuck in his gullet and he choked so violently that Loveday had to pat him on the back and pour him out a fresh cup of tea. When he spoke again his face was absolutely scarlet, not only with the choke but with rage and jealousy and exasperation.

'You dare do such a thing!' he exploded. 'You—Maria—you—if you marry a London man I'll wring his neck!'

'Robin! Robin!' expostulated his mother in horror. 'I've never seen you in a temper like this before. I did not know you had got a temper.'

'Well, you know now,' said Robin furiously. 'And if she marries that London fellow, I'll not only wring his neck, I'll wring everybody's necks, and I'll go right away out of the valley, over the hills to the town where my father came from, and I won't ever come back here again. So there!'

Maria said nothing at all in response to this outburst. She just continued to drink her tea and look more demure than ever. And the more demure she looked the angrier Robin became. His eyes flashed fire, and his chestnut curls seemed standing straight up all over his head with fury. Maria was quite sure that if she had been standing behind him she would have seen the twist of hair in the nape of his neck twitching backwards and forwards like a cat's tail. She drank her tea with maddening deliberation and spoke at last.

'Why don't you want me to marry that London boy?' she asked.

Robin brought his fist down on the table with a crash that set all the china leaping. 'Because you are going to marry *me,*' he shouted. 'Do you hear, Maria? You are going to marry *me.*'

'Robin,' said his mother, 'that's not at all the way to propose. You should go down on one knee and do it in a very gentle voice.'

'How can I go down on one knee when I'm in the middle of my tea?' demanded Robin. 'And how can I do it in a gentle voice when I feel as though I had a roaring lion inside me? If I didn't roar, I should burst.'

'You can stop roaring, Robin,' said Maria. 'You can stop, because for the sake of peace and quiet I have suddenly made up my mind to marry you.'

Robin's curls flopped down on his head again and the crimson tide receded from his forehead. 'That's all right then,' he said with a great sigh of relief. 'That's settled. I'll have some more parkin, please, Mother.'

After that they ate and drank and laughed, and talked of other things, while the fire leaped up, the white kitten purred, the kettle hummed louder and louder, and happiness seemed all about them like a radiance and a singing that they could almost see and hear. But something seemed still troubling Robin very slightly, and at last he burst out: 'Maria, who *is* this London boy you were thinking of marrying?'

'I have never had the slightest intention of marrying any London boy,' said Maria.

'But you said—'

'I said, a boy I *knew* in London,' said Maria. 'That boy was you.'

The last remnant of Robin's jealousy and rage evaporated. He threw back his head and laughed and laughed, roaring not this time with anger but with mirth, and something about that genial roaring reminded Maria abruptly and surprisingly of Sir Benjamin.

'Now listen, children,' said Loveday, getting up from the table and standing and looking down on them with sudden deep seriousness, 'you are laughing now; but a little while ago Robin was angry and Maria was being as aggravating as she knew how to be. You might have quarrelled very badly. *And you must never quarrel.* If you do, you will wreck not only your own happiness but the happiness of the whole valley.'

Then she gathered the tea-things together, stacked them in a corner of the room beside her washing-up bowl, folded up the tablecloth and put it away, and went up the stairs to her own room. She was not crying, but Maria had the feeling that had she not been so proud a woman, she would have been.

'I shouldn't wonder,' said Maria to herself, 'if she wasn't loving that fine gentleman she didn't marry all the time she was quarrelling with him, but she was too proud to make it up. Poor Loveday!'

After that she was silent for a moment, watching Robin

feeding the kitten and remembering how all the Moon Princesses quarrelled with the men they loved and had to go away from Moonacre Manor, remembering that she did not want to go away herself, remembering that she and Robin had very nearly had a bad row a moment ago, remembering that she had said to Old Parson that perhaps if Paradise Hill was given back to God these quarrels would not happen any more.

'Robin,' she said, 'before we drive out the wickedness of the Black Men, we've got to give Paradise Hill back to God. Sir Wrolf stole it, you know. We must give it back.'

Robin looked round from the saucer of milk he was setting before the fire. 'Very well,' he said. 'But how?'

Maria, still sitting at the table, cupped her determined chin in her hands and considered. How indeed? She would have liked to ask the advice of the monks from whom Sir Wrolf had originally stolen it, only they had been dead for centuries. The nearest thing to a monk that she knew of in these parts was Old Parson. Would he know what to do? 'I'll ask Old Parson,' she said to Robin.

'All right,' said Robin. 'Only whatever Old Parson tells us to do we'd better do it at once, so that we can make a start on the Black Men. There's no time to waste, you know. They're getting worse and worse. Animals are being caught in traps every day, and more and more chickens and geese and ducks and sheep and cows are getting stolen. Six cows disappeared last week.'

Maria got up. 'I'll go to Old Parson at once,' she said. 'On my way home.'

Robin got up, too, and faced her across the table. His eyes

were sparkling, and she knew that he, too, was exulting in the hugeness of the adventure that lay before them.

'Robin,' she said, 'how did you know that you and I together had to drive out the wickedness of the Black Men? The very first day I saw you here, you said we'd have to do it. How did you know?'

'It was because of Serena,' said Robin. 'No one before has ever been able to save anything from the Black Men, but you and I saved Serena. I knew then that we could save the whole valley. I knew it more than ever, when we saved the sheep.'

'There's another thing I don't understand,' said Maria. 'How did you manage to come and play with me in the Square garden in London?'

'I went to you when I was asleep,' said Robin. 'Sometimes I'd be keeping the sheep on Paradise Hill or weeding the manor-house garden, and suddenly I'd feel sleepy, and I'd curl round on the grass or among the flowers and doze off; and then I'd find myself in London. Or I'd suddenly feel sleepy while I was scrubbing the Merryweather Chantry, and I'd lie down on top of Sir Wrolf, with my head on the dog, and doze off. Or I'd feel sleepy while I was here with Mother and I'd sit down on the floor and fall asleep with my head on her lap. I asked Mother about it once and she said that we are really all of us two people, a body person and a spirit person, and when the body person is asleep the spirit person, who lives inside it like a letter inside an envelope, can come out and go on journeys.'

'I see,' said Maria. Then she asked another question. 'Robin, Loveday told me that Sir Benjamin does not know she lives here. But if you are his shepherd boy and garden boy, he must know that *you* live here?'

'Yes, of course he does,' said Robin. 'But he thinks I am the adopted child of old Elspeth who used to live in this house. Mother told the villagers to tell him that because she doesn't want him to know that old Elspeth is dead and that she lives here now. She keeps hidden when he's anywhere around.'

'But why, Robin?' demanded Maria, aflame with curiosity. 'Why?'

'I don't know,' said Robin indifferently, pouring out a fresh saucer of milk for the kitten.

'Robin, haven't you *any* curiosity?' Maria demanded almost passionately. 'Haven't you asked Loveday?'

'No,' said Robin. 'Why should I? It isn't any business of mine. How I could manage to visit you in London was my business, and so I asked Mother about it. But it was nothing to do with me about her not wanting Sir Benjamin to know she lives here.'

Maria heaved a great impatient sigh. Truly the non-curiosity of men was beyond her comprehension. As for herself, she felt that if she did not get to the bottom of what was between Loveday and Sir Benjamin before she slept tonight, *her* curiosity would most certainly be the death of her. But it was no use asking any more questions of Robin.

'I'm going upstairs to take this dress off, Robin,' she said, gathering up her own clothes from before the fire. 'And then I'll go home by way of the Parsonage and ask Old Parson about Paradise Hill.'

'All right,' said Robin cheerfully. And then, as she went up the steps to Loveday's room, he called after her, 'Next time you put that dress on it will be to marry me.'

'So it will, Robin,' said Maria. And she laughed. It would be great fun to marry Robin.

She had expected to find Loveday upstairs, but there was no sign of her, and as she took off the lovely wedding dress and laid it away again in the oak chest she had the feeling that Loveday had gone up through Robin's room and climbed the steps inside the hill, and gone out through Paradise Door to Paradise Hill, and was wandering there where once the Moon Princess had wandered, trying to find comfort because she had quarrelled with the man she loved.

•: 2 :•

When she had changed and gone downstairs again Robin let her out through the Back Door, and she ran all the way through the gathering dusk to the Parsonage and knocked at the old front door. Old Parson let her in at once with a welcoming smile and shut the door behind her. It was warm and cosy and pretty in his little room, for he had drawn his curtains and lighted his candles and kindled a bright fire on the hearth, and his pink geraniums were glowing gloriously. Sitting beside him on the settle, warming her toes at his fire, for it had turned quite chilly after the storm, she told him that she wanted to give Paradise Hill back to God but she did not know how.

'I'll show you how,' said Old Parson. 'Come to the church very early tomorrow morning, at the hour when the children are playing there, and you and I and the children will all go up to Paradise Hill together and give it back to God. But there's another thing that you must do, Maria, and you must do it tonight.'

'Yes?' asked Maria.

'Sir Benjamin makes a lot of money out of selling the wool that grows on the backs of those sheep of his that he keeps on Paradise Hill, but if the hill is to be given back to God then after tomorrow morning the wool is God's wool, not Sir Benjamin's. You must explain that to him.'

Maria looked at him a little doubtfully. 'Couldn't *you* explain it?' she asked. 'You could walk home with me now.'

'I could not,' said Old Parson firmly. 'I shall be much occupied for the rest of the evening. Now you'd better go home, Maria, for it's getting dark and you don't want to be out by yourself in the park in the dark.'

Maria got up at once. She certainly did not. Alone in the dark was a state of affairs she did not relish with these Black Men about. When Old Parson had shut his front door behind her and she saw how much darker it had grown while she had been with him, she felt downright frightened. He might have come with her, she thought. He might have come with her to look after her. . . . And what was that great shadow there, outside the gate? Was it a Black Man? . . .

She gave a little stifled cry of fear, which changed midway to a cry of joy, as the supposed Black Man lifted a tail and waved it in the air, and she saw that the shadowy shape was Wrolf. She went down the garden path, patted his great head, and marvelled to think that once she had been afraid of him. And then together they went down the village street, and through the broken gate into the park.

That walk through the park with Wrolf was a thing that Maria never forgot. It was almost dark now, and had she been alone she would have been afraid, but with Wrolf pacing along beside her, the embodiment of courage and strength, she felt as safe as houses. She walked slowly, the fingers of one hand twisted in his great furry ruff, and smelt the sweet scents of wet earth and flowers and moss, and lifted her head to watch for the first pricking forth of the stars in the sky above the treetops.

It was so still after the storm that she could hear a dog barking miles away and the rustle of birds going to bed. Now and then she looked up the shadowy glades on each side of her, but not with any sense of expectation, only to think how beautiful they were. She did not really expect to see the little white horse now, because she had looked for him so often and had never seen him again. Sometimes she wondered if she ever *had* seen him, or if what she had seen on the first night had been only a stray moonbeam.

No, it wasn't because of anything that she saw that that walk home was so lovely. It was because of Wrolf. Since this afternoon there seemed a new and very strong bond between them. She thought he was pleased because of what she and Robin had decided to try to do. He wanted her to succeed and not to fail like the other Moon Maidens. He did not want her to have to leave Moonacre Manor. Perhaps he did not want to have to leave it himself? For it seemed that the tawny dog always had to go back to the pine-wood when the Moon Maiden quarrelled with her lover. It was as though he were a sort of picture of the fine qualities of Moonacre men—strong and brave, loving, warm and ruddy—so that when the Moon

Maiden parted with her man she had to part with the tawny dog too.

And the little white horse, Maria thought suddenly, had all the Moon Maiden qualities, the white beauty, the shining purity, the still pride. Only the tawny dog and the little white horse had a perfection to which individual sun and moon Merryweathers would never attain. . . . They were ideals. . . . It was because of these thoughts that went through her head, as well as because Wrolf was so pleased with her, that Maria so enjoyed that walk home.

It was not until they were in sight of the manor-house, and she saw a light shining out from her tower window, as though someone had lit a light there to guide her home, that she suddenly wondered whether Sir Benjamin and Miss Heliotrope were dreadfully anxious about her. She was very penitent, for she had not given a thought to them for hours.

'Quick, Wrolf,' she said, tugging at his ruff. 'Hurry! Hurry!'

But Wrolf refused to be hurried, and gazing up into her face he gave her a reassuring look. . . . He knew they were not anxious.

And when they reached the lighted hall the spectacle presented by Sir Benjamin and Miss Heliotrope, seated at the table in front of the fire devouring pork chops and onions, baked apples, and custard, while Wiggins and Serena lapped bread and milk from bowls set upon the hearth, was not one that suggested anxiety.

'Safe home,' said Sir Benjamin, but not as though he had doubted that she would be. And he was wearing his best waistcoat, she noticed, the one embroidered with yellow roses and crimson carnations, and his great ruby ring. People don't bother to put on their best clothes when they are anxious.

'You're late, dear,' said Miss Heliotrope, but not as though she minded.

In spite of the big tea she had eaten Maria found that her Merryweather appetite was still functioning quite nicely, and she was sorry to see that Sir Benjamin, who had been concentrating upon the pork and onions, had left very little for her to concentrate upon, and that Miss Heliotrope, before whose place the baked apples and custard had been set, was evidently not suffering from indigestion tonight. But she need not have worried, for the kitchen door now opened a crack and the heads of Marmaduke Scarlet and Zachariah the cat appeared one above the other in the aperture.

'Should the young Mistress and the dog Wrolf deign once more to enter my humble apartment they will find within it two small collations designed respectively for the satisfaction of the inward cravings of a high-born young female and her faithful canine attendant,' said Marmaduke.

Maria and Wrolf deigned, with speed. The kitchen, lighted by the glow of the great fire, was gloriously cosy. The canary, as yet uneaten by Zachariah, was singing lustily. On the table was set a roasted pigeon in a silver dish, an apple dumpling, and a pot of cream. On the floor was a huge mutton bone. Wrolf fell to without more ado, but Maria, though her supper smelled so delicious that it set her nose quivering like a rabbit's, went first to the wide hearth and looked in the ashes.

Yes, there was another series of pictures drawn there. First came a picture of Serena, leaping along on three legs, her ears streaming behind her with the wind of her going, then came once again that outline of the sickle moon that stood for herself, and then the outlines of two small square solid houses such as a child draws.

Maria laughed out loud in delight. Serena had brought the message and Zachariah had written it on the hearth. 'Serena says Maria is safe as houses.'

'Oh, clever Serena!' cried Maria. 'And clever Zachariah!'

Zachariah walked round and round her in circles, his tail held as usual in three coils over his back, pressing against her skirts, and purred and purred and purred.

·: 3 :·

But the discovery of the pictures on the hearth was not the last of Maria's discoveries that day. There was still one more to come.

When she had finished her delicious supper and gone back to the hall she found it empty, but candlelight shining from beneath the parlour door told her where she would find everybody. And there they all four were, Wiggins and Serena sleeping before the fire and Sir Benjamin and Miss Heliotrope beside them, seated one on each side of the small table that usually stood against the wall with the chessmen and workbox upon it. . . .

And they were playing chess. . . . Those frozen chessmen were being used again at last. The little red dogs and white horses were prancing over the black and white squares, and the kings and queens and knights and bishops were all drawn up in battle array, and they were not frozen any more. In the glow of the firelight and candlelight they were made not of ivory but of opal and pearl. They were alive.

'Oh!' cried Maria in delight. 'You're using the chessmen again!'

Sir Benjamin looked up, and Maria saw that his face was redder than ever and that his brown eyes had a very startled expression in them, as though he were doing something that he had never expected to find himself doing again.

'I haven't played chess for more than twenty years,' he said hoarsely. 'I used to play chess with—well—that's an old story—'

'Whatever made you do it now?' demanded Maria.

'When we came into the room they looked so unused,' said Sir Benjamin. 'Not like the harpsichord, which looks somehow quite different since you came. Before I knew what I was saying, I had suggested to Miss Heliotrope that we should have a game.'

'Where's the workbox?' demanded Maria. 'The workbox that stood on the table beside the chessmen? That's unused too. What have you done with the workbox?'

'Was there a workbox?' asked Sir Benjamin vaguely.

Miss Heliotrope gazed about her over the top of her spectacles. 'I think I put it on the floor somewhere,' she said.

'On the floor!' exclaimed Maria indignantly. Then she saw it down in the corner and pounced on it. 'If you're using the chessmen, I'm going to use the workbox,' she said.

'Certainly, my dear,' said Sir Benjamin. But he was intent on the game, and she doubted if he had heard what she said. Nevertheless, she had his permission, the permission to open the workbox that had not been given her the other day. She carried it over to the window-seat, sat down and held it for a little while in her lap, sniffing the lovely faint scent of the cedarwood. Then she lifted the lid and looked inside.

The box was lined with quilted ivory satin, and fastened against the inside of the lid by loops in the satin were a beautiful little silver thimble and a pair of scissors. Inside the box was a half-finished piece of embroidery, neatly folded. Maria took it out and unfolded it, and it was a waistcoat of white satin embroidered with white moon-daisies with yellow centres like little suns, each daisy backed by green leaves so that it showed up against the white satin. It was nearly finished. There were only a few leaves not yet completed.

Maria set the workbox on the seat beside her, and spread the waistcoat out on her lap. Then she looked across at Sir Benjamin, sitting opposite her, too absorbed in his chess to notice what she was doing. The candlelight gleamed upon the beautiful embroidered waistcoat he was wearing. Maria looked from one piece of work to the other. The flowers were different, but the design was the same. One could not doubt that the same hand had worked them both—and—and —yes—the same stitches had been used in the embroidery of the flowers upon the lavender bags that Loveday had made for Miss Heliotrope. . . . Loveday had worked both these waistcoats.

Maria sat very still, thinking very hard. The waistcoat in her lap looked, she thought, as though it had been made of the same satin as the wedding dress that she had been wearing only that afternoon. It looked as though it, too, had been made for a wedding. Moon-daisies with centres like yellow suns. Moon and sun.

Suddenly she remembered something Marmaduke Scarlet had said on the day she had first visited him in the kitchen and he had praised Miss Heliotrope. 'A distinct improvement upon the other duenna who resided here once before with the other young mistress.'

And then she remembered what Loveday had said about old Elspeth, who had once lived at the manor-house, but had quarrelled with Marmaduke and refused to live there any more. Sir Benjamin had made her porteress, and then she had quarrelled with him too. But she must have been friends with Loveday, for Loveday had known when she died and had taken her place in the gatehouse inside the hill.

Maria suddenly saw it all. Her curiosity was satisfied. Loveday as a girl had lived here with her governess, even as she, Maria, was living here now with hers. And Loveday and her governess had driven about in the little pony-carriage. And Loveday had ridden Periwinkle and loved Wrolf. And she would have married Sir Benjamin, but they quarrelled, and she went away. Maria remembered that Old Parson, when she had breakfast with him, had talked about the tune that Maria had liberated from the harpsichord, and said: 'It must have been the last one she played before she shut the harpsichord. Yes, I remember that she played it that night. It was her last night at the manor. That was twenty years ago.'

Maria had not known then who he was talking about. It was Loveday, of course. Loveday and Sir Benjamin had quarrelled that night and Loveday had gone away to the town beyond the hills and married the lawyer, Robin's father, instead. . . . And Wrolf had gone back to the pine-woods. . . . But she loved this valley so much that when her husband died she had to come back to it.

But she had been too proud to let Sir Benjamin know she had come back, too proud to try to make it up. What had Sir Benjamin and Loveday quarrelled about, Maria wondered? Whatever it was, it was time they made it up, now that Sir Benjamin's and Marmaduke's dislike of women had been slightly mollified by the good behaviour of herself and Miss Heliotrope.

'I must make them make it up,' said Maria to herself with great determination.

But first there was Paradise Hill to give back to God. That was the next thing. Maria folded up the waistcoat and put it away, tucked the workbox under her arm, and went quietly towards the tower stairs. For she must go to bed early because she had to be up early in the morning for her next adventure. There was, however, one more thing that must be done before bed.

With her hand on the latch of the tower door she said in commanding tones, 'Sir Benjamin! Sir!'

Her relative looked up, considerably startled, for never before had he been addressed in his own house in quite such a royal manner.

'Sir Benjamin,' said Maria, 'you have no right to the money that you get from selling the wool that is sheared from the backs of the sheep you keep on Paradise Hill.'

'Indeed, Maria!' ejaculated Sir Benjamin. 'And why not, pray?'

'Sir Wrolf stole Paradise Hill from God,' said Maria firmly.

'And tomorrow Old Parson and all the children and I are going to give it back to God. It won't be yours any more.'

'Dear me,' said Sir Benjamin.

'You must give me your word, Sir,' said Maria, 'that you will not keep the money for yourself any more, but will give it to the poor.'

'My income will be considerably depleted,' said Sir Benjamin in rather dry tones.

'You could eat less,' suggested Maria helpfully.

'Maria!' ejaculated Miss Heliotrope in horror. 'What a way to speak to your cousin!'

'I'm speaking to him for his good,' said Maria.

Sir Benjamin suddenly flung back his head and roared with laughter, the same genial roaring that Robin had indulged in earlier in the evening. 'Very well, Maria,' he said. 'Your Highness's commands shall be obeyed.'

Maria went up to bed happy in the knowledge that her curiosity upon many subjects had been completely satisfied that day. . . . But she still did not know where Marmaduke Scarlet slept.

Chapter Nine

·: 1 :·

Loveday Minette kept her promise and next morning Maria was awakened by a kiss upon her cheek, light as the touch of a butterfly's wing, and opening her eyes looked up into what she thought for a moment was an angel's face. Then she saw who it was and smiled.

'Mother Minette,' she said.

Loveday laughed. 'I've been called by many names in my life,' she said, 'but that's the best of all. Now get up quickly, Maria! You've a lot to do this morning.'

Maria jumped up at once, and Wiggins, who happened to be lying on her feet, was sent catapulting into the air to land flat on his back on the floor in no very good temper. He lay there, growling crossly, all four legs in the air, until Loveday took a sugar biscuit from the tin on the mantelpiece and placed it on his chest. Then he catapulted right way up again, ate the biscuit and was happy.

'You knew just where to find that biscuit, Mother Minette,' said Maria, as she washed herself in the silver basin. 'When you were a girl and slept in this room, did Marmaduke Scarlet make them for you too?'

Loveday Minette, in the middle of lifting Maria's riding-habit from the chest, paused in astonishment. 'What makes you think I slept here when I was a girl?' she demanded.

'I just guessed,' said Maria, getting into her petticoats. 'After all, where else could you have slept? Sir Benjamin and his mother had the rooms in the other tower. Your governess Elspeth would have had the big bedroom in this one, just as Miss Heliotrope does now. Did you sit here a great deal? Or did you sit mostly in the parlour? Where did you sit when you were making your wedding dress? And Sir Benjamin's waistcoat?'

'Maria!' cried Loveday in consternation. 'Has anyone been talking to you about me?'

'No,' said Maria. 'I've just been putting two and two together.'

'You are so good at arithmetic, Maria, that you frighten me,' said Loveday.

'I've sense,' said Maria, gently taking her habit from Loveday and putting it on. 'And I shouldn't wonder if I'm not the first Merryweather to have it. I must have got it from my mother, because my father had none. And I don't believe you and Sir Benjamin have any, either. If you had you wouldn't have quarrelled. Why *did* you quarrel?'

'It's too long a story to tell you now,' said Loveday hastily.

'You'll have plenty of time to tell me as we go through the park to the village,' said Maria. 'Mother Minette, you *must* tell me. Loving mothers and daughters don't have secrets from each other.'

Loveday Minette made no answer. She handed Maria her feathered hat, flung her own grey shawl round her shoulders, and led the way through the little door that was just the size for Moon Maidens and dwarfs, and down the tower stairs to the hall, Wiggins following after.

In the hall they found Wrolf and Serena waiting for them and—most astonishing—Zachariah also.

'Is Zachariah coming?' asked Maria in surprise. 'I thought he never went anywhere with anybody.'

'This is a very great occasion in Moonacre history,' explained Loveday. 'And so all the animals who take a special interest in you are rallying round you. Periwinkle is outside. I saddled her for you. Robin is at the church with the other children.'

They went out and down the steps, and found Periwinkle waiting patiently by the mounting-block.

'You ride Periwinkle and I'll ride Wrolf,' said Maria. 'It won't matter that you have no habit. She goes very quietly.'

'I know that,' said Loveday softly, as she mounted expertly from the mounting-block. 'My darling Periwinkle!'

Periwinkle whinnied softly and affectionately, and then looked lovingly at Maria, lest she should be jealous.

'The Merryweather animals all seem to live to a very great age, don't they?' said Maria, as she mounted upon Wrolf's back and noticed the grey hairs in his ruff.

'They know they are needed,' said Loveday.

'Yes, they've sense,' said Maria thoughtfully. The guidance and protection of their animals, she was realizing more and more, was absolutely essential to the not-very-sensible Merryweathers.

It was still so early that the moon was hanging like a lamp in the sky above the cedar-tree and the stars twinkled very faintly. But in the east, behind Paradise Hill, the sky was like a rose, and in the west over the sea a bank of pearly clouds was outlined with pure gold. There was plenty of time, and the two Moon Maidens rode slowly along the moss-grown road beneath the trees. Periwinkle's hoofs made no sound on the moss and Wrolf's padded feet were always silent. Serena, Zachariah, and Wiggins, coming along behind, were talking to each other, but so quietly that their conversation was not audible. It was just the right sort of still moment for the telling of tales.

'Tell me now, Mother Minette,' pleaded Maria.

·: 2 :·

'Like you, I was not born at Moonacre Manor,' said Loveday. 'I was born in Cornwall, where the sea thunders against the great rocky cliffs and the geraniums are the loveliest in the world. I lived there until I was ten years old, when my parents died, and I came to Moonacre Manor with my governess Elspeth, to be brought up by Lady Letitia Merryweather, my aunt by marriage and the mother of Sir Benjamin. She had been widowed early in her married life, but she was a capable woman and brought up her son so well and managed the estate so skilfully that Moonacre flourished under her rule. She was strict and severe, and I did not love her, though I am sure now that she must have meant to do her best for the little penniless orphan that I was, arriving at Moonacre possessing nothing in the world but the clothes on my back and ten flower-pots with cuttings of geraniums in them, those glorious salmon-pink geraniums that are the pride of Cornwall.'

'So that's why there are so many geraniums in your house,' murmured Maria.

'Yes,' said Loveday. 'The ones at my house, and Old Parson's also, are all the descendants of those original ten cuttings. If I brought sorrow to Moonacre, at least I brought geraniums too.'

'Go on,' prompted Maria softly.

'My father and Sir Benjamin's father and your grandfather were brothers,' said Loveday. 'There were only the three of them, and each of them had only one child; Sir Benjamin, myself, your father; and so now the Merryweathers are a very small family, just Sir Benjamin and myself and you.'

'Well,' said Maria stoutly, 'what we lack in quantity we make up in quality. You couldn't find three nicer people. And how two such nice people as you and Sir Benjamin came to quarrel I cannot imagine. . . . Go on about the quarrel, Mother Minette. . . . What *did* you quarrel about?'

'The geraniums,' said Loveday in a very small voice.

'The *geraniums*!' gasped Maria. 'But how in the world could you have such a dreadful lifelong quarrel just about geraniums?'

'Looking back, I really don't know how we could,' said Loveday, 'but at the time those geraniums seemed the most important thing in the world. That's the way with quarrels, Maria, especially Merryweather quarrels. They begin over some quite little thing, like pink geraniums, and then the little thing seems to grow and grow until it fills the whole world.'

'Go on,' said Maria.

'When I arrived at Moonacre,' said Loveday, 'I was a very unhappy little girl. I had loved my parents, and they were dead, and I had loved my Cornish home, and it was gone from me. The only things I had to remind me of my parents and my home were my pink geraniums. I have no words to tell you, Maria, how I adored those pink geraniums. I was given the little tower room for my own as soon as I arrived, and I filled it with geraniums; and then as the geraniums multiplied I stood them in pots all up the tower stairs. . . . And then it was that the trouble began. . . . For Lady Letitia had two intense dislikes, geraniums and the colour pink—especially salmon-pink. There wasn't a geranium in the manor-house garden or a scrap of pink inside the house. It was she who furnished the manor-house parlour and worked those chair-seats, and you'll remember that the roses are red and yellow, but not pink.'

'I know,' said Maria. 'One of the things I like about the parlour is its pinklessness, for I'm like Lady Letitia, Loveday, I don't like pink either.'

'What?' cried Loveday. 'You ride there beside me, Maria, and dare to tell me that you don't like pink?' And Loveday drew herself up, and her eyes flashed cold fire and she seemed to be freezing all over. She looked like a woman who had received some mortal insult; and Maria thought she was being so ridiculous that she too drew herself up, and her eyes flashed, and her mouth opened to make some snappy remark. But before she had time to make it there was a low growl from Wrolf and a warning whinny from Periwinkle, and instead of snapping she laughed.

'Don't let's quarrel,' she said. 'You like pink and I don't, and we'll agree to differ.'

Loveday quieted down and smiled. 'That's what Lady Letitia and I somehow could not do,' she said. 'We quarrelled ceaselessly. She would not let so much as one geranium overflow from my tower into the house, and she would not let me wear so much as a bit of pink ribbon in my hair. And I was terribly bitter, because to me an insult to my geraniums was an insult to my parents. I was very unhappy. I think I should have died of my unhappiness had it not been for my governess, old Elspeth, who was a cross-grained old thing but who always took my part, and for the great kindness of Sir Benjamin. When I was a child of ten he was a splendid young man of twenty-five, and, as I said, he was kind to me and I loved him; even though he shared his mother's dislike for pink geraniums. For he was not like his mother, always talking about the things he disliked; he just kept his mouth shut and did not mention them. He was always giving me things to make up for his mother's strictness. He was a skilled carpenter in his young days, and it was he who made for me all the pretty furniture that is in your room now. And he taught me to play chess. We were always playing chess together. I cannot tell you how much I loved him, Maria. And he loved me, too. . . . Though he loved his mother more.'

'That must have made you very jealous of his mother,' said Maria.

'Yes, it did,' said Loveday. 'I was a horrid girl in those days, Maria; jealous and proud and passionate in a cold sort of way that was quite different from Lady Letitia's hot anger, and that annoyed her very much. Yet Sir Benjamin loved me, and when I grew up he asked me to marry him, and I said yes.'

'Was Lady Letitia upset?' asked Maria.

'Very upset,' said Loveday. 'But she was a just woman. Sir Benjamin was over thirty by that time, and she realized he had every right to marry me if he wanted to. So she made the best of it. But she disliked me very much indeed and she was very unhappy because of our betrothal, and I think her unhappiness must have weakened her because that winter she caught a cold and died of it before any of us had time to turn round. And Sir Benjamin was heartbroken, because he had adored his mother. I did my best to comfort him, and he seemed to love me more than ever, and we arranged to get married in the spring, and he and I and Elspeth set to work to get the house all shining and polished and ready for the wedding. And I worked hard at my embroidery. I had already made Sir Benjamin a beautiful waistcoat, a pale-blue one embroidered in yellow and crimson because those are the sun colours that he likes; and now I started on another for our wedding. And I made my own trousseau dresses and my wedding dress. . . . And then, Maria, one spring evening just before our wedding day, I did a very stupid thing.'

'I can guess exactly what you did,' said Maria. 'By that time the tower was so overflowing with pink geraniums that there was scarcely an inch of space where you could put another pot, and so one day when Sir Benjamin was out riding you brought them all down and filled the house with them.'

'That's exactly what I did,' said Loveday. 'Especially I filled the parlour with them, for Old Parson was coming to supper and I wanted to make it look as gay as I could. And I put on one of my trousseau dresses—a pink one. And I decorated the supper table with pink flowers. And then Old Parson arrived. And then, rather late, because he had been delayed out riding, Sir Benjamin arrived, and saw what I had done.'

'What did he say?' demanded Maria.

'He didn't say anything then,' said Loveday, 'because Old Parson was there. He played the courteous host all the evening, but I could see that he was very angry. And I think Old Parson saw it too, because to make things easier after supper he asked me to play and sing to them, and I sang a song that had been written by some Merryweather centuries ago and that Sir Benjamin liked because the girl in the song reminded him of me.'

'Yes,' whispered Maria to herself. 'I know that song.'

'But he didn't seem to like it that night,' said Loveday, 'and when Old Parson had gone he told me exactly what he thought of me. He has the Merryweather temper, you know, even though he is so sunny and genial, and when he was a young man he could behave like a roaring lion. And he raged and stormed that night until his anger nearly lifted the roof off. He said that I had insulted the memory of his saintly mother and that I was not worthy to follow in her footsteps. And he said other things that made me very angry, so that I said hard things too. Among other things I said that his mother had not been a saint at all, but a very wicked woman to be so severe with a little girl as she had been with me over my love of pink. And no saint hates geraniums, I said. Saints love all the flowers that God has made, especially the salmon-pink geraniums of Cornwall, because God never made lovelier flowers than those. . . . And at that Sir Benjamin picked up all the pots of geraniums within reach and flung them out of the window into the rose-garden.'

'And what did you do?' demanded Maria.

'I went up to my tower room and I took off the silk dress I had on and put on a walking dress. And I wrote a little note to old Elspeth, my governess, saying that I was going away for ever but that I would be quite safe and she wasn't to worry, and I slipped it under her bedroom door. And then, when it was quite dark and the house was quiet, I took a big workbag that I had and I crept out of the house and into the rose-garden, and I gathered up out of the wreckage of their smashed pots all the geranium plants that I could manage to find in the darkness and filled my bag with them, and then I walked through the park and out through the tunnel and the big door and up the road that leads out of the valley. I walked all night, and when the dawn came I found myself out in a world that I did not know at all; and it seemed like a foreign country to me, and I felt very strange and forlorn in it. But I did not weaken or turn back. I followed the road to the market-town and knocked at the door of the first nice-looking house I came to, and asked if they would take me as a maid-servant. And they did. And the son of the house, a young lawyer, fell in love with me on sight, and I married him as soon as it could possibly be arranged, because he was kind and I liked him, and in my pride and anger I wanted to put it beyond Sir Benjamin's power to get me back again.'

'Did he try to get you back again?' asked Maria.

'Yes, he did. He and Old Parson and Elspeth did not rest until they had discovered where I was, and Sir Benjamin sent

Old Parson to tell me that he would forgive me and take me back again. But he did not come himself. . . . I expect he was still too hurt and proud and angry. . . . And he did not send any apology for throwing my geraniums out of the window. And so I was angrier than ever, and sent back a message by Old Parson asking to have all my clothes sent to me, and saying that I was going to marry my lawyer as soon as I could and live in the town, and never set foot in the valley ever again.'

'But you did,' said Maria.

'Yes, I had to. I loved it too much to keep away and, country-bred girl that I was, I hated the town. When Elspeth was installed as porteress I used to visit her at the gatehouse, and when she died, and my husband died too, I collected all my belongings, including all my pink geraniums, and went secretly to live there, as I told you. . . . Like the first Moon Princess.'

'Why!' gasped Maria. 'Did she live there?'

'I think so,' said Loveday. 'When Robin and I went to live at the gatehouse, no one had used the little cave-room that is now Robin's. It was full of earth and stones and rubbish that had fallen in through the hole that is now the window. Robin and I cleared away the rubbish and found the little door into the hillside with the horse-shoe knocker on it, and we found also, right underneath the rubbish, the silver mirror with the galloping horse over it that now hangs in my room. Who could it have belonged to if not to her? I believe she lived there all her life after she left the manor, with her little white horse put out to pasture on the slopes of Paradise Hill.'

'I expect she did,' said Maria. 'Loveday, the legend says she took her string of pearls away with her when she left the manor-house. Did you find them too?'

'No,' said Loveday. 'I've looked often, but I've never found them. The great ruby ring that the Moon Princess gave Sir Wrolf is safe, and Sir Benjamin wears it sometimes; but the pearls seem quite lost. It's a pity, because you would have looked lovely in them on your wedding day.'

'To think, Loveday,' said Maria, 'that you have lived at the gatehouse all these years and never even tried to make it up with Sir Benjamin!'

'Why should I?' said Loveday in a cold hard voice. 'He has never tried to make it up with me.'

'But he did! He sent Old Parson to you at the lawyer's house.'

'That wasn't a proper make-up,' said Loveday. 'For he never said he was sorry for losing his temper, and he never apologized for throwing my pink geraniums out of the window. And all the other pink geraniums, the ones he didn't throw out of the window, he must have burned, because I've never heard of a pink geranium being seen either in the manor-house or the garden.'

Maria said nothing, but she suddenly remembered that mysterious room over the tunnel that led from the stable-yard to the kitchen garden, and the pink geraniums she had seen in its window. She resolved there and then to look into the matter of those pink geraniums at the first opportunity. But just now the business in hand was this matter of giving Paradise Hill back to God, and they had reached the broken gate leading to the village.

'I've not time now, Mother Minette, to tell you how dreadfully silly I think you and Sir Benjamin have been,' she said severely, 'but I'll tell you later. I suppose we'd better leave the animals at the lych-gate while we go inside the church?'

'No, we'll take them inside,' said Loveday. 'Old Parson does not mind animals inside the church. He says that dogs and cats and horses are much the best-behaved of God's children, much better behaved, as a general rule, than men and women, and he never can see why they should be kept out of God's house.'

'Nor can I see either,' said Maria.

They rode along the village street, which still seemed asleep at this early hour, though the stream that flowed down from Paradise Hill was tinkling merrily beneath the little bridges before each garden gate, and through the lych-gate and up through the churchyard. At the porch Loveday and Maria dismounted and walked into the church hand in hand, with Wrolf and Periwinkle, Zachariah and Serena, following behind two by two, Wiggins bringing up the rear waving his tail like a banner in the air.

·: 3 :·

The church was full of sunshine, children, and music. Old Parson was standing at the chancel steps with his fiddle tucked under his chin, playing one of the loveliest tunes that Maria had ever heard, and sitting all round him on the steps were all the children of Silverydew, in their gay clothes like flowers, singing as the birds sing in the dawn, with all their power and joy.

Old Parson did not stop playing as Loveday Minette, Maria,

Wrolf, Periwinkle, Zachariah, Serena, and Wiggins joined the group of singing children, but he called out to them: 'Take your places and pick up the words and the tune of this new song as quickly as you can.'

Loveday and Maria sat down on the steps with Wiggins and Serena on their laps, and Wrolf and Periwinkle standing patiently and reverently beside them, and set themselves to the learning of this new song. . . . But Zachariah leaped over the top of the door that led into the Merryweather pew, and sat himself down inside upon the cushions as though he were all the Pharaohs who had ever lived combined into one magnificent purring personage.

The words of the new song that Old Parson had written for this historic occasion were easy to pick up, and Loveday and Maria were soon singing them as lustily as any child present.

SPRING SONG

Praised be our Lord for our brother the sun,
Most comely is he, and bright.
Praised be our Lord for our sister the moon,
With her pure and lovely light.
Praised be our Lord for the sparkling bright stars
Encircling the dome of night.

Praised be our Lord for the wind and the rain,
For clouds, for dew and the air;
For the rainbow set in the sky above
Most precious and kind and fair.
For all these things tell the love of our Lord,
The love that is everywhere.

Praised be our Lord for our mother the earth,
Most gracious is she, and good,
With her gifts of flowers and nuts and fruit,
Of grass and corn and wood,
For she it is who upholds us in life
And gives us our daily food.

Praised be our Lord for the turn of the year,
For new-born life upspringing;
For buds and for blossoms, for lambs and babes,
For thrush and blackbird singing.
May praise, like the lark, leap up from our hearts,
To Heaven's gate upwinging.

'That will do, I think,' said Old Parson, when everyone was singing to his satisfaction. 'Maria, will you please go to the Merryweather Chantry, and see whether Robin has finished the task that I set him there.'

Maria put down Serena, who was in her lap, and hurried to the chantry. Robin was seated cross-legged on the floor, his back against Sir Wrolf's tomb. Sir Wrolf's great cross-handled sword was laid across his knees and he was scrubbing it vigorously with emery paper. When he saw Maria he looked up and grinned. 'I can't make the steel come really clean and bright,' he said, 'it's too old. But it's better than it was. We're to take it with us, Old Parson says.'

Maria dimpled with pleasure. That was a good idea of Old Parson's! Sir Wrolf himself couldn't come with them to restore the property that he had stolen, but at least they could take his sword!

Robin got up and dusted himself, put the emery paper

neatly away with his scrubbing-brush and pail in the corner of the chantry, and he and Maria together carried the sword to Old Parson. When they got back to the chancel steps again Old Parson had put away his violin and hitched up his cassocks, and Loveday Minette was lifting the statue of the Lady and the Child down from its niche, and the children were taking the Bell from its place by the pulpit.

'Are we taking them?' asked Maria.

'Of course,' said Old Parson, 'they are monastery property, and we are going to restore them to where they belong.'

Some of the children were a bit tearful. 'We shall miss the Lady dreadfully,' they lamented.

'Nonsense,' said Old Parson. 'You can take your gifts to her on Paradise Hill just as well as here. From this day on we shall be going there often to praise God. Now come along, all of you. We are going there in procession this very moment. I will go first and the rest of you, animals and children, will follow me two by two, singing that song of praise that I have just taught you, at the tops of your voices. You can take it in turns to carry the Lady and the Bell.'

'We shall look like the animals going into the ark,' said Maria.

'We could not look like anything better,' said Old Parson. 'Come along, now. Robin, give me the sword.'

Robin gave him the great cross-handled sword and, holding it aloft like a processional cross, Old Parson went striding down the aisle with it and out into the sunshine, singing at the top of his voice. And close behind him, side by side, went Wrolf and Periwinkle, and behind them went Maria and Robin, with Wiggins and Zachariah making a pair behind them, and then came Loveday Minette leading little Peterkin Pepper, followed by Prudence Honeybun and all the other children, carrying the Lady and the Bell, lustily singing the song Old Parson had taught them.

By the time they reached the steep lane the sun was high in the sky and it was the most glorious spring morning ever seen. As they climbed upwards, still singing, though rather breathlessly now, the children picked the ferns and periwinkles and primroses and made them into great bunches. And all about them the birds were singing too, carolling so loudly that the noise they made nearly drowned the children's singing. When they came out from the lane on to Paradise Hill the sun seemed to blaze more gloriously than ever, and, climbing the hill, they all felt very happy, making their way in and out between the sheep and the frisking lambs, over the bright green grass and purple violets, past the blossoming thorn-tree, up and up to where the beech-trees reared their silver and green against the blue sky. When they were nearly at the summit Old Parson made them stop and get their breath back, and then, singing once again, they made their way beneath the branches of the beech-trees and through the doorway in the broken wall and into the paved court beyond.

As soon as they got inside Maria understood why it was that Old Parson had not offered to walk back with her through the park last night. . . . He had had something more important to do. . . . As soon as she had left him he must have climbed up here in the gathering twilight, and by the light of the moon and stars he must have laboured half the night. For the paving-stones had been cleared of all the rubbish, the weeds and brambles, and had been washed and scrubbed so that they reflected the sun's light like slabs of pearl. And the well and the channel through the paving-stones had been cleared of dead leaves, so that the spring bubbled up clear and strong and then ran away quickly and easily, as bright as silver, through the low archway beneath the rowan-tree. The tree looked glorious in the morning sunlight, its berries bright as lighted candles, and beneath its branches Old Parson had piled up the stones that he had cleared from the court into a little altar. The whole place looked fresh and clean and lovely, and utterly made new, and when Old Parson had thrust Sir Wrolf's sword into the branches of the rowan-tree, so that it stood behind the stone altar like a cross, with the children's flowers piled before it, and the statue of the Lady and her Child had been set in the empty niche above the low stone archway, and the Bell had been hung from a branch of the old holly, the whole place was ready for the prayers and praises which Old Parson proceeded to offer there.

First, standing before the altar with Loveday, the children and the animals grouped about him, with as many of the sheep and lambs as had been able to squeeze their way into the already overcrowded little court, he said a very long prayer, though as it was such a lovely morning nobody minded. He prayed for forgiveness for Sir Wrolf, who had stolen this place from God—and at this point the living Wrolf gave a deep penitent growl. And then he prayed for forgiveness for all the Merryweathers who during succeeding generations had neglected to give it back—and here Loveday Minette and Maria and Robin bowed their heads and said they were sorry. And then he prayed for further forgiveness for the Merryweathers because they kept for themselves the money they had got from selling the wool off the backs of the sheep who were pastured on this holy hill—and at this point all the sheep baaed distressfully. And then he prayed that for ever and ever this place should now be a holy place, and that no wickedness should be done here any more. And then they all said Amen, and the sheep baaed low and mysteriously, and Robin went to the holly-tree and set the Bell swinging, and its deep voice sounded out loud and clear to tell the people in the valley below that once more Paradise Hill belonged to God. And then Robin took his shepherd's pipe from where it still lay beside the entrance to Paradise Door, and to its accompaniment they sang 'The Lord is my Shepherd' and 'The Old Hundredth', and the Bell Song and the Spring Song, and all the praising things they could think of. And then at last, reluctantly, because it was so lovely up here on the hill, they turned themselves about and went in procession back to the village, singing all the way.

And when they got to the village they found that the sound of the Bell, and of the joyous singing, had brought all the grown-ups out into the village street, and they were laughing and talking and crying all together because they were so happy. For the spring had come and Paradise Hill had been given back to God, and they felt that they were all in a fair way now to live happy ever after.

Chapter Ten

·: 1 :·

For some little while now Maria did not see either Robin or Loveday, and as no clothes were put ready for her in the mornings she guessed that no adventures were demanded of her just at the moment. Wrolf, too, seemed out a good deal, and seemed to think she could look after herself just for a while. It was glorious spring weather, with the trees and flowers bursting into leaf and blossom and the birds singing at the tops of their voices.

Maria, when she got up in the mornings, ran first to the south window of her room to look at the daffodils that made glorious rivers and pools of light against the sombre darkness of those sinister black men and black cocks.

And then she would run to the west window and look down into the rose-garden that was now all a soft mist of tender green leaves where the bright colours of the birds' wings flashed like fire.

And then she would go to the north window, and look long and seriously at the dark mass of the pine-woods beyond the tumbled roofs. Several times, in the early dawns, she thought she heard a cock crowing out there in the woods, and the sound was a challenge.

'Well?' it said. 'Cock-a-doodle-do. What are you going to do-do-do about it? What are you going to cock-a-doodle-do?'

But as she had not the least idea what she was going to do about the wickedness of the Black Men, she could not answer the challenge. She could only wait. But she was not idle while she waited, because she was holding herself in readiness for whatever it was that she would have to do. She was trying not to be frightened in her mind, and she found that that sort of waiting and thinking really keeps a person quite busy.

And then she had her lessons with Miss Heliotrope, and almost every day she rode up to Paradise Hill and admired the sheep and lambs, which were now no longer Merryweather sheep and lambs, and talked to the children whom she found playing in the paved court under the beech-trees. For the children of Silverydew had now adopted the monastery as a second nursery. It had not ousted the church in their affection, but they had decided to keep the church for wet or cold days and Paradise Hill for when it was fine and warm. They were not afraid to be there. They knew by instinct that now that Paradise Hill had been given back to God, the Black Men would not come there ever again.

Robin, Maria thought, must feel like the other children, because he was not protecting the sheep any more. Never once did she see him there. She missed him, but she guessed he was doing something useful somewhere, and she would see him again soon if she was patient.

The little paved court was getting to look less like a ruin and more like a loved and lived-in church every day. The feet of the children, and of the grown-ups who often came up here now when the day's work was over, had made a path beneath the beech-trees to the doorway in the wall.

Old Parson had put two big pots of pink geraniums on the stone altar before Sir Wrolf's great cross-handled sword, and one on each side of the doorway; and the Lady and her Child always had their gifts of flowers, just as they had had them in the church down below.

The village carpenter had fixed up a bench upon which panting grown-ups could sit and rest themselves after they had toiled up the hill. The village mason had repaired the wall in many places, and the village thatcher, reputed to be the best thatcher in the whole countryside, had already fixed the posts and beams that were one day to support the thatched roof, which was to be erected over the little court to protect it from raindrops dripping from the trees.

And unknown people had brought various treasures; an earthenware pot to put the Lady's flowers in, a string of horse-chestnuts to look pretty hanging on the wall, and a fine new rope to pull the Bell with. Whenever anybody said their prayers in this place they pulled the Bell, just as the monks had done, to let the people in the valley below know what they were doing.

One day, when she was out riding with Sir Benjamin, Maria took him to Paradise Hill to see what had been done there. When he saw the sheep and remembered that he was not going to make any money out of them any more, he looked very gloomy; but as soon as Maria led him into the paved court he cheered up. He took off his hat, as he did in church, and looked about him in delight, and when they left he paused beside the pots of geraniums at the door and sniffed.

'They have a good smell,' he said. 'A wholesome sort of smell.'

'I used to hate pink,' said Maria, 'but now—these look so nice here—I rather think I'm changing my mind.'

'Don't rather think—do it,' said Sir Benjamin abruptly, almost crossly. 'Don't waste hate on a pink geranium. All colour is of the sun, and good. Keep your hatred for black things —evil things. Now come along home for goodness' sake. You've kept me dawdling here a good hour, and now we're going to be late for dinner.'

All the way home he was quite snappy, a thing Maria had not known he could be, but she did not mind because now she knew that he too, as well as Loveday, regretted that quarrel. And after a good dinner of roast beef, gravy, Yorkshire pudding, roast potatoes, greens, horse-radish sauce, apple-tart, sugar, cream, cheese, plum cake, and beer he was quite himself again.

•: 2 :•

The next morning Maria's waking dream was that the carved sickle moon over her head had flown down like a butterfly and kissed her on the nose. And when she woke up she saw that her riding-habit had been put ready for her, so it must have been Loveday who had kissed her. At breakfast Sir Benjamin noticed that she was wearing her habit and smiled broadly.

'Lovely day,' he said. 'Grand day. Too good to waste over

lesson books. Give her the day off, Miss Heliotrope. Let her run wild today—go where she likes—do what she likes. You might take a look at the orchard, Maria. I've turned some sheep in there, and they're a pretty sight.' Then he sighed gustily. 'I'm going to keep more sheep than I did, now that owing to your meddlesome ways those on Paradise Hill are a dead loss.'

But when Maria looked at him she saw that he was not really cross with her about the sheep, because his eyes were twinkling.

She was a little surprised, though, that he should be in such a good mood, because there had been a minor tragedy this morning. Marmaduke Scarlet had left the larder door open and Wrolf had gone in and devoured the whole of the leg of mutton intended for dinner, the whole of the beef-steak and kidney pudding intended for supper, and the whole of the ham intended for tomorrow's breakfast. . . . He had never been known to do such a thing before.

Miss Heliotrope agreed about the day off, and as soon as she had finished her breakfast Maria, with Serena, Wiggins, and Wrolf, went to the stable to saddle Periwinkle, for she thought she would take her pony into the orchard too, and afterwards she would ride to—wherever it was she was supposed to ride to today. Then, leading Periwinkle and followed by the other animals, she went through the tunnel into the kitchen garden, where all the fruit-trees were just coming into blossom and the great mulberry-tree was robed in green. She paused on one of the narrow paths, between the box hedges, and looked up at the window over the tunnel, and as before it was a blaze of salmon-pink geraniums.

'I'll look into it later,' said Maria to herself. 'After I've finished with the Black Men.'

Then she went on to the door in the east wall, unlocked it, and went through into the orchard. She had not been here for some while, and she gasped in delight when she saw the pink-and-white blossom that made a canopy fit for a queen over her head. It had been so warm lately that the fruit blossom was out much earlier than usual, and there were still clumps of primroses growing about the gnarled old trunks of the trees.

A rollicking spring wind was swaying the apple blossom, and carried to Maria a thread of merry music from the other end of the orchard. She followed it, and found Robin sitting on the grass beneath the largest and loveliest of the blossoming trees, his back against the trunk, playing his pipe. The branches above him were crowded with birds, robins, blackbirds, thrushes, tits, wrens, finches, all singing away fit to burst themselves. There were several rabbits skipping about, looking as though they were dancing in time to the music, and Serena began dancing too, and Wiggins rushed round and round, chasing his tail as he had done when he was a puppy. Wrolf and Periwinkle were too dignified to dance or skip, but Wrolf wagged his tail and Periwinkle whinnied on a high note of delight.

'Robin, you're a kind of enchanter, like Orpheus,' said Maria. 'I believe animals and birds would follow your music anywhere.'

'Yes, they do,' said Robin. Then he smiled up at her, and asked, 'Well, are you ready?'

Maria's heart began to beat. 'Today?' she whispered.

'Yes,' said Robin. 'Now. I've spent the last few days exploring the pine-woods with Wrolf. He showed me where the Black Men's castle is, and I found out the way to get inside it. It won't do to ring at the door in the ordinary way, of course. They wouldn't let us in. We must get inside secretly.'

'But, Robin,' whispered Maria, 'what do we do when we *are* inside?'

'I don't really know,' said Robin. 'I suppose we just walk up to the Black Men and tell them not to be wicked anymore. We could try that, anyway.'

Maria thought this plan, though simple, sounded dreadfully dangerous, and she went prickly all over with fright; but she answered his cheerful grin with a gay smile.

'Just one moment, young Mistress and young Master Robin,' called out a squeaky voice, and turning round they saw Marmaduke Scarlet ambling along towards them through the trees, carrying two bulging leather bags, one in each hand, and followed by Zachariah.

'Hearing through the chink of the kitchen door, slightly ajar at breakfast, that today was to be a festal day unclouded by the shadows of education, I have taken the liberty of packing up a small picnic repast,' he said. 'It will allay the pangs of hunger should your peregrinations delay longer than had been foreseen that safe return to the ancestral mansion which is so eagerly anticipated by your well-wishers. The bags have straps that can be slipped around the neck, and if supported in the small of the back the weight of them will not prove an inconvenience. Good-day, young Mistress; good-day, young Master Robin.'

Then he handed them the bags, waved aside their thanks,

and bowed low. In the act of turning away he paused and fixed his bright blue eyes upon Zachariah.

'Zachariah,' he said solemnly, 'go with them and do your duty this day.' Then he turned and ambled away through the orchard again.

'Now,' said Robin, when they had slung the bags round their necks as instructed, and Maria had put her foot in his outstretched hand and vaulted up on Periwinkle, 'come along, all of you, and may God defend the right!'

The procession, with Wrolf leading, Maria following on Periwinkle with Robin beside her, and Wiggins, Serena and Zachariah, with his tail held in three coils over his back, coming along behind, made its way to the far end of the walled orchard and out through another door into that part of the park where Maria had gone the first morning of all. But they did not go towards Primrose Hollow and the sea, they turned north towards the pine-woods.

A wooden fence separated the park from the pine-woods, but at one point there was a break in it, and through this they made their entrance.

'Sir Benjamin is always mending the fence, but They always break it down again,' said Robin.

The moment they were inside the pine-woods the bright spring sunshine was shut away and they were in a twilight world. The trunks of the great trees soared all about them like the pillars of some vast cathedral, and, far above, the branches spread out and interlaced and made a vast canopy of darkness over their heads. A thick carpet of pine-needles deadened all sound beneath their feet, and the silence was deep and strange. The pillared aisles of this vast wood seemed all alike, but Wrolf knew the way. His great shaggy figure went loping along, deeper and deeper into the wood, on and on. Robin and Periwinkle, Serena, and Zachariah seemed tireless, but Wiggins got sore feet quite soon, and felt scared and complained, so Maria carried him. He was trembling a little and, cuddling him close in her arms, she felt much braver. There's nothing like protecting someone more frightened than one is oneself, she thought, to make one feel as brave as a lion . . . as brave as . . . Wrolf. . . . She looked at Wrolf going on ahead.

'Robin!' she whispered suddenly, 'I don't believe Wrolf is a dog at all; I believe he's a lion!'

'Of course,' said Robin.

'But Sir Benjamin always calls him a dog!'

'It wouldn't do to alarm people,' explained Robin.

'Well!' marvelled Maria. 'Well—I—never! I'm glad I got to know him before I realized what he was.'

She looked at Wrolf, marching on ahead of them, and though she could not have felt for him any more respect than she did already, she felt now awe as well as respect. . . . A lion!

A little later Wrolf sat down suddenly beneath a giant pine-tree, whose roots poked their way up out of the earth and curved this way and that in a way that invited one to sit down and lean against them. A small clear stream ran beside it, hurrying east towards the sea.

'Dinner!' said Robin.

Maria dismounted, and she and Robin settled themselves comfortably among the supporting roots, while the five animals lay gratefully down on the soft carpet of pine-needles beside them. Maria opened the two bags, unfolded the snowy napkins inside, and exclaimed in delight at their contents. Marmaduke Scarlet had surpassed himself. It was amazing what he had got into a small space. Ham sandwiches. Jam sandwiches. Sausage rolls. Apple turnovers. Gingerbread. Saffron cake. Sugar biscuits. Radishes. A small crystal bottle of milk. Two little horn cups and two horn saucers. The children's eyes sparkled, the animals licked their lips and they all set to with a will. Zachariah had ham sandwiches and milk lapped from one of the saucers. Serena ate the radishes. Wiggins chose sausage rolls and sugar biscuits. Periwinkle crunched happily at apple pasties. Maria and Robin ate everything that was left. Wrolf, when offered sausage rolls, disdained them, and had a good drink from the stream instead.

'He ought to eat something. He ought to keep his strength up,' said Robin.

'He kept it up at breakfast,' Maria said. 'He had a leg of lamb, beefsteak and kidney pudding, and a ham. I wondered at the time how he could be so greedy; but now I understand.'

'Lions like to do that,' Robin explained. 'They have a huge feed and then go all day on the strength of it.'

When they had all eaten and had a good drink from the stream, Maria folded up some sandwich papers that they did not need any more and pushed them down out of sight beneath the roots they had been leaning against. But Wrolf did not seem to approve of the spot she had chosen, for he fished them out again with his paw, picked them up in his mouth, carried them round to the other side of the tree, and dropped them there.

'But they must be out of sight, Wrolf,' said Maria. 'I hate litter.' And she gave them a vigorous push beneath a root. To her surprise, as she pushed the ground gave way beneath her hand and she nearly fell forward on her nose.

'Look, Robin!' she cried. 'It's just space down below!'

Robin came and knelt beside her and, peering down, they saw that there was a great hollow beneath the pine-tree. It would be quite possible for a small person to push his or her way between the roots and creep inside it.

'Well!' said Robin. 'One could live down there, and nobody would know where one was. Now we'd better go on again. Wrolf seems ready.'

So they went on as before, Wrolf leading, on and on into the dark depths of the wood, which got deeper and darker the farther they penetrated, until at last it was so dark that they could hardly see their way at all. And then it got a little lighter, and at last Robin said: 'Look, Maria!'

They had come to the edge of a clearing in the wood, a desolate place like a quarry strewn with boulders, with stagnant pools of water between the rocks. On three sides the rock rose up sheer like a wall, and crowning the wall the way they were facing was a castle built four-square like a tower, so old that it looked like part of the rock upon which it was built. Upon each side of it, except just this side where its great gate looked down upon the clearing, the pine-trees closed about it with the darkness of night. . . . It was a terrifying castle. . . .

And the only way to reach it, so far as Maria could see, was to climb up the flight of steps that had been cut in the cliff beneath; and to do that they would have to leave the shelter of the pine-trees and cross the clearing under the eyes of whoever might be looking out of that window above the gate.

'There's another way,' whispered Robin. 'Wrolf showed it to me when we were here before. Look, he's leading us that way now.'

They went back among the pine-trees, turned to their left in a wide half-circle, and began to climb steeply upwards, climbing over the rocks that had pushed themselves out of the ground between the pine-trees, and pushing their way through thickets of bramble bushes. Maria had to dismount and lead Periwinkle, and Robin carried Zachariah and Wiggins one under each arm, so that their thick fur should not catch in the brambles. Then they swerved round to the right again, and they had come right round to the back of the castle. Its frowning walls rose sheer up above them. But there was no door here. No windows even. Nothing but the great high wall, as high as the tallest pine-tree, with battlements along the top.

'We climb up the tallest tree, and then on to the battlements,' explained Robin airily. 'I tried it the other day to see if it could be done, and it's quite easy.'

'I don't believe Wrolf will find it easy,' said Maria.

'Oh, the animals won't be able to get up,' said Robin cheerfully. 'We'll have to go alone.'

Go inside there without Wrolf? Maria's heart sank right down into her shoes. But she didn't say a word. She just tucked up her habit and prepared to follow Robin up the pine-tree. The branches grew low down on the trunk, and if she put her feet where Robin told her it would not be difficult.

But Wiggins wasn't going to be left behind with Wrolf, not if he knew it. Wrolf might eat him. Before Maria was two feet off the ground he stood up on his hind legs against the tree and began to whimper pitifully.

'Robin,' said Maria, 'I can't leave Wiggins behind. He always goes where I go.'

'Pass him up to me, then,' said Robin good-humouredly. 'I can hold him with one hand and climb with the other quite easily.'

So they descended, picked up Wiggins, and started once again. When they were half-way up Maria, feeling safer, dared to look down. Wrolf and Periwinkle and Serena were standing side by side at the foot of the pine-tree, with expressions of bland satisfaction and approval upon their furry faces. But Zachariah, Maria was astonished to see, was climbing up the tree just behind her. . . . He was coming, too. . . .

Somehow the presence of Zachariah made Maria feel much safer. He might be only a cat, but he was no ordinary cat.

The topmost branch of the pine-tree stretched like a bridge from the tree-trunk to the battlements, and had it not been for the awful drop below it would have been perfectly easy to wriggle along it. Had there only been a few feet between the branch and the ground Maria would have thought nothing of it. As it was, Robin seemed to think nothing of it. He wriggled across, with Wiggins under one arm, in the most carefree manner possible.

But when it came to Maria's turn, she felt that she just

simply could not do it. There seemed miles and miles of space beneath her. She just could not. When Robin, safely across, laid his free hand upon the battlements, she was still at the other end of the branch, swaying where she sat, sick and dizzy. She dreaded the moment when Robin would turn round and see that she was afraid. . . . But she just could not do it. . . . And then something black leaped over her shoulder to the branch in front of her, and she found a large black furry tail tickling her nose. With a gasp of relief she seized it with one hand as though it were a rope, shut her eyes, wriggled forward, and was towed by Zachariah along the branch to Robin, who was leaning over the battlements with arms outstretched to receive her.

·: 3 :·

When she opened her eyes again, the four of them were sitting together on the stone roof of the Black Men's castle. It was like a courtyard, quite empty except for a sort of square stone box in the centre of it with a door in the wall. They sat and got their breath back, and then Robin walked to the door and opened it. Inside was a spiral stone staircase leading down into darkness. Without a word he picked up Wiggins and led the way down, Maria following with Zachariah at her heels.

The light from the open door behind them did not last long, and soon they were in pitch blackness. They went on, feeling their way, until Robin came up against another door. He fumbled for the latch, lifted it, and cautiously opened the door an inch. A vertical beam of light shone in the crack and he opened the door a bit wider and peeped round.

'Come on,' he whispered to Maria.

They crept through the door and shut it noiselessly behind them. They were standing in a small stone gallery from which a narrow stone staircase led to the great hall of the castle down below. It was evidently kitchen as well as hall, for a log fire was burning in the great hearth and huge chunks of meat were roasting on spits before it.

'That will be Sir Benjamin's beef,' Robin whispered to Maria. 'His best bull was stolen a few days ago, you know.'

'No, I didn't know,' said Maria.

'Well, it was,' said Robin. 'And Peterkin Pepper's father had all his eggs stolen yesterday. And Prudence's father missed a barrel of cider last Wednesday, and all Mrs Honeybun's bread disappeared.'

There was a trestle table in the centre of the hall, and in the centre of it was a large dish of hard-boiled eggs. There were loaves of bread, too, and jugs of cider.

But Maria was not so much interested in the food as in the human beings in the hall. Two fierce-looking men, with black hair and beards, and leather aprons tied round their middles, were turning the chunks of meat on the spits and two more were setting plates and mugs on the trestle table. Another was blowing at a brazier of coals with a bellows, and yet another was sitting on a stool and sharpening a lot of horrible-looking knives on a whetstone, and she didn't like the look of any of them.

'They are going to have dinner,' she whispered to Robin. 'They have their dinner very late.'

'They have it when they've finished being wicked for the day,' explained Robin. 'We'll wait until they've got Mr Honeybun's cider inside them and are feeling good-tempered, and then we'll go down.'

A door at the far end of the hall opened, and a very large Black Man, taller than the others, with a huge black cock on his shoulder, came in with a gun in his hands and a couple of dead rabbits dangling from his belt. He was the man from whom they had rescued Serena. He was followed presently by five others, carrying baskets of beautiful fresh fish. They gave some of it to the man at the brazier, and he set to work to clean it and cook it over the coals. Then the Black Men proceeded to pull off their boots and take their ease upon the benches that were set against the wall.

Maria counted. There were twenty of them altogether. Twenty large Black Men and one large black cock, against two children, a very small dog, and a cat.

As soon as the meat and fish were cooked the meal began. The Black Men pulled the benches to the table and fell to with zest, and it made the children's blood boil to see how they enjoyed their stolen food. The fish smelt delicious. They never had lovely fresh fish like that at the Manor. Even Zachariah's fish-heads had to be brought by Digweed from the market-town and were of inferior quality. Zachariah particularly seemed to feel this very much, for as soon as the Black Men started on the fish he began to spit and swear softly under his breath.

Someone had once told Maria that stolen food and drink are never enjoyed, but she soon saw that this statement had been incorrect, for never had she seen anyone enjoy a meal as did the Black Men—not even herself and Sir Benjamin. They had started the meal rather bad-tempered, but as it went on and more and more of Sir Benjamin's beef and Mr Honeybun's cider and eggs and bread, and the beautiful fish from Merryweather Bay, went down their throats, they got jollier and jollier, until at last they were all talking at the tops of their voices, and laughing and singing and thumping the table. They made such a noise that the black cock flew up and sat on one of the beams and began to crow, and his crowing accompanied the words of the song they were singing.

COCK SONG

We are the men of the northern woods,
Of the moor, the hill and the sea,
Huntsmen, trappers and fishermen wild
Riding ways that are fierce and free.

We are the men of the great black cock
Who roosts so high on the tall pine-tree,
Crying cock-a-doodle, a-doodle,
Do! Do! Black cock on the tall pine-tree.

We are the sons of thunder and storm,
The frost and the wind and the snow,
We are tumult, the fear of the night,
And darkness wherever we go.
We are the men of the great black cock,
With inky feathers and sable crest,
Crying cock-a-doodle, a-doodle,
Do! Do! Black cock with the sable crest.

We are the men of dungeon and wall,
Of axe and of helm and of shield.
We are the men of cudgel and sword,
The fighters who never will yield.
We are the men of the great black cock,
Who crows so loud on the castle keep,
Crying cock-a-doodle, a-doodle,
Do! Do! Black cock on the castle keep.

And so did the music of Robin's pipe, which he took from his pocket and began to play. When he had got the tune correctly he whispered to Maria, 'Now!'

And then he marched off down the stone staircase, playing as he went, and Maria came next with Wiggins in her arms, and Zachariah followed, still spitting and swearing, with his huge tail uncoiled and waving angrily.

They advanced bravely up the hall towards the Black Men, but they were nearly at the table before Robin's sweet music penetrated the noise and made the Black Men look round. And then their astonishment was so great that they did not do anything awful, they just stopped singing and thumping the table and sat and stared, while Robin, still playing to the accompaniment of the crowing cock on the beam, came and stood on the left hand of the leader of the Black Men, where he sat at the head of the table, and Maria came and stood upon his right.

'Good singing, good Sir!' cried Robin in his clear voice, and so lovely was his playing that first one Black Man and then another took up the song again until at last they were all singing once more.

As soon as that astonished silence came again Maria sat

herself down on the bench beside her host, pulled a clean plate towards her and said in her clear silvery voice, 'Please may I have some fish?'

And Robin also sat down, and said, 'Me, too, please.'

And, scarcely seeming to know what he did, the leader of the Black Men stretched out his fork, speared two fish from the dish in front of him, gave one each to Maria and Robin, and at the prompting of a savage 'Miaow!' behind him cut off the fish-heads and flung them over his shoulder to Zachariah.

'It's delicious fish, Sir,' said Maria, eating daintily.

And indeed it was delicious, and in spite of the big meal she had eaten in the woods she found she had quite an appetite for it, and felt less and less frightened the more she ate. By the time she was quite full she was also quite brave and, laying down her knife and fork, she dared to look right up into the face of the man beside her.

It was a face like an eagle's, dark and wicked, with a cruel hooked nose and flashing black eyes that looked at one very directly but had no softness in them. His black eyebrows beetled alarmingly, and what could be seen of his mouth between his black moustache and thick black beard was like one of his own cruel traps. Yet his eyes, though hard, were startled, and Maria knew by instinct that if you get people thoroughly startled you can do a lot with them.

'Monsieur Cocq de Noir,' she said very courteously, 'I have long desired the pleasure of your acquaintance.'

At this she had her host more startled than ever. His eyes positively bulged. 'What makes you give me the name of Cocq de Noir?' he asked.

'Because it is your name,' said Maria. 'I know who you are.

You are the descendant of that little son of Black William's who was supposed to have been murdered by Sir Wrolf. But he wasn't. His mother took him away to safety in the far country beyond the valley. He never came back to the valley, but his sons did, and all of you here now are the descendants of his sons.'

The astonished silence that greeted this statement told Maria that she and Old Parson had put two and two together quite correctly.

'My ancestor, Sir Wrolf, was very wicked to try to take Black William's land away from him,' went on Maria. 'But he was not any more wicked than you are, poaching and stealing in the way you do.'

'My land is unproductive,' snapped Monsieur Cocq de Noir. 'We cannot rear livestock in a pine-wood. Upon what am I and my men to live if we do not poach and steal?'

'You should trade with the valley people,' Robin piped up suddenly. 'We never have any fresh fish in the valley. We're longing for it. You should sell us your fish, and we would sell you our meat and eggs and poultry.'

Monsieur Cocq de Noir snorted with contempt. 'It would be quite impossible for a Cocq de Noir to support himself in his ancestral castle with the dignity befitting his rank by selling fish,' he said with an indignation that raised his voice gradually from an angry mutter to a shout of rage. 'Where's that string of pearls that my ancestress the Moon Maiden took with her to Moonacre Manor? Those pearls are the property of my family. Had I those pearls, I could sell them and live virtuously upon the proceeds until the end of my days. Wickedness has no attraction for me provided I can get what I want without it. . . . Your family stole those pearls.'

'We did not!' said Maria indignantly. 'Those pearls have not been seen since the Moon Maiden disappeared. She lost them, or she hid them, herself. *We* didn't do anything with them.'

'Give me those pearls,' said Monsieur Cocq de Noir, 'and I might seriously consider the mending of my ways.'

'How can I give you what was lost hundreds of years ago?' asked Maria angrily. And then she remembered what Loveday had said about not getting angry and she tried to speak more calmly. 'We ought not to quarrel,' she said. 'If you will forgive Sir Wrolf for trying to get his land away from Black William, Sir Benjamin will forgive you for all your poaching and stealing, and then if you will promise not to be wicked any more, we can all be friends for ever after. . . . For we are distant cousins, you know. The Moon Maiden is my ancestress too.'

But Monsieur Cocq de Noir was getting angrier and angrier. 'Though Sir Wrolf did not murder Black William's son, he murdered Black William,' he stormed. 'And that is a sin that will not be forgiven while any Cocq de Noir lives.'

'Sir Wrolf did *not* murder Black William,' said Maria stoutly. 'Black William just got bored with everything suddenly, like wicked men do, and went off by himself somewhere. And then I believe he just got into a boat and sailed away into the sunset.'

'Prove it,' shouted Monsieur Cocq de Noir, banging on the table with his fist. 'Get me those pearls, prove to me that Black William was not murdered, and I'll be a model of virtue till the end of my days.'

It was no good. Monsieur Cocq de Noir was being so utterly unreasonable in his demands that Maria simply could not keep her temper. Even though Robin leaned forward and made a warning face at her, and Zachariah miaowed a great reproving 'Miaow!', she simply boiled over.

'You're the most unreasonable man I ever met,' she stormed, 'as well as the wickedest! And if Black William was anything like you, I wouldn't have blamed Sir Wrolf if he *had* murdered him—though of course he didn't. And I'm ashamed to be your distant cousin, I am indeed.'

At this pandemonium broke loose. All the Black Men leaped to their feet and shouted and waved their cudgels and guns, and the black cock on the beam crowed like mad, and Monsieur Cocq de Noir yelled at the top of his voice. 'These are the most insolent children I have ever met. Put them in the dungeon and let them starve on bread and water. No sausages or apple-pie—only bread and water.'

Robin leaped to his feet. 'Run for it!' he shouted to Maria. 'Quick! Run for it!'

He dived beneath the table, scooped up Wiggins, who all this time had been scrunching a delicious bone at Maria's feet, and then they ran for it, making a dash for the stone staircase leading to the little gallery before the Black Men quite realized what they were doing.

But the minute they did realize, they were after them, and the children could not possibly have escaped had it not been for Zachariah, who covered their retreat in the most masterly manner.

Swelling himself out to twice his in any case considerable size, he advanced backwards behind Maria and Robin, spitting and scratching savagely, and shooting out such terrifying flames of fire from his great green eyes that the Black Men were just for the moment daunted, and the four adventurers ran up the stairs and into the gallery, and through the little door into the friendly darkness of the tower stairs.

'Go on running,' gasped Robin. 'Only another five minutes, Maria, and we'll get away on Wrolf and Periwinkle.'

The children had only just reached the roof when they heard the Black Men pounding up the stairs. They scrambled over the battlements and on to the branch of the friendly pine-tree and wriggled their way across, Maria going first, so much more afraid of the Black Men than of the drop below her that this time she gave it no thought at all; Robin following after with Wiggins in his arms and Zachariah bringing up the rear. They reached the pine-tree and scrambled down it, and then, when they reached the ground, they had what they afterwards agreed was the worst shock of any that they had that terrifying day.

For Wrolf and Periwinkle were not there.

·: 4 :·

Then Robin grinned at Maria and took her hand. 'We'll do it on our legs,' he said. 'Run, Maria. Pull up your skirts and run. The Black Men won't dare scramble along the pine-tree branch, but they'll come out of the main doorway and down the rock.'

They ran, and when they reached the clearing and Maria looked back over her shoulder, she saw that Robin was quite right. The Black Men were pouring out of the castle door and running down the flight of steps cut in the rock below.

'Run! Run!' urged Robin, but there was rather a despairing note in his voice, and indeed it was difficult to see how they could escape, for they were out of breath already, they were not sure of the way, and Maria was impeded by her skirts and Robin was burdened with Wiggins. Only Zachariah, leaping easily along, seemed unhurried and unafraid. And then, suddenly, despair was turned into joy, for a beam of sunlight, piercing through the darkness of the trees, shone upon a beautiful, silvery, long-eared form leaping along ahead of them.

'It's Serena!' gasped Maria. 'Serena to show us the way!'

After this they were not afraid any more, even though they soon heard the Black Men pounding behind them. They followed Serena, and ran and ran, until at last they saw looming up before them the great pine-tree where they had eaten their dinner. Serena bounded towards it, jumped between two of the great roots and disappeared.

'She's gone right down inside!' gasped Maria. 'Down into the hollow place underneath that Wrolf showed us!'

'She means us to go down inside, too,' said Robin.

Maria went first, squeezing herself between the roots and crawling through on hands and knees, and Robin pushed Wiggins and Zachariah in after her and then followed himself. They could only just do it. Had they been a very little bit fatter they would have stuck. And they were only just in time. One minute later and the first Black Man to reach the pine-tree would have caught hold of Robin's leg as he disappeared.

Down in the warm, safe darkness below the pine-tree roots they found themselves slithering down what seemed a steep bank of earth, and then they fell. But they did not hurt themselves because they landed comfortably on a soft bed of dried pine-needles.

For a moment they lay there panting, getting their breath back, seeing at first nothing at all in the darkness. And then, as their eyes grew accustomed to it, a beam of light filtering through the pine-tree roots far above their heads showed them a little of their surroundings, and they sat up and looked about them. They were in a little cave in the earth. They were sitting on soft ground, but the lower walls of the cave were of rock. And then, as they were able to see better, they made a startling discovery. . . .

Once upon a time this cave had been lived in. . . . A hollow place in the wall was blackened, as though a fire had been lit there, and standing on a flat rock beside it was an iron pot that must have been used to cook stew in. And lying on the rock beside the pot were a huntsman's knife in a metal sheath and a tarnished silver mug. Maria and Robin picked them up and looked at them, holding them close to their eyes in the dim light, and lo and behold, the sheath that held the knife was beautifully made in the shape of a cock, and upon the silver mug also there was traced the outline of a cock.

'Someone lived here once,' said Robin.

'Black William lived here once,' said Maria triumphantly. 'I expect the pine roots were not so thickly twisted in his day, and there was quite a large opening. It's just as I said, Robin. He got bored with all the quarrelling and came and lived here in the woods by himself.'

Robin opened his mouth to reply, but suddenly there was an alarming noise above, the noise of an axe on wood, and they discovered that they were not safe after all, and up they jumped. The Black Men, too large to push their way through the small opening that had admitted the children, were hacking at the tree roots.

'Look!' cried Robin, whose eyes were now so accustomed to the dimness that they could see quite well. 'Look at Zachariah!'

On the other side of the cave, opposite them, was the jagged three-cornered entrance to what looked like another cave, and Zachariah was standing there making frantic beckoning movements with his tail. They darted in after him, and it wasn't a cave at all, it was an underground passage leading right down into the earth, very like the one that led down from Paradise Door to Loveday's house. But they had no lantern now, it was all pitch dark.

However, Zachariah was as good as any lantern. Maria took firm hold of his tail, as she had done when she crossed the pine branch, and Robin came behind her holding to her skirt with his right hand and carrying Wiggins under his left arm, and Serena lolloped after. They went stumbling away into the darkness, down and down, stubbing their toes against stones in the path, grazing their elbows against the sides of the rock passage, but led, sustained and supported by Zachariah's tail.

Behind them they could hear a rending sound, and knew that the Black Men had made their way into the hiding-place, and then a silence, as though they were taking a look at what they found there, and then a clanging of nail-shod boots on stones which told them that the Black Men were following them down the passage.

'But they won't get along as quickly as we're getting along,' said Robin encouragingly. 'They haven't got Zachariah's tail.'

So they stumbled on in good heart, and presently a strange beautiful sound came up the passage to meet them, now loud, now soft, like music that swells and then dies away again, and then swells once more.

'Whatever is that?' asked Maria.

'It's the sea,' said Robin. 'I do believe, yes, I do believe, that we are going to come out in Merryweather Bay.'

Maria could not speak. Her excitement at the thought of being close to the sea at last absolutely choked her.

Presently there was a dim green light in the tunnel, and she could see Zachariah's ears and whiskers outlined against it, and all the time that lovely sound of the sea was growing all about them. And then the tunnel widened out and they were in another larger cave, with opposite them upon its farther side an opening that framed a bit of dim yet lovely daylight. Zachariah was making for the daylight, but Maria halted him with a vigorous pull at his tail. 'Look!' she cried. 'There's Black William's boat!'

They stopped and looked. It was lying on the floor of the cave, narrow and long, rather like a Viking's ship. The wood had rotted away in places, but the ribs were still there, stout and strong and beautifully shaped, and the prow of the boat was carved in the shape of a great cock with wings outspread.

'There!' cried Maria triumphantly. 'That's the boat in which Black William sailed away into the sunset.'

'Then why is it here?' asked Robin. 'It ought to have been in the sunset.'

'After Black William landed in the sunset, the little white horses who live in the sea brought it back to the land again,' said Maria. 'And one of them pulled it in here.'

Robin laughed the sort of laugh that says, 'I don't believe a word you're saying'; and they might have stopped to argue about it, but Zachariah, who wasn't interested in Black William's boat but only in getting them to safety, pulled vigorously on his own tail and hurried them along towards that patch of daylight. Going through it they found it was the entrance to yet another cave, with a sandy floor strewn with shells, that led them straight out into Merryweather Bay.

'Oh! oh! oh!' cried Maria. 'Stop, Zachariah! Robin, stop! Look, Wiggins! Look, Serena!'

And even though they knew the Black Men were after them, they all stopped and stared.

Merryweather Bay was shaped like the crescent moon. Beautiful rocky cliffs, full of caves, enclosed a little beach of coloured pebbles, and then a strip of golden sand scattered over with rocks that held pools full of scarlet sea anemones, and shells, and coloured seaweeds like satin ribbon. Beyond the bay the sea was deep blue, flecked with white-capped waves that looked like galloping horses, hundreds of white horses stretching to the horizon in a glory of sparkling light that made Maria want to shout aloud for the very wonder of it. Within the bay this glorious sea came to meet them in wave after shining wave that curved and broke and fell, flinging showers of bright foam and rainbow-coloured bubbles to lie like tossed flowers at her feet.

The salt smell of the sea, the cool breath of it, seemed to be sending great surges of strength through her tired body, and over her head the seagulls wheeled in splendour and cried their strange strong cry.

An ancient stone jetty was built out into the bay, and on it fishing nets had been laid to dry, and some ugly little black fishing boats, with dirty black sails furled around their masts, were rocking on the blue water. At sight of these fishing boats Maria felt suddenly angry. Black! Ugly little black boats on that sparkling sea. They should have been blue boats, red boats, green boats, yellow boats, with white sails like the wings of birds. . . . And so they would be, when the blackness of the Black Men was banished from this place.

But at the present moment it wasn't, and her efforts at banishment had been a complete failure, and Robin was pulling at her skirt with a warning cry. She looked round and saw the Black Men coming pouring out of the cave like horrible black beetles out of their lair.

'Run!' cried Robin.

A steep dangerous little path wound up the rock to the top of the cliff above, and they ran for it, Serena leaping ahead and Zachariah coming behind. Unused as she was to rock climbing, Maria found the scramble very difficult, and Robin did not find it any too easy with Wiggins under one arm. He tried to put Wiggins down and make him climb by himself, but Wiggins wasn't used to rocks either and refused to budge, so he had to pick him up again. It was a horrible climb, because very soon they heard the feet of the Black Men behind them, gaining on them fast.

It was like a nightmare. And Maria wondered if when they got to the top they would be able to run fast enough to get away from the Black Men. Why, oh why, had Wrolf and Periwinkle deserted them? But they never would get to the top, she thought. In a very few moments now they would feel the hands of the Black Men closing round their ankles. She knew they were terribly close because of the way Zachariah was spitting and swearing in the rear.

'Go on!' gasped Robin behind her. 'Faster! Faster!'

But poor Maria couldn't go faster. Her limbs seemed to have turned to lead, and her hands were sore and bleeding from holding on to the sharp rocks. The only way she could get along at all was by fixing her eyes upon the white blob of Serena's tail, bobbing up the rock in front of her, and the hare's two long ears waving like flags in the air. There was something very soothing in the sight of that blob of a tail, something invigorating in those cheerfully waving ears. Serena was apparently quite serene. On and on went Maria, seeing nothing at all now except Serena.

And suddenly the hare gave a great leap and disappeared, and Maria's sore hands were clutching not rock but tufts of heather, and she was looking straight up into the brown furry face of Wrolf. They had reached the top of the cliff, and Wrolf and Periwinkle were waiting there for them. She should not have doubted those beloved animals. 'Wrolf! Wrolf!' she cried, and flinging her arms round his neck she kissed him passionately upon his cold black nose.

'Don't waste time kissing him!' cried Robin behind her in exasperated tones. 'Get on him!'

She got on him, Zachariah leaping up behind her, and Robin and Wiggins got on Periwinkle, and with Serena leaping ahead they rode like the wind for home, the seagulls wheeling and crying triumphantly over their heads. The pine-trees sped by them, and the clumps of golden gorse. Up hill and down dale they rode, and presently they reached Primrose Hollow, where they had found Serena, and then the pine-trees gave way to the oaks and beeches, and they saw the apple blossom waving over the orchard wall, with the towers of the manor-house rising beyond. They were safe now, with home in sight and the Black Men left far behind, and the galloping of Wrolf and Periwinkle changed to a gentle trotting. Maria and Robin could get their breath and smile at each other, and be happy because they were safe.

'Well, it's been a grand day!' said Robin.

'Yet we haven't done what we meant to do,' said Maria. 'The Black Men are just as wicked as ever and angrier than they were before. We haven't made them better, we've made them worse.'

'Yet I don't seem to mind, do you?' asked Robin.

'No, I don't,' said Maria. 'I suppose we couldn't expect to succeed at the first try. But there has to *be* a first try, and now we've had it, and it's behind us.'

'And it was a jolly good adventure,' said Robin. And then he looked up at the sky and saw that it was flushed with colour. 'Why, it's sunset,' he cried. 'We've been out all day. I must run home or Mother will be anxious.'

He jumped off Periwinkle, handed the reins to Maria, put

down Wiggins, and sped away through the park in the direction of the gatehouse, turning round once to wave his hand to Maria. The sunset light lit up the long green feather in his hat and his rosy laughing face. Then he was gone, the trees gathering him in to themselves as though he were their child.

•: 5 :•

Maria rode slowly through the formal garden and into the stable-yard, where she found Digweed waiting. He did not say anything, but gave her a broad and comforting sort of smile, as though to say, 'Never mind! Better luck next time!' And then he led off Periwinkle to give her a good rub down and a good feed. Wrolf, too, when Maria had slipped off his back, gave her a reassuring, consoling look, and then he and Zachariah and Serena and Wiggins went slowly up the stone steps to the kitchen, in search of rest and food. They all looked very tired, Maria thought. . . . All except Wiggins, who was leading the procession with the air of a conquering hero. . . .

But then Wiggins had done nothing at all the entire day except get in the way and be carried. His was the triumphant mien of the military commander who has taken no active part in the dust and heat of the battle, yet marches very actively indeed at the head of his troops when they return victoriously home.

Only we aren't victorious, thought Maria, and now that Robin was not with her any more she did, after all, feel a little discouraged. She felt as though she could not go indoors and face Sir Benjamin, who would see at once in her face that she had had an unsuccessful day. She sat down on the stone parapet of the well, and thought that she would rest for a little while first.

It was lovely and peaceful here in the stable-yard, with the white doves cooing about her and the blue sky over her head flecked all over with little pink clouds like curling feathers. She bent over and looked in the well and saw her own face looking back at her from the dark water; it looked white and tired and a little sad, and somehow not quite the face she was accustomed to. It looked, she thought, as the face of the first Moon Maiden might have looked when she rode away from the manor-house for ever. Perhaps, before she saddled her little white horse, she too had sat here on the parapet of the well for a little, and had seen her face reflected in the water with her lovely golden hair about it and her moony pearls shining about her neck.

'What *did* she do with those pearls?' wondered Maria.

A high squeaky cough, a please-look-round-and-see-me cough, interrupted her thoughts, and looking round she saw Marmaduke Scarlet standing at the top of the kitchen steps. He nodded and smiled at her, and he too seemed quite undisturbed by the failure of this first day's effort.

'I am about to prepare an omelette for your delectation at supper,' he said, 'and I require the butter, which I put to cool this morning within the well. May I trouble you, young Mistress, to put your hand within the aperture just below you, to withdraw the required condiment and to bring it with you when you come within to make your toilet in preparation for the assimilation of the nourishment of which by this time you must stand in dire need?'

At the conclusion of these remarks Marmaduke Scarlet bowed and withdrew, and Maria immediately prepared to do his bidding, for she knew his long speech meant in plain language; 'You're keeping supper waiting. Hurry up.'

She leaned over the well again, reaching her hand and arm down through the ferns, and groping for those attractive hidden cupboard places in the wall of the well that Sir Benjamin had shown her on her first day here, and that she had thought would make such a splendid hiding-place for jewels. In the first little cupboard she could find only cheese, but the second she tried had the butter. It was rather a small pat, she found, when she had pulled it out, and she wondered if it would be enough, for Marmaduke Scarlet's delicious omelettes were always very large and very buttery indeed. Perhaps there was a second pat farther inside. She leaned right over the parapet of the well this time, as far as she could, and groped with her hand right to the very back of the little cupboard.

She could not find any more butter, but her fingers touched what felt like a small metal box, and she took hold of it and pulled it out. It *was* a box, and she sat on the parapet of the well again and put it in her lap. It was very old, but she could still make out the cock upon the lid. The box was not locked and she opened it. Inside was a bit of discoloured, rotting silk, that seemed to fall almost to dust when she touched it, and folded within it was a string of gleaming pearls.

Maria sat motionless, holding them in her fingers, her lips parted in amazement at the beauty of them. Over her head the sunset sky had changed from blue and pink to gold, and the white doves strutting around her had gold-tipped wings. The wind had dropped and it was utterly still. Very slowly Maria lifted her hands and twisted the pearls round her neck, then she leaned over the well again and looked once more at her reflection. The sunset must have got into her sandy hair, as well as into the doves' feathers, for she saw it this time shining like pure gold about her white face; yet more full of light than the pearls about the column of her white throat. She smiled at her face in the water and the face smiled back at her, and so still and lovely was the moment that it seemed as though the whole world held its breath.

Maria sat up again and thought about the pearls. As though the first Moon Maiden had told her, she understood how they had come to be hidden in the well. The Moon Maiden *had* sat here for a little while on the night she went away, and she had wondered who the pearls belonged to, whether they were her own because her father had given them to her, or her husband's because they were the only dowry she had brought to Moonacre. She had not been able to decide, and not wanting to take away what was not hers, nor yet to give her husband wealth to which he had no right, she had hidden the pearls in the well.

A squeaky voice once more sounded forth loudly and a little indignantly from the top of the kitchen steps, 'Young Mistress, the hour is late—'

Maria loosened the pearls a little, pushed them inside her coat and buttoned it up on top of them. Then she took the pat of butter and slowly and sedately walked up the kitchen steps into the house.

Chapter Eleven

·: 1 :·

Maria that night slept very deeply for a few hours, and then woke up abruptly to find her little room as bright as day. At first she thought that the morning had come, and then she realized that the most brilliant moon she had ever seen was shining in through her window and flooding her room with light. The silver waves of it came washing in through the uncurtained window rather as the waves of Merryweather Bay had come rolling in to break at her feet in welcome.

There was something very friendly about this moonlight, as though tonight's moon loved her and claimed her as a sister, and was lighting up the world for her alone. She unfastened the moony pearls, that were still wound about her neck, and held them up in her hands almost as though she were offering them as a gift, and the moon, shining upon their loveliness and making it ten times more lovely, seemed to be accepting the gift.

And yet Maria did not want to give those pearls away. She loved them far too much. She did not want to give them even to the lovely moon, and as for giving them to the Black Men —well—she just couldn't do it. And yet she had to do it. Monsieur Cocq de Noir had promised that They would stop being wicked if she could give him proof that Black William had not been murdered by Sir Wrolf but had withdrawn to a hermit's life by his own choice, and if she would give him the pearls.

That first condition was already fulfilled, for when he was pursuing her and Robin he would have seen Black William's hermitage with his own eyes; and the pearls he would have, too, if she could bring herself to give them to him. . . . And then he would not be wicked any more, and complete happiness would come to the Moonacre Valley. . . .

Somehow Maria did not doubt that if she kept her part of the bargain, Monsieur Cocq de Noir would keep his. The wickedest of men have good in them somewhere, and, remembering the direct look in his eyes, she felt quite sure that he was not a man who would break his word. Yet she felt she could *not* give him these pearls, that she had found herself and that seemed already a part of her.

'If I could only give them to *you,*' she said to the moon. 'But I don't want to give them to that ugly Black Man.'

And then it struck her suddenly that if she gave her pearls to Monsieur Cocq de Noir she would, in a way, be giving them to the moon. For the moon belongs to the night, and what was more like night than Monsieur Cocq de Noir and his black pine forest? And the first Moon Princess had come out of the night-dark pine-wood, bringing the pearls with her. The pearls belonged far more to the Black Men than they did to the Merryweathers.

'I'll do it,' said Maria, and unable to lie still any longer she got out of bed and went to the south window and looked through the branches of the great cedar-tree at the formal garden below.

It was all black and silver, as it had been on the night of her arrival. The daffodils had had their gold stolen from them by the witchery of the moon, and each of them held up a silver trumpet on a slender silver spear. And the yew-tree men and the yew-tree cocks were as black as night, and looked so alive that Maria felt that if the daffodil trumpets were to sound they would immediately begin to move. . . . One *was* moving, and Maria caught her breath.

But she was wrong, it wasn't one of the Black Men who was moving out from the shadows beside the silver shield of the lily pond, it was a shaggy four-footed creature who stalked slowly across the garden and came beneath the window and stood there under the cedar-tree and looked up at her. . . . It was Wrolf.

She leaned out of the window and spoke to him. 'Yes, I'll do it, Wrolf,' she said, 'and I'll do it now. Wait for me there.'

She dressed as quickly as she could, trying to make no sound, because she did not want to wake Wiggins. Dearly though she loved him, she felt that she would probably get along faster tonight if she had no companion except Wrolf. Wonderful Wrolf! She saw now why he and Periwinkle had left her and Robin to escape from the castle unaided. If they hadn't, Monsieur Cocq de Noir would never have seen Black William's hermitage.

Maria put on her riding-habit and then twisted her pearls once more round her neck. And then she stood and considered for a moment. She did not want to wake Miss Heliotrope as she went down the stairs, nor did she want Sir Benjamin to see her. He went to bed very late sometimes, and she did not know what the time was. . . . It might be still not far past midnight. . . . Could she climb down the cedar-tree? Surely she could. She had noticed her very first evening how easy it was to climb; much easier than the pine-tree. And Marmaduke climbed it.

Without giving herself time to feel afraid, she climbed out of her window and on to the great friendly branch beneath it, and so steadily down from branch to branch, until at last her groping right foot felt beneath it not hard wood but the soft strength of Wrolf's back. With a sigh of content she settled herself there and took firm hold of his furry ruff.

'I'm ready, Wrolf,' she said.

He was off at once at a steady pace through the black-and-white magic of the moonlit formal garden. With his paw he lifted the latch of the gate that was never locked, and they were out in the park going in the direction of the pine-wood. Maria gazed in delight at the beauty of the moonlit world. It was utterly quiet and still. Not a bird cried, not a leaf stirred.

Yet in spite of the peace of the night, when they had left the park behind them and passed into the pine-wood she suddenly felt desperately afraid, not of the Black Men but of the darkness. The moonlight could not penetrate the thick canopy of the pine branches overhead, and the inky blackness was like a pall muffling not only movement and sight but breath too. Wrolf was going very slowly now, and she could not imagine how he was to find the way. And she was afraid, too, that the unseen trees would strike at her. And not only the trees, but hobgoblins and sprites who perhaps lived in these woods and had the hours of darkness for their own.

She found herself riding with one arm raised to protect her face and her mouth suddenly dry with fear. Once, when an unseen twig plucked at her hair, she thought it was a hand that plucked, and when a bramble caught at her skirt she felt that hands were trying to pull her off Wrolf's back, and she had hard work not to cry out. And then she had a feeling, just because she could not see him, that Wrolf had left her. It was not Wrolf she was riding, but some horrible nightmare beast who was carrying her deeper and deeper into fear. 'If there's never any light, I don't think I can bear it,' she thought. And then she said to herself that she *must* bear it. All things come to an end, even the night. Resolutely she lowered the arm she had raised to protect herself, straightened her shoulders and smiled into the darkness.

And then, almost as though her smile had been a flame that set a lantern shining, she found that she could see a little. She could distinguish the shaggy head of her mount, and he was her own dear Wrolf. And she could dimly see the shapes of the trees. And then the silvery light grew even stronger, and was in itself so lovely that she knew no evil thing could live within it. 'It must be moonlight,' she thought, but yet she knew that no moonlight could get through the canopy of darkness overhead, and that not even the moon had quite so wonderful a radiance.

And then she saw him. A little white horse was cantering ahead of them, leading the way, and from his perfect milk-white body, as from a lamp, there shone the light. He was some way ahead of them, but for one flashing moment she saw him perfectly, clear-cut as a cameo against the darkness, and the proud curve of the neck, the flowing white mane and tail, the flash of the silver hoofs, were utterly strange and yet utterly familiar to her, as though eyes that had seen him often before looked through her eyes that had not until now looked steadily upon his beauty; she was not even surprised when he turned his lovely head a little and looked back at her and she saw a strange little silver horn sticking out of his forehead. . . . Her little white horse was a unicorn.

After that they travelled with speed, Wrolf managing to keep the little white horse in sight. But they never caught up with him, and Maria didn't again see him so clearly as she had in that first moment of vision; for the rest of the way he was just a steady shining, a moving shape of light whose outline was not again clear-cut against the darkness. Yet she was content with what she saw, content even when the trees thinned out and the darkness faded, and against the growing splendour of moonlight beyond the radiance of the little white horse slowly dimmed; content even when it vanished. . . . For now she had seen him twice over, and the fact of him was a thing that she would not doubt again. And perhaps she would see him once more. She had a strong feeling that she was going to see him just once more.

·: 2 :·

And now she and Wrolf were out in the clearing looking up at the Black Men's castle, and over the top of it the moon hung in the sky like a great shield and emblazoned upon it was the outline of a man bent nearly double by the burden that he carried on his back.

'Poor man!' said Maria. 'It's Monsieur Cocq de Noir up there in the moon, Wrolf, and he's carrying his wickedness on his back like Christian in the *Pilgrim's Progress.* He'll be glad when he's thrown it away.'

But this remark was only answered by Wrolf with a contemptuous snort as he crossed the clearing to the foot of the steps that had been cut in the rock. Here he stopped as a hint to Maria that they would find it easier to climb them if she were to get off his back. So she got off, and they began to climb, Maria going first and Wrolf following.

Up and up they went, and the way was so long and so steep that Maria felt as though they were climbing up to the man-in-the-moon himself, on an errand of mercy to relieve him of his burden. But they got to the top at last, and she stood breathless before the great doorway of the castle, with Wrolf beside her leaning his great shaggy head against her shoulder to give her courage. An iron bell hung high above them, with a long rusty chain hanging from it, and she took hold of the chain and pulled with all her strength, and the bell tolled out once in the silence of the night as though it were one o'clock, and the beginning of a new day.

Almost at once the window over the great door swung open and a dark eagle face looked out. Monsieur Cocq de Noir regarded Maria and Wrolf in silence, but the lift of his eyebrows and the scornful twist of his lips were not encouraging. Maria did not say anything either, but she unwound the pearls from her neck and held them up in the moonlight for him to see, and then Monsieur Cocq de Noir's eye flashed with sudden brilliance, and he shut the window and disappeared from sight. After a great grinding and creaking of bolts the heavy door swung open, and he stood there confronting them, a lantern held high over his head and his great black cock sitting on his shoulder.

'You may come inside, Moon Maiden,' he said. 'But the tawny dog can stay outside.'

'Certainly not,' said Maria firmly. 'Where I go my dog goes too.' And before Monsieur Cocq de Noir could say anything more she stepped inside, Wrolf keeping close beside her, and the door had clanged shut behind them. They were in a small square stone room with stone seats on each side of it, and a second door that Maria guessed led into the great hall. The room had no window and felt cold and clammy like a vault, and was lit only dimly by the lantern that Monsieur Cocq de Noir now set upon one of the seats. The black cock kept flapping his great wings in a frightening sort of way, and Maria would have felt very scared had it not been for Wrolf's warm strong body pressed close against her. She flung her left arm round his neck, while with her right hand she held the pearls against her chest. Monsieur Cocq de Noir stretched out a strong lean brown hand, with curved fingers like an eagle's claws, and would have snatched at the pearls, but Wrolf growled savagely and he withdrew his hand.

'Monsieur,' said Maria, 'I have fulfilled both your conditions. When you followed me into the hollow beneath the pine-tree you saw that it was Black William's hermitage, to which he withdrew when he was tired of the world. And when you went down the passage to the cave below, you saw the boat in which he sailed away into the sunset. . . . So now you know that Sir Wrolf did not murder Black William. . . . And, as you see, I have the pearls. I found them by accident inside the well at home. The Moon Maiden must have hidden them there the night she went away. I know that you are a man of your word, Monsieur. I know that now that I have kept my side of the bargain, you will keep yours.'

'I do not consider that you have fulfilled my conditions,' retorted Monsieur Cocq de Noir. 'You have the pearls, certainly, but the knife and the drinking cup are merely evidence that the hollow beneath the pine-trees was at one time used by Black William, not that he withdrew there to live at the time when Sir Wrolf was suspected of causing his death. And as for your fairy-tale about his sailing away into the sunset in that boat in the lower cave—well, Moon Maiden, how did the boat get back from the sunset into the cave again?'

It was the same question that Robin had asked, and Maria gave it the same answer. 'The white horses who live in the sea brought it back to land,' she said. 'And one of them pulled it into the cave.'

The black cock crowed long and loud in derision, and Monsieur Cocq de Noir roared with laughter. 'A fine story!' he mocked. 'Do you expect an intelligent man to believe that tale? Moon Maiden, you cannot throw moon dust in the eyes of a Cocq de Noir. Give me these pearls, that are my rightful property, and be off. I'll not harm you this time, but if you ever come near my castle again, you'll be clapped in that dungeon I spoke of.'

But Maria held her ground. 'What I told you was no fairy-tale but the truth,' she said steadily.

And once again the cock crowed and his master laughed.

'Show me the white horse that pulled the boat into the cave after its journey back from the sunset and I'll believe you,' he said.

'Very well,' said Maria steadily. 'Come with me into the pine-woods and I will show him to you.'

The moment she had spoken she was struck dumb with astonishment and fear. Astonishment because until the words were actually out of her mouth she had not known that she was saying them, and fear because she was afraid that what she had said might not prove true. She might take Monsieur Cocq de Noir out into the pine-woods and they would see nothing at all. . . . Then Wrolf pressed himself reassuringly against her, and she knew that it was all right.

'Shall we go now?' she said to Monsieur Cocq de Noir, and letting go of Wrolf for a minute she wound the pearls round her neck again.

For answer he laughed once more, picked up his lantern and opened the door. 'But mind you,' he said, 'I'm not going to spend the entire night wandering round and round in the woods chasing the fantasy of your imagination. If I don't clap my eyes on this white horse of yours by the time we reach the pine-tree I've won and you've lost—and you hand me over those pearls and I go on with my poaching and stealing exactly as before.'

'And if we *do* see the horse,' said Maria, 'I've won and *you've* lost. I give you the pearls, and you and your Black Men stop being wicked from this day on.'

'Done,' said Monsieur Cocq de Noir, and he held out his hand, and Maria took it, and as they shook hands and she looked up into his face and met his steady glance she knew that he would keep his word. Though it was evident that he did not expect for a moment that he would have to keep it. He was laughing, and the cock was crowing derisively, all the time he was opening the door.

•: 3 :•

The four of them went down the steps in the cliff together in the bright moonlight, and when they got to the bottom Maria mounted once more upon Wrolf and they crossed the clearing and came again into the pine-wood. Monsieur Cocq de Noir held his lantern high to light their way, but it shed only a fitful gleam upon the great darkness all about them. But Maria was not frightened of the darkness now, and not frightened any more of the tall man striding along beside her. . . . Somehow she was coming rather to like Monsieur Cocq de Noir. . . . He might be a wicked man, but he knew how to laugh and how to strike a bargain.

Then her feeling of pleasure in this dawn of friendly feeling began to be swallowed up in anxiety, for they must be coming near to the pine-tree now and there was no lightening of the darkness all about them, no sign at all of what they had come to seek. She had, she thought now, taken leave of her boasted common sense when she had told that story about the white sea-horses which had brought Black William's boat back from the sunset, and the one white horse which had pulled it up into the cave. It was, of course, just a fairy-tale that she had made up. . . . Yet the funny part was that when she had told it to Robin and to Monsieur Cocq de Noir, she had believed it. . . .

Well, she didn't believe it any more, and as they went on and on through the darkness her heart sank lower and lower, and if she had not been so strong-minded she would have cried because for the second time it was all going to end in failure. She did not know when she had felt so unhappy. And the darkness now was dense and so was the silence, and Monsieur Cocq de Noir's lantern was flickering as though it meant to go out.

And then suddenly it did go out, and it felt to Maria as though the darkness and silence had fallen down on their heads, smothering them. And Monsieur Cocq de Noir must have felt the same, or else he had barked his shin against a tree-trunk, for he began muttering angrily into his black beard, and though she could not hear what he was saying she had a strong feeling that it was all most uncomplimentary.

Yet Wrolf kept steadily on.

'If you were to take my hand,' Maria said timidly to Monsieur Cocq de Noir, 'I think you would be less likely to hit yourself against things, because Wrolf seems to be finding the way all right.'

So he took her hand, but the grip of it was like a steel trap and did nothing to reassure her, and he still went on muttering angrily into his beard, and the darkness and silence seemed to get heavier and heavier. And then the great black cock, which had been riding all this time silently upon his master's shoulder, suddenly crowed. It was not a crow of derision this time, it was that triumphant trumpet call with which cocks usher in a new day, and Maria remembered a saying she had heard somewhere, 'The night is darkest towards the dawn.'

'I believe the night is nearly over,' she said to Monsieur Cocq de Noir.

'The moment I can see my way I go straight home,' he said nastily. 'And I advise you to do the same, young lady, and to keep out of my way in future lest worse befall you. What induced me to come out on this wild-goose chase I cannot imagine. You must have infected me with your own moon madness. You must have—'

He broke off abruptly, for something was happening in the woods. They could see the faint shapes of the trees about them and the outline of each other's faces. And it was not only that the darkness was yielding, for the silence was broken too. Far off, faint and mysterious, they could hear the sound of the sea.

'Wrolf must have brought us the wrong way,' said Maria. 'We must have come down to the seashore.'

'No,' said Monsieur Cocq de Noir. 'The woods end before you come to the seashore. You can only hear the sea in the woods on windy nights, and there's no breath of wind.'

His voice sounded queer and husky, as though the great Monsieur Cocq de Noir was actually a little scared.

But Maria did not feel scared, only awed. 'Let's stop and watch the dawn come,' she said. 'Stop, Wrolf. Look, oh look!'

They were motionless as statues now, the girl and the lion and the man and the cock, as though turned to stone by the beauty of what they saw. To the east, where was the sunrise and the sea, light was stealing into the woods, like a milk-white mist, and as the light grew so did the sound of the sea grow too. And then it seemed as though the light was taking form.

It was still light, but within the light there were shapes moving that were made of yet brighter light; and the shapes were those of hundreds of galloping white horses with flowing manes and poised curved necks like the necks of the chessmen in the parlour, and bodies whose speed was the speed of light and whose substance seemed no more solid than that of the rainbow; and yet one could see their outline clear-cut against the night-dark background of the trees. . . . They were the sea-horses galloping inland, as Old Parson had told Maria that they did, in that joyful earth-scamper of theirs that ushered in the dawn.

They were nearly upon them now, and there was the roaring of the sea in their ears and blinding light in their eyes. Monsieur Cocq de Noir gave a cry of fear and shielded his head with his arm, but Maria, though she had to shut her eyes because of the brightness of the light, laughed aloud in delight. For she knew the galloping horses would not hurt them; they would just wash over them like light, or like the rainbow when one stands in the fields in the sun and the rain.

And it happened like that. There was a moment of indescribable freshness and exhilaration, like a wave breaking over one's head, and then the sea-sound died away in the distance and, opening their eyes, they saw again only the faint grey ghostly light that showed them no more than just the faint shapes of the trees and the outline of each other's faces. The white horses had all gone . . . all except one.

They saw him at the same moment, standing beneath the giant pine-tree to their right, with neck proudly arched, one delicate silver hoof raised, half turned away as though arrested in mid-flight. And then he, too, was gone, and there was nothing in the woods except the normal growing light of dawn.

There was a very long silence, while they stood looking at the pine-tree, with the great gaping hole among its roots where the Black Men had forced their way through the day before, sad and desolate because they both knew they would never again see the lovely thing that had just vanished. Then the black cock crowed again and the spell was broken. Maria sighed and stirred.

'Well?' she said.

'You've won,' said Monsieur Cocq de Noir. 'Tomorrow I shall think this is a dream—but you've won and I will keep my word.'

Maria took off the pearls and handed them to him. 'These aren't a dream,' she said. 'And it won't be a dream when you come to Moonacre Manor tomorrow to make friends with us all. You will come, won't you?'

'Moon Maiden,' said Monsieur Cocq de Noir. 'I foresee that for the rest of my life I shall be obeying Your Highness's commands. I will present myself at the manor-house tomorrow about the hour of five.'

Then he bowed and left her, his black cock still on his shoulder, and Maria and Wrolf rode swiftly homewards in a wonderful dawn that changed from grey to silver, and from silver to gold, and blossomed as they came out of the pine-woods into one of those rosy dawns edged with saffron and amethyst that usher in the blue of a happy day.

Wrolf carried Maria not to the formal garden again but to the door in the wall that led to the orchard, and here he stopped and shook himself as an indication that she should get off him. He was tired now, his shake said, he'd had enough of her on his back. She got off obediently, kissed him, and thanked him for all that he had done for her that night. He gave her a kindly look, a push towards the orchard door, and then went off on his own affairs.

·: 4 :·

Maria went into the orchard, where the sheep and lambs were still sleeping beneath the pink-and-white blossoming trees, with the morning dew sparkling like silver on their woolly backs, and through into the kitchen garden. She was, she discovered, very tired now, and ravenously hungry. As she walked down the path between the box hedges she thought she had only two ideas in her head, breakfast and bed, but a sudden gleam of pink, like a banner flourished before her eyes, made her look up and planted a third idea between the bed and breakfast ones. . . . The pink geraniums in the window of that room over the tunnel. . . . she could see them more clearly than usual today, because the window, that had until now always been closed, had been flung wide open to the dawn.

She stood still and looked up at them, and she found herself rejoicing in their beauty. After all, though pink was not her favourite colour, it *was* a colour and, as Sir Benjamin had said, all colour is of the sun, and good. And pink is the colour of dawn and sunset, the link between day and night. Sun and moon alike ought both to love pink, because when one is rising and the other setting they so often greet each other across an expanse of rosy sky.

And then, to Maria's astonishment, as she stood there looking up at the pink geraniums, an arm appeared holding a watering-can and a bright shower of silver drops descended upon the flowers. And there was no mistaking that long thin arm in its bright sleeve. It was Marmaduke Scarlet's arm.

'Marmaduke!' called Maria softly. 'Marmaduke!'

The geraniums were parted and Marmaduke Scarlet's rosy, bearded face looked out. He was nodding and smiling, and seemed delighted, but not surprised, to see her. 'Young Mistress,' he said, 'I am about to partake of a light repast before going across to the manor-house to begin the labours of the day. Will you do me the honour of stepping up and sharing it with me?'

'I'd love to, Marmaduke,' said Maria, 'for I'm dreadfully hungry. But how *do* I step up?'

'Look behind the water-butt,' said Marmaduke.

Maria ran to the big green water-butt that on her very first day she had noticed to the left of the tunnel, and quite hidden behind it was a little green door in the wall, a door no larger than the one that led into her own little room in the tower. She lifted the latch and opened the door, and found herself facing a steep flight of narrow stone steps just suited to a very little person. She went up them, opened another door and found herself in the room of the pink geraniums.

'Welcome, young Mistress, to my humble abode,' said Marmaduke Scarlet.

'So *this* is where you live, Marmaduke?' cried Maria, her curiosity upon this point satisfied at last.

'This is where I live when not engaged upon my domestic labours,' said Marmaduke Scarlet.

It was the oddest room Maria had ever seen, long and narrow like the tunnel below. At one end of it the window, with the pots of geraniums standing on the sill, stretched from wall to wall, and at the opposite end was Marmaduke's little wooden truckle bed, neatly covered with a checked counterpane of scarlet and white. In the middle of the room was a little wooden table with two wooden three-legged stools standing before it, and they were all of the right size for a dwarf.

The table was covered with a checked red-and-white tablecloth that matched the counterpane, and upon it was set a blue dish full of apples, a yellow jug of milk, a purple plate upon which were piled buttered scones, two green plates and two mugs to match. But what made Maria give a cry of astonishment was neither the deliciousness of the food nor the variety in colour of the china, but the appearance of the long north and south walls, for all along their length from floor to ceiling ran wooden shelves, and standing upon the shelves were pots and pots of salmon-pink geraniums.

What with all those geraniums, and the gay counterpane and tablecloth and china, and Marmaduke's bright clothes, the room was such a blaze of colour that one would have been almost blinded by it had it not been that there was only the one window, and that so filled up by geraniums that the light filtered through a lattice-work of pink petals and entered the room considerably subdued, though very pink.

'Oh, Marmaduke!' cried Maria. 'Are those the geraniums that Loveday Minette left behind when she went away?'

'Cuttings from the original plants,' said Marmaduke, motioning courteously that Maria should seat herself upon one of the stools.

'So you love pink too?' said Maria, sitting down.

'Can't abide it,' said Marmaduke, seating himself opposite her and pouring milk into the two mugs. 'But neither can I abide waste. No good cook can. So when at the time of that unfortunate disagreement twenty years ago my master bade me remove from the house by way of the door all those geranium plants which had not actually been cast forth by himself by way of the window, I did not throw them away, I brought them here. They might, I thought, one day come in useful.'

Maria, munching away at apple and scones spread so thickly with yellow butter that there was almost as much butter as scone, suddenly had an idea. She was silent for a little, thinking it out.

'Marmaduke,' she said at last. 'I think I know how they might come in useful. I think I have just had rather a bright idea.'

'I don't doubt it, young Mistress,' said Marmaduke courteously.

'Marmaduke,' said Maria, 'could I have a tea-party tomorrow afternoon? A party for seven people?'

'Certainly, young Mistress,' said Marmaduke. 'But if you wish Sir Benjamin to be with you, I doubt if you have chosen a suitable day. Tomorrow morning he rides to the market-town to sit on the Bench. He is a magistrate, you know.'

'Won't he be back by tea-time?' asked Maria.

'He is not usually back by tea-time,' said Marmaduke. 'The exhaustion of sitting on the Bench generally necessitates a subsequent visit to the local inn, a large meal and some refreshment of a liquid nature.'

'I'll ask him to come straight home from the Bench,' said Maria, 'and we'll give him a large meal and lots of liquid refreshment here at home.'

'Very well, young Mistress,' said Marmaduke. 'Mulled claret goes well with afternoon tea.' And then laying down the apple at which he was daintily nibbling, and with the fire of inspiration suddenly lighting up his whole face, he fixed his bright eyes upon the north-west corner of the ceiling and murmured under his breath, 'Plum cake. Saffron cake. Cherry cake. Iced fairy cakes. Eclairs. Gingerbread. Meringues. Syllabub. Almond fingers. Rock cakes. Chocolate drops. Parkin. Cream horns. Devonshire splits. Cornish pasty. Jam sandwiches. Lemon-curd sandwiches. Lettuce sandwiches. Cinnamon toast. Honey toast. . . .'

'But, surely, Marmaduke, seven people won't eat all that!' interrupted Maria.

'I always like to be prepared for more guests than are actually expected,' said Marmaduke. 'Also I gathered from the tone of your voice that this tea-party was to be a great occasion, and great occasions need to be greatly celebrated. The mere suggestion of meanness, upon a great occasion, is much to be deprecated. The bodily sustenance of the inner man as well as the aesthetic satisfaction of the outward eye should be on a lavish scale.'

Maria did not quite know what his last sentence meant, but she felt it had something to do with floral decoration, and it encouraged her to ask, 'Please, Marmaduke, may I borrow all these geraniums to decorate the house for my party?'

'Certainly, young Mistress,' said Marmaduke.

'Robin will help us carry the pots into the house,' said Maria. 'And, oh, Marmaduke, will you be seeing Robin today, when he comes to look after the sheep in the orchard? And if so, will you give him a letter from me?'

For answer Marmaduke waddled across to his truckle bed, dived beneath it and came back carrying an ink-horn, a quill pen and a beautiful piece of parchment.

'Dear Robin,' Maria wrote. 'Last night Wrolf took me to have a second try, and it was successful. I don't think the Black Men will be wicked any more. Please forgive me, dear Robin, that I had to have the second try without you. I could not help it. And I could not have done it the second time if you had not helped me the first time. I cannot tell you about it in a letter, but I will tell you when I see you. I want to see you very badly, so please will you come to tea tomorrow? I would like you to be here at half past three. And please, Robin, will you ask Loveday to come tomorrow too, at half past four. Tell her she *must* come, please. If she does not come, then everything will be ruined. Tell her that. I know, of course, that she will not want to come into the house at that time of day, but if she will wait in the rose-garden I will come to her there. Tell her that tomorrow Sir Benjamin rides to the market-town to sit on the Bench. That will make her feel quite happy about coming. Oh, and please will you see Old Parson and tell him to come too, at a quarter past four. Dear Robin, you and Loveday *must* both come, and Old Parson too.'

This letter Maria folded and gave to Marmaduke. Then she

got up and curtsied and thanked him for the delicious little meal.

'I trust it has not spoilt your appetite for breakfast?' he asked anxiously.

'Not in the least, thank you,' Maria assured him.

She went down the stairs and through the stable-yard and the formal garden to the house. She found as she looked at them that she was no longer afraid of the yew-tree men and cocks. It was as though some living evil in them had been withdrawn, and now they were not presences any more but just yew-trees clipped into amusing shapes.

In the hall she met Sir Benjamin, just coming down. He gazed at her in astonishment, for with her white tired face, and the pine-needles sticking to her skirt, it was obvious that she had been having a night out, and he opened his mouth to ask her where in the world she had been. Then, looking at her with love and trust, he shut his mouth and held his peace, as though he knew.

'I'm too sleepy to tell you today, Sir,' she said. 'But I'll tell you some time soon. . . . Please, Sir, may I have a small tea-party tomorrow? I want to ask Old Parson to tea. And will you come too? Dressed in your best?'

'It's my day for the Bench,' said Sir Benjamin.

'But if you come straight home, and don't go to the inn, you'll be in time for my tea-party,' said Maria. 'And there'll be lots to eat and lots to drink at my tea-party. Please, *please,* dear Sir!'

He could not refuse her white pleading face. 'Have it your own way,' he said. 'But if your "lots to drink" is tea, I don't want it. Of all the wishy-washy, insipid beverages—'

'It isn't,' Maria hastened to reassure him, 'it's mulled claret.'

Sir Benjamin's face brightened. 'You can rely on me,' he assured Maria. 'And I'll come dressed in my best.'

'And may I have floral decorations at my party?' asked Maria.

'God bless the child!' he ejaculated. 'Of course you may if you want to, though it seems to me you're making a great to-do about entertaining Old Parson to tea.'

'And will you give me your solemn word that if you don't happen to like my floral decorations you won't throw them out of the window?' said Maria.

Sir Benjamin's eyes popped slightly, but he only replied gravely, 'My solemn word.'

'That's all right, then,' said Maria with satisfaction. 'Now I'm going to get tidy for breakfast, and after breakfast I'm going to sleep and sleep and sleep.'

'You look as though you needed it,' her relative assured her. 'I never saw a clearer case of the morning after the night before.'

Chapter Twelve

·: 1 :·

Maria spent most of that day, and the whole of the next night, fast asleep, and the whole of the next morning finding it exceedingly difficult to concentrate upon her lessons. She found it difficult, also, to pacify Miss Heliotrope, who was full of anxiety about the peculiarity of her behaviour. 'It's quite all right, Miss Heliotrope,' she kept saying. 'Once the tea-party this afternoon is safely over, I will explain everything.'

'But who is coming to this mysterious tea-party?' asked Miss Heliotrope.

'Apart from us, and Old Parson, a very unhappy lady, a very wicked man, and that little boy I used to play with in the Square garden in London,' said Maria.

'But, my dear Maria, I've told you time and again that there's no such person!' ejaculated poor Miss Heliotrope.

'You won't say so any more after this afternoon,' said Maria.

'And an unhappy lady and a wicked man!' said Miss Heliotrope. 'It all sounds most unsuitable.'

'But after this afternoon she'll be happy and he'll be good,' said Maria. 'And Marmaduke Scarlet knows all about my party.'

'Ah well, if Marmaduke Scarlet knows,' said Miss Heliotrope, and cheered up. She now had the very highest opinion of Marmaduke, owing to the excellence of his housekeeping and the fact that he was graciously allowing her to attend to all the neglected household mending.

After dinner Maria dispatched Miss Heliotrope to her room to rest, with orders to stay there until fetched, and Digweed to intercept Sir Benjamin at the gatehouse and bring him quietly through without ringing the bell. Digweed also had instructions to conduct Sir Benjamin to his room with his eyes shut, and tell him, too, to stay there until fetched. Then she and Marmaduke collected together all the beloved animals that they might help in the preparations for the happy ending that they had laboured so hard to bring about—Wrolf, Wiggins, Zachariah, Serena, and Periwinkle. Marmaduke demurred about bringing Periwinkle actually into the house, but she was led up the steps and stood at the open front door where she could watch all that went on. It might have been argued that the part taken by Wiggins in the animals' labour had not been worth mentioning, but Wiggins today was looking so wonderfully beautiful that everyone forgot that perhaps his behaviour did not always match his looks.

At this point Robin appeared, his russet clothes beautifully brushed, his shoes polished till they shone like glass, the green feather in his hat waving merrily, and his round rosy face shining with soap and water, happiness and excitement.

'Old Parson is coming, and Mother will be at the far end of

the rose-garden at half past four,' he assured Maria. 'She promised. I'd hard work to make her promise, but she did.'

'Thank you, Robin,' said Maria. 'And you didn't mind that I had to finish things without you?'

'Not in the least,' Robin assured her cheerfully. 'Not provided you tell me all about it.'

'I'll tell you all about it while we get ready for the party we're going to have,' said Maria. 'All my life Robin, I'll always tell you all about everything.'

'And I'll tell you,' said Robin. 'If I didn't you'd ask so many questions that life would not be worth living.'

Then they set to work. Wrolf, a large basket held in his mouth, helped Maria and Robin carry all the geraniums from Marmaduke's little room to the house. There were many more than Maria had realized. She and Robin filled the parlour with them, putting them all along the window-seat so that from outside in the rose-garden the window should look a blaze of pink, and they filled the great hall with them, and the windows of Maria's tower room as well. And then after that they helped Marmaduke Scarlet set out the tea on the hall table. It looked wonderful when it was all put ready, with lighted candles all down the centre of the table, flanked by vases of the choicest geranium blooms, the best Crown Derby cups and saucers and crystal goblets, and all the eatables in silver dishes. The tea in a silver urn and the great jugs of mulled claret would be brought in by Marmaduke later.

And then Maria went up to her tower room to put on her very best dress, her London party frock that she had not worn yet at Moonacre Manor; a dress of primrose silk with blue forget-me-nots embroidered all over it. It had a large hanging pocket, and into this she slipped the little book with the heliotrope cover that she had borrowed from Old Parson on the day she had first visited him, and the green-covered book of French verse that Louis de Fontenelle had given to Jane Heliotrope. While she was dressing she saw Sir Benjamin and Digweed come back, and Sir Benjamin was led up the steps with his eyes shut. Maria knew she could trust him not to peep when he got inside the hall. He was a thoroughly trustworthy man.

Punctually at ten minutes past four Maria fetched Miss Heliotrope and led her downstairs, dressed in her purple bombasine with one of Loveday's lovely mobcaps on her head, and one of the fichus.

'Now, Miss Heliotrope,' she said, throwing open the parlour door and disclosing Robin bowing hat in hand in the middle of the room, 'this is Robin. I have known him nearly all my life, and I am going to marry him, so that there won't ever be a time when I shan't know him. I love him very much, and I love you very much, so you must love each other.'

'Dear me!' said Miss Heliotrope, gazing at Robin in utter astonishment over the top of her spectacles. 'Dear me! What a very unusual, brightly coloured boy.'

'Isn't he just as I described him to you in London?' asked Maria.

'Yes, he is,' said Miss Heliotrope. 'Only larger.'

'Madam, I have grown since then,' said Robin, and he bowed again, very politely, his hat with its peacock's feather flourished in his right hand and his left hand on his heart, in the gallant manner that had been in fashion when Miss Heliotrope was young. And it was obvious that now that she was recovering from her first shock of surprise, Miss Heliotrope's heart was warming towards him.

'Dear me!' she said again, but she said it very cordially.

Robin came to her and took her hand and kissed it. 'Your servant, Madam,' he said, 'until my life's end.'

And at that Miss Heliotrope's heart melted entirely and she bent and kissed him. 'You're a nice boy,' she said. 'Whether or not you are the boy Maria imagined in London—well—I shouldn't like to say. But you're a nice boy, and if you're good to Maria you'll have no more faithful friend than Jane Heliotrope.'

A step sounded and there was Old Parson, with a pink geranium stuck in one of the buttonholes of his cassock.

'Oh, Sir!' Maria cried to him, 'will you please take Miss Heliotrope for a little stroll in the kitchen garden? It's nice and warm there in the sun, and the fruit blossom is very pretty. And there's a nice bench under the mulberry-tree. Would you like to sit there and read aloud to Miss Heliotrope for a little? She likes being read aloud to—especially poetry. She'd like this book of English verse you lent me, and the French one too.' And Maria took the two little books from her pocket and handed them to him. 'Tea is at five,' she finished.

Old Parson, a twinkle in his eyes, took the books, bowed to Miss Heliotrope and offered her his arm. 'Madam, may I have the honour?' he said to her. And to Maria he said, 'Your Royal Highness, the deep-laid schemes of managing women have never until now commended themselves to me. But in yours I willingly entangle myself. For the witchery of the moon is in them, and so brave is the moon, confronting so great a darkness with so small a face, that a man who does not count himself her willing slave is a born fool.'

And with this handsome tribute Old Parson led Miss Heliotrope from the room, and Maria and Robin were alone together. 'Robin,' she said, 'I want you to go up to Sir Benjamin's room and fetch him down. Bring him here to the parlour window, looking out on the rose-garden, and engage him in conversation.'

'And how long for?' asked Robin. 'And what about?'

'Until I come back,' said Maria. 'I won't be long. Talk about sheep. Sir Benjamin would stand for hours in one position talking about sheep.'

Then she climbed out of the parlour window and ran across the rose-garden to the farthest hidden end. Loveday had not failed her. She was there, in her grey dress, sprigged with pink, her proud little head bare to the spring sunshine. She was standing very upright, and she looked very regal in spite of her tiny stature, and the briars of the roses were flaunting their new fresh green.

'Mother Minette,' cried Maria, flinging her arms round her, 'the Black Man is coming to afternoon tea.'

Loveday gave a cry of joy and hugged Maria hard. 'Then you've done it, Maria?' she asked. 'Oh, you lovely brave little Moon Maiden! But how did you do it, Maria?'

'It'll take me hours and hours to tell you everything,' said Maria. 'So I'll have to tell you later. Now, please, Loveday, I want you to take a look through the parlour window at my floral decorations.'

'Have you made me walk all this way just to look at floral

decorations?' asked Loveday. But she was not annoyed, only amused.

'What you'll see in the parlour window will be worth the walk,' Maria assured her. 'Now shut your eyes, please.'

Loveday shut them, and being, like Sir Benjamin, an utterly trustworthy person, she did not even peep through her eyelashes as Maria led her towards the house. The two looked very beautiful coming through the rose-garden hand in hand in their flowered dresses, with the sunshine lighting their fair hair to silvery gold, and a cloud of little birds accompanying them with their bright wings fluttering and their cascading song like showers of light in the blue air. The man and the boy standing in the parlour window stopped talking about sheep and caught their breath in wonder.

'Now!' said Maria, and Loveday opened her eyes.

And what she saw was a mass of salmon-pink geraniums, those geraniums that are the pride of Cornwall. They filled the window and the parlour beyond, just as they had done on that evening years ago, before her lover lost his temper and flung them out of the window. And he was standing there in the middle of them dressed in his best cauliflower wig, his Sunday coat and the waistcoat that she had made for him long ago, and gazing at her as though she were the sun and the moon and the stars all rolled into one.

'Loveday!' he cried with a great roar of delight, 'forgive me, for the love of heaven, for having thrown those darned geraniums out of the window, and come in here at once and never go away again!'

And Loveday stepped in through the open window on to the window-seat, and was lifted up into his arms like a child, and Maria ran away like the wind through the formal garden and up the steps to the hall.

'That's all right,' she cried to Robin, who had also fled like the wind from the parlour. 'That's one good job done. Shall you mind Sir Benjamin marrying your mother, Robin?'

'He can if he likes,' said Robin. 'I don't care who marries who so long as *you* marry *me*.'

And he suddenly bellowed with joy in much the same way as Sir Benjamin had done, and flinging his arms round Maria enveloped her in a great bear hug that nearly took her breath away. And all the animals, Wrolf, Zachariah, Serena, Wiggins and Periwinkle (who had now come right into the hall), gathered round them in a circle and roared and miaowed and squeaked and barked and whinnied with joy, while Marmaduke Scarlet stood in the kitchen door with arms akimbo and smiled the very broadest of his smiles, the one when the ends of it ran into his ears and disappeared.

•: 2 :•

And then through the noise they were all making there penetrated the sound of trotting hoofs, not the hoofs of one horse but of many. It seemed that a great company of horsemen was approaching from somewhere. Maria and Robin let go of each other and ran to the door, with Marmaduke Scarlet and the animals crowding behind them. The formal garden was absolutely full of Black Men on black horses, some of them quite still and the rest trotting forward two by two, and the still ones were the yew-trees and the moving ones were Monsieur Cocq de Noir and all his retinue. There were black cocks, too, in the garden, though all were still except the one which flapped his wings and crowed upon his master's shoulder.

'They've all come!' gasped Maria in dismay. 'I invited Monsieur Cocq de Noir, but they've all come!'

'Have no fear, young Mistress,' came Marmaduke's voice soothingly behind her. 'There is enough. There is sufficient plum cake, saffron cake, cherry cake, iced fairy cakes, éclairs, gingerbread, meringues, syllabub, almond fingers, rock cakes, chocolate cakes, parkin, cream horns, Devonshire splits, Cornish pasty, jam sandwiches, lemon-curd sandwiches, lettuce sandwiches, cinnamon toast and honey toast to feed twenty and more. Have no fear, young Mistress; when Marmaduke Scarlet is cook there is always enough.'

'But the mulled claret!' cried Maria.

'Of that also,' said Marmaduke, 'there is an unlimited supply.'

So Maria and Robin stood at the top of the steps hand in hand, like a Prince and Princess, and cried out 'Welcome!' And the Black Men, dismounting at the mounting-block and leaving their black horses to wander companionably among the yew-tree horses in the garden trooped up two by two, bowed before Maria and Robin, and passed on through a guard of honour formed by the animals into the hall, to be welcomed by Sir Benjamin and Loveday Minette, who were now standing like a King and Queen in front of the great fireplace.

It was to the credit of Sir Benjamin and Loveday that, drawn from the parlour to the hall by the row going on there, they were able immediately to emerge from their private happiness and assume the roles of host and hostess to twenty men whom they had hitherto regarded as their enemies without any appearance of stupefaction. . . .

'In the future, Sir Benjamin,' said Monsieur Cocq de Noir, bowing low, 'you will find me all that a neighbour should be.'

'I don't doubt it, Sir,' said Sir Benjamin. 'We will let bygones be bygones and start afresh from today.'

After that the tea-party went with a swing, Marmaduke Scarlet was persuaded to sit down at the great table with Sir Benjamin and Loveday, Maria and Robin, and the twenty Black Men. Wiggins sat on Maria's lap, Zachariah shared Marmaduke's chair and the black cock sat on his master's shoulder, and Periwinkle and Wrolf stood one on each side of Sir Benjamin's chair at the head of the table. They ate and drank and laughed and sang songs, and when at last the Black Men rode away singing into the sunset, there was not a crumb of food or a drop of anything to drink left upon the table; nor a drop of hatred in any heart nor a crumb of bitterness in any mind. Everything was explained and forgiven, and the future stretched before them with a fair promise.

•: 3 :•

A fair promise that was fulfilled, because they all of them lived happy ever after.

It may have been noticed by the intelligent reader that Old Parson and Miss Heliotrope did not put in an appearance at the tea-party. That was because they forgot to.

After they had strolled up and down the paths of the kitchen garden for a little while, enjoying the sunshine and each other's conversation, because from the moment when they had seen each other in church the first Sunday they had been extraordinarily attracted to each other, Old Parson remembered Maria's commands and led Miss Heliotrope to the seat beneath the mulberry-tree, and opened the two little books to see which would be the nicest to read aloud to her.

And at that very moment a sunbeam striking through the green spring leaves above their heads lit upon them, and Miss Heliotrope saw the name of her one-time lover written upon the flyleaf of one book in her own handwriting, and Old Parson saw the name of the only woman he had ever cared about written upon the title page of the other in *his* handwriting. And at that very same moment another sunbeam lit up the locket she was wearing, and Old Parson recognized it as the locket he had given her years ago when they were young, with a lock of his hair in it.

And after that they had a great deal to say to each other, because however old you are you never forget the time when you were young, or the people you loved when you were young; indeed, the older you get the more clearly you remember the times and the more dearly you love the people. . . . So it wasn't to be wondered at if Miss Heliotrope and Old Parson forgot to come in to tea.

Sir Benjamin and Loveday's wedding took place a month later. Though it was very quiet, taking place very early in the morning, with only the people who really loved them attending it, because Sir Benjamin and Loveday felt shy about getting married at their age, it was nevertheless very lovely. Loveday finished embroidering the wedding waistcoat, and Sir Benjamin wore it; and Loveday wore her wedding dress, and they both looked splendid. Old Parson married them, and did it beautifully.

Old Parson and Miss Heliotrope's wedding took place a month later still, and was even quieter, but lovely too; the only drawback to it being that Old Parson could not marry himself, and a fat little parson from beyond the hills had to come and do it. But he was a nice little parson, so it didn't really matter. And Old Parson and Miss Heliotrope lived at the Parsonage together and were happier than they had either of them known they could be; and Miss Heliotrope did not have indigestion any more, because her indigestion had originally been the result of her grief at her separation from Louis de Fontenelle, and now that she was married to him there wasn't any point in having indigestion.

Robin and Maria were not married until the following spring, because their elders thought they ought to have another year of learning to control their Merryweather tempers before they lived together for good. But in the following spring, on a glorious warm April morning, their wedding took place, and it was not at all quiet, it was the noisiest, happiest, as well as the loveliest wedding that had ever happened in the old church of Silverydew. Maria wore Loveday's wedding dress, and she carried a big bunch of primroses tied with gold and silver ribbon, and wore a wreath of primroses on her hair. Robin wore a brand-new jerkin made of the brightest emerald green, with primroses in his button-hole, and he carried in his hand a green hat trimmed with a cockade of gold and silver ribbon and a bunch of cock's feathers that Monsieur Cocq de Noir had with his own hand pulled from the tail of his big black cock, as a sign that there was now undying friendship between the Black Men and the Merryweathers.

They rode from the manor-house to the church for their wedding, not in the carriage but upon the backs of Wrolf and Periwinkle, with Zachariah, Wiggins, and Serena following behind with bows of gold and silver ribbon tied round their necks, and they were met at the lych-gate by all the children of Silverydew dressed in their best, with their arms full of flowers, singing the Bell Song to the accompaniment of the bells pealing out overhead.

When Maria and Robin walked up the aisle to be married by Old Parson at the chancel steps, the devoted animals followed two by two behind them, and all the children followed behind the animals. Sir Benjamin and Loveday (who was now Lady Merryweather) and Miss Heliotrope (who was now Madame de Fontenelle) and Monsieur Cocq de Noir and Marmaduke Scarlet were sitting in the manor-house pew dressed all in their best, and so happy that they felt they would burst, and behind them the church was packed to the doors with all the people of Silverydew, and all the Black Men, singing in a way that nearly lifted the roof off. The church was beautifully decorated with flowers, primroses and apple blossom and daffodils and violets and snowdrops and crocuses, which that particular year had decided to bloom all at the same moment, so that they could all be present together at Maria's wedding. The tomb of Sir Wrolf Merryweather was an absolute bower of flowers, and when Maria and Robin had put the final touches to Sir Wrolf's floral decorations the evening before, they had fancied that they had seen a flicker of a smile pass over the carved stone countenance of their disreputable ancestor.

'Only he's not disreputable any more now,' Maria had said to Robin. 'He won't haunt Paradise Hill any more, because he's got into the real Paradise and he's riding on a white horse through the fields of lilies beside the flashing stream.'

When the wedding was over, Maria and Robin mounted once more upon Wrolf and Periwinkle and rode back to the manor-house through the sunshine and the new spring green of the lovely park, with everyone who had been in the church following singing behind them, to the wedding breakfast that Marmaduke Scarlet had prepared.

It was such a superlatively wonderful feast that even Marmaduke himself was inclined to think it the crowning achievement of his distinguished culinary career. The white-iced wedding-cake was the size of a cartwheel at its base and was six feet tall, mounting up like a pyramid. It was decorated with sugar flowers and fruit and birds and stars and butterflies and bells, and at the very top there was a tiny sickle moon and a tiny sun enclosed within a silver horseshoe. There were lots of other kinds of cakes, of course, and every possible sort of sugar biscuit and iced bun, and all the different kinds of sandwiches that it is possible to think of, and dishes of candied cherries and crystallized ginger and sugared almonds and chocolates. And there were jellies and creams and syllabubs and ices, and hot coffee and iced coffee, and tea and lemonade and sherbet, and mulled claret and champagne.

Everybody had lots to eat and drink, and everyone enjoyed it, but nobody ate or drank too much, because they did not want to spoil this happy day by having aches in their insides later on; they wanted this day to be happy right through to the end.

And so it was. And all the days that followed were happy too, and the months and the years. Monsieur Cocq de Noir kept his promise, as Maria had known that he would, and he and his Black Men sold their fish to the valley people and traded with them for the things that they wanted, and did not poach or steal any more. And they left off wearing black clothes and wore gay colours like the valley folk, and painted their black fishing boats red and green and blue, and gave them white wings like birds. And the children of Silverydew could go and play on the shore at Merryweather Bay, and the Black Men did not mind; indeed, they played with them, and helped them collect sea-shells to take as gifts to the Lady on Paradise Hill.

The Black Men were happy in their castle in the pine-woods, and in the gatehouse that Sir Benjamin gave to them for their own, to use when they felt in need of a little change.

And Sir Benjamin and Loveday, and Maria and Robin, and Digweed and Marmaduke Scarlet, and all the animals were happy in the manor-house; and Miss Heliotrope and Old Parson and all the people of Silverydew were happy in their houses in the village; and up on Paradise Hill the sheep were happy and the birds sang and the little shrine was a beloved place of pilgrimage for all the countryside. Happy were the days of sunlight, and happy the moonlit nights, too, and full of sweet dreams.

But in this world nothing stays still, and in the fullness of time Miss Heliotrope and Old Parson became very old indeed, and tired of life in this world, so they took off their bodies and laid them aside and went joyfully away into the next.

And after many long years Sir Benjamin and Loveday did the same, and then Maria, who was Sir Benjamin's heiress, inherited Moonacre and ruled there with her husband Robin. He was the brave soul and she was the pure spirit of their family motto, and one in heart, merry and loving, they inherited the kingdom together.

And they never quarrelled, as other Merryweather lovers had done, so Wrolf did not have to leave them, but remained with them always. They had ten children, and the ten of them kneeling with their father and mother on the twelve hassocks in the Merryweather pew in the church were a goodly sight, and when Maria looked down the row she felt she had nothing left to wish for . . . at least, only one thing. . . .

For sometimes in her dreams at night she stood beneath the branches of a mysterious wood, and looked down a moonlit glade, her eyes straining after something that she could not see. And when she woke up, there would be tears on her cheeks because her longing had been unsatisfied.

Yet she was not unhappy because of this dream. She knew that one day, when she was a very old woman, she would dream this dream for the last time, and in this last dream of all she would see the little white horse, and he would not go away from her. He would come towards her and she would run towards him, and he would carry her upon his back away and away, she did not quite know where, but to a good place, a place where she wanted to be.